D1395223

DEATH AND THE
JOYFUL WOMAN

DEATH AND THE JOYFUL WOMAN

Ellis Peters

Macdonald

A Macdonald Book

Copyright © 1961 Ellis Peters

First published in Great Britain in 1961 by Collins
This edition published in 1990 by Macdonald & Co (Publishers) Ltd
London & Sydney

British Library Cataloguing in Publication Data

Peters, Ellis *1913–*
    Death and the joyful woman.
    Rn: Edith Pargeter   I. Title
    823.912 [F]

    ISBN 0 356 19487 6

Printed and bound in Great Britain by
Biddles Ltd, Guildford and King's Lynn

Macdonald & Co (Publishers) Ltd
Orbit House
1 New Fetter Lane
London EC4A 1AR
A member of Maxwell Macmillan Pergamon Publishing Corporation

CHAPTER I

THE FIRST TIME Dominic Felse saw Kitty Norris she was dancing barefoot along the broad rail of the terrace at the Boat Club, in a cloud of iris-coloured nylon, a silver sandal dangling from either hand. It was the night following the Comerbourne Regatta, the night of the mid-season Club dance, when such acrobatic performances were not particularly surprising, though the demonstrators were usually male. It was also the eve of Leslie Armiger's wedding day, though Dominic was not aware of that, and wouldn't have understood its significance even if he had been.

He was on his way home from his music lesson, an inescapable boredom which beset him weekly; and because the night was fine and warm he had let the bus go without him and set out to walk the mile and a bit to Comerford by the riverside road. At the edge of the town it brought him close beneath the club-house terrace. The strains of the band floated out to meet him, and a babel of voices was blown across the wooden balustrade with the music; and there along the railing, ten feet or so above his head, floated Kitty in her extravagant dress, hands spread wide dangling the absurd contraptions of cobweb straps and three-inch spike heels she called shoes. Several voices, all male, were calling on her entreatingly to come down and be sensible; two young men were threading a hasty way between the tables on the terrace to intercept her, and one of them in his extreme concentration had just failed to see a waiter with a loaded tray. Shrieks of consternation and a flurry of dispersing flounces marked the area which was now awash with short drinks. Kitty danced on, unheeding; the table lights illuminated from below a face set in child-like concentration, the tip of her tongue protruding at the corner of parted lips. Dominic had never seen anyone so incandescent with gaiety.

His first thought had been a mildly contemptuous: " If they're this high by a quarter to ten, what on earth will they be like by one o'clock in the morning? " But that was the automatic reaction of his youthful superiority, and tempered already by curiosity. He had experimented with tobacco so frequently during the last year and a half, unknown to his parents, that he had worn out its novelty without discovering its attractions; but now that he was beginning to contemplate alcohol hopefully from afar he did so with the same incorrigible conviction that it must be wonderful, since adults took such delight in it, and reserved it so jealously for their own use. These antics going on over his head were part of the rites; Dominic curled his lip at them, but stopped in the darkness beneath the terrace to take a longer look at the bacchanalia from which he was barred. And having seen Kitty he lost sight of everything else.

She was the centre of the din, but she herself was silent, and perhaps that contributed to the overwhelming impression of disembodied beauty. She was of no more than medium height, but so slender that she looked tall, and taller still because of being poised swaying above him against the dark-blue sky. She looked pale, too, white almost to transparency, though in fact she was sturdy and sun-tanned and as robust as a bull-terrier. Almost everything about her swam, like her body, in diaphanous clouds of illusion, but in the heart of the phantasm there was Kitty, a reality.

He stood gaping in his shadowy place below her, holding his breath for fear she would fall. One of the young men, a flash of magpie black and white lunging over the rail, made a grab for her, and she whirled round perilously and eluded him, her full skirts swirling about her. Dominic, staring upwards fascinated, caught a glimpse of long, slim legs, a smooth, pale golden thigh. He averted his eyes hastily, but made even more haste to raise them again. After all, who could see him? She wouldn't know. Nobody was looking at him, nobody knew he was there.

"Kitty, you'll fall! Don't be a fool!" implored the terrified young man above, catching at her hand as she drew back from him. She uttered a sudden high squeak of protest, and dropped one of her sandals plump into Dominic's startled hands; and there in microcosm was the solid reality that harboured within the iris-coloured cloud. A bit of silver nonsense it might be, but it was made for a healthy, modern, size six foot. Dominic stood holding it gingerly before him as though it might be charged with the incalculable properties of enchantment, so stupefied that it took him several seconds to realise what a quietness had fallen overhead. When at last he looked up it was to see three or four heads leaning over the wooden balustrade and staring down at him. Only one of them had any significance for him, he didn't waste any time looking at the others.

"I'm terribly sorry," said Kitty. "I hope it didn't

hurt you? If I'd realised there was anyone there I wouldn't have been behaving so badly."

A clear, round voice she had, direct and disconcerting, and so polite that it confused him even more than her former extravagances had done. She wasn't drunk, after all, she wasn't even elevated. As soon as she was aware of him she spoke to him as a punctilious child speaks to a stranger. And where was the gaiety now? She looked down at him from the shadow of her long, smooth, light-brown hair with large, plaintive violet eyes, and her expression didn't change when she had weighed up the person with whom she had to deal. Dominic was used to the look of indulgent condescension that visited so many faces when confronted with his want of years, but Kitty continued to gaze at him with the wondering, wary, courteous look of an equal and a contemporary.

He couldn't find his tongue, there wasn't anything for him to say that wouldn't sound idiotic, and he didn't know how to break out of the constricting moment. Disgusted with himself and crimson to the ears, he stood in a sweat of shame, wishing he'd gone straight home, wishing the night could be darker, wishing the morons up there with her would stop grinning, or better still, go away.

" You can throw it," said Kitty simply. " It's all right, really, I can catch."

And she could and did. He measured the distance carefully, and tossed the sandal gently up into her out-stretched hands, and she lifted it out of the air as lightly as thistledown, held it up for him to see, in something between a wave and a salute, and stooped to put it on. And that was the end of the incident. One of the young men put his arm round her, and she let herself be led away towards the dance-hall. There was just one instant when she looked back, a last glance of reluctance and regret, as though she knew she had disastrously disturbed the peace of a fellow-creature who was in no case to defend himself. The oval face with its clear, generous features had a honeyed glow in the shadow of the burnished hair; the violet eyes were wide and dark and full of a rueful wonder. He had never seen anyone look so sad. Then she was gone.

She stayed with him, however, all the way home, and upset his life and all his relationships for months. His term results suffered a downward lurch from first place to fifth, his co-ordination on the Rugby field that winter went to pieces and he didn't get into his house fifteen. He couldn't talk about Kitty to anyone; his best friends, without malice, would have made his life a misery, and his parents were out of the question, for his mother was after all a woman, and he instinctively knew better than to confide in her about another woman whose image was elbowing her out of sole possession of his heart, while his father was a man, and good-looking enough and young enough to be in some degree a rival. Even if he had wanted to unburden himself to them, Dominic wouldn't have known what to say; he didn't understand himself what was happening to him.

At fourteen love can be an overwhelming experience, all the more so for being totally incomprehensible. But Dominic was as normal as his own predicament; his appetite didn't fail him, if anything it increased, he slept well, he enjoyed most of what happened to him, however disquieting, and he got over it. By the time he saw the girl again, more than a year later, he was back at the top of his class, mad about sports cars, and engaged in a campaign to induce his father to let him have a motor-bike as soon as he was old enough. He had almost for-gotten what Kitty looked like. He had never discovered who she was, indeed he had never tried, because any inquiries, in whatever quarter, would have involved a certain degree of self-betrayal. She was just Kitty, a recollection of absurd, melancholy beauty, already growing shadowy.

The occasion of their second meeting was the autumn visit of the mobile Blood Transfusion Unit to Comer-bourne Grammar School in the last week of September. Dominic had stayed late for football practice, and after his shower had remembered something he wanted to look up for his history essay, and lingered an extra hour in the library. When he finally crossed the forecourt on his way to the side gate it was already dusk, and he saw the unit's van drawn up close to the gymnasium block, and a nurse trotting across from the rear doors with an armful of documents and equipment. The session was a quarterly occurrence, and he had never paid the least attention to it before and would not have done so now but for the dark-red Karmann-Ghia which was just turning into park in the narrow space behind the van. The car brought him up standing, with a gasp of pleasure for its compact and subtle beauties, and when its door opened he could scarcely drag his eyes from that chaste thoroughbred shape even to satisfy his curiosity about its lucky owner. But the next moment even the car was in eclipse. A girl swung long, elegant legs out of it, and walked slowly across the concrete to the door of the block, as if she was a little dubious of her errand or her welcome when it came to the point. And the girl was Kitty.

Dusk or daylight or unrelieved midnight, Dominic would have known her. She had only to put in an appearance, even after fifteen months, and everything that had to do with her acquired a significance so intense as to blot out the rest of the world. The parked van, the lighted windows behind which the nurses moved busily, the whole apparatus of donating blood suddenly became a vital reality to Dominic, because Kitty was a donor. He knew he ought to go home and tackle his homework, but he couldn't bring himself to move from the spot, and when finally he did compel his legs into action he found that they were carrying him towards the gymnasium block instead of towards the gate.

In any case he'd probably missed the bus he'd intended to take by now, and there was twenty-five minutes to wait for the next. If he went away now he might never have such an opportunity again. She wasn't with a party this time, she wasn't on a terrace ten feet above him; anybody could go in there and join her at the mere cost of a pint of blood. After all, it was a good cause, and even if they did have a list of regular donors they surely wouldn't turn down another one. I really ought to think about these services more, he said to himself virtuously, especially with Dad being in the position he is, it's up to me to do him credit, actually. It's now or never, warned some more candid demon at the back of his mind, she's on her own as yet because she drove herself here, but if you don't make up your mind pretty smartly the official transport will be there, and you won't have a dog's chance of getting near her. *And* you'll have tapped off a pint of blood for nothing, it added spitefully, demolishing the pretence that he was contemplating the sacrifice out of any impulse of public-spiritedness. But he was beyond noticing the intricacies of this argument within him, for he was already pushing open the swing-door and shouldering his way through into the hall.

She was sitting alone on one of the chairs ranged along the wall, looking a little perplexed and a little forlorn, as if she wondered what she was doing there at all. She wore a dark green jersey suit with a skirt fashionably short and tight, and the magnificent legs which had made his senses swim gleamed smoothly golden from knee to ankle, so perfectly tanned that he couldn't tell whether she was wearing nylons or not. She looked up quickly as he came in, pleased not to be alone any longer. The heavy coil of honey-coloured hair swayed on her smooth cheek, the disconcerting eyes smiled at him hopefully.

" Hallo! " she said almost shyly, almost ingratiatingly.

She didn't recognise him, he saw that at once, she was merely welcoming him as a fellow-victim. " Hallo! " he said with a hesitant smile. He stacked his books on a window-sill, and sat down several places away from her, afraid to make too sudden a claim upon her attention merely because she found his company preferable to being alone.

" We're early," said Kitty. " They're not ready for us yet. I hate waiting for this sort of thing, don't you? Is it your first time? "

" Yes," said Dominic rather stiffly, because he thought for a moment that she was making an oblique reference to his youth.

" Mine, too," she said, cheered, and he saw that he'd
been misjudging her. " I felt I ought to do something
about *something*. Every now and again it gets me like that.
I'm not much use at anything much, but at least I've got
blood. I hope! Was yours a case of conscience, too? "

She grinned at him. There was no other word for it,
it was too wry and funny and conspiratorial to be called
merely a smile. He felt his stiffness melting like ice in
sunlight, and with it the marrow in his bones.

" Well, it was sort of on the spur of the moment," he
admitted, grinning back shyly, he who was seldom shy
and frequently a good deal too cocky. " I just happened
to be late leaving and I saw the van here, and I thought
maybe I ought—well, you see, my father's a policeman——"

" No, really? " said Kitty, impressed. The big eyes
dilated; they weren't really the colour of violets, he saw,
but of purple-brown pansies.

" Well, a detective actually," said Dominic punctiliously, and then blushed because it sounded dramatic,
and in reality he knew that it was normally nothing of the
kind. The very name of the profession carries such
artificial overtones, you'd never dream how humdrum
is the daily life of a member of the County C.I.D.

" Gosh! " said Kitty, eyes now enormous with pleased
respect. " I see I must keep in with you. Who knows
when I may need a friend? What with all these fifty limits
around at week-ends, and no parking allowed anywhere
less than a mile from the middle of town, I could be run
in almost any minute." She caught his fixed and fascinated eye, and laughed. " I'm talking an awful lot,
aren't I? You know why? I'm nervous of this thing

we've got coming along. I know it's nothing, but some-how I don't like the idea of being tapped like a barrel."

"I'm scared of it, too," said Dominic.

It wasn't true, he hadn't given the actual operation a single thought; but it was generously meant, and it never occurred to him how difficult he was making it for her to hit upon a reply which would be equally graceful to his self-esteem. But she managed it, some natural genius guiding her. She gave him a pleased look, and then a doubtful one, and then a wonderful smile.

"I don't believe you," she said confidently, "but it's jolly nice of you to say it, anyhow. If I yell when they prick my ear for a sample, will you promise to yell, too, so I won't feel alone in my cowardice?"

"I shall probably be the first to yell," he said gallantly, hot with delight and embarrassment.

A door opened with a flourish upon their solitude, and a plump young nurse put her head out into the hall. "My, my!" she said, with that rallying brightness which is almost an occupational hazard in her profession. "Two of us here before time! We *are* eager to help, aren't we?"

"Yes, aren't we?" said Kitty like a meek echo, dragging her eyes away from Dominic's before the giggles could overwhelm them both.

"If you'd like to get it over with, folks, you can come in now."

They went in to the sacrifice together. A row of narrow camp-beds and two attendant nymphs waited for them expectantly, and an older nurse shuffled documents upon a small table, and peered up at them over rimless glasses.

" Good evening! " she said briskly. " Names? " But she beamed at Kitty and didn't wait for an answer. " Oh, yes, of course! " she said, ticking off one of the names in her list. " This is a very nice gesture you're making, we do appreciate it, my dear. It does me good to see you young people setting an example."

She was being very matey indeed, Dominic thought, evidently Kitty was really somebody; but then, a girl who drove a Karmann-Ghia was bound to be somebody. But if only the old battle-axe had let her give her name! He tried to read the list upside down, and was jerked out of his stride as the blue-grey eyes, bright and knowing, pin-pointed him and sharpened into close attention. " Name, please? "

He gave it. She looked down her list, but very rapidly, because she was only verifying what she already knew. " I haven't got your name here, apparently we weren't expecting you." She looked him up and down, and the hard, experienced face broke into a broad and indulgent smile.

" No, I just came in——" he was beginning, but she wagged an admonishing finger at him and rode over him in a loud, friendly, confident voice which stated positively: " *You're* never eighteen, ducky! Don't you know the regulations? "

" I'm sixteen," he said, very much on his dignity, and hating her for being too perceptive, and still more for trumpeting her discoveries like a town-crier. She had made eighteen sound so juvenile that sixteen now sounded like admitting to drooling infancy, and his position was still further undermined by the unacknowledged fact that he had been sixteen for precisely one week. This formidable woman was perfectly capable of looking at him and deducing that detail to add to her score. " I thought it was from sixteen to sixty," he said uncomfortably.

" It's from eighteen to sixty-five, my dear, but bless you for a good try. We can't take children, they need all their strength for growing. You run along home and come back in a couple of years' time, and we'll be glad to see you. But we shall still need your parents' consent, mind."

The younger nurse was giggling. Even Kitty must be smiling at him under cover of the gleaming curtain of her hair. Not unkindly, he had sense enough to know that, but that didn't make the gall of his humiliation any less bitter. And he really had thought the minimum age was sixteen. He could have sworn it was.

" Are you *sure*? It *used* to be sixteen, didn't it? "

She shook her head, smiling broadly. " I'm sorry, love! Always eighteen since I've been in the service. Never mind, being too young is something time will cure, you know."

There was absolutely nothing he could do about it, except go. Kitty craned round the nurse's shoulder from her camp-bed and saw him turn towards the door, crushed and silent. The old fool needn't have bellowed at him like that. The poor kid was so mortified he wasn't even going to say good-bye.

" Hey, don't go! " said Kitty plaintively after his departing back. " Wait for me, and I'll give you a lift." She made it as near a child's wail for company as she decently could, to restore him to a good conceit of himself, and threw in the bribe to take his mind off his injuries, and the sudden reviving gleam in his eyes as he looked round was full repayment. She put it down to the car, which was intelligent of her though inaccurate. " You could at least come and talk to me," she said. " I was counting on you to take my mind off this beastly bottle."

Nobody believed in her need to be amused and distracted, but girls like Kitty are allowed to pretend to as many whims as they please.

" Well, if you really want me to——" he said, recovering a little of his confidence.

" That's all right," said the matron, beaming benevolently, " by all means wait, my dear, nobody wants to drive a willing lad away." He gave her a look she was too complacent to understand; she couldn't even pat a child on the head, he reflected bitterly, without breaking its neck, the kind of touch she had. But she was no longer so important, now Kitty had called him back.

" Here you are," said the young nurse, planking a chair down beside Kitty's camp-bed. " You sit down and talk to your friend, and I'll bring you both a nice cup of tea afterwards."

Dominic sat down. Kitty was looking at him, and studiously avoiding looking at the bottle that was gradually filling up with her blood; but not, he observed, because she felt any real repugnance for it. She was shaking with giggles, and when his slender bulk was interposed between her and the official eyes she said in a rapid, conspiratorial whisper: " These people *kill* me!"

That made everything wonderful by standing everything on its head. He made a fool of himself and she

B

didn't seem to notice; they behaved according to their kind, only slightly caricaturing themselves, and they killed her.

"I really did think it was all right at sixteen," he said, still fretting at the sore place, though he couldn't help grinning back at her.

"Sure," said Kitty, "I know you did. I never thought about there being a limit at all, but it's only sense. Am I done yet? You look, I don't like to."

He didn't like to, either; the thought of her blood draining slowly out of the rounded golden arm gave him an almost physical experience of pain. "Nearly," he said, and averted his eyes. "Look out, here comes our nice cup of tea."

It wasn't a nice cup of tea, of course, when it came; it was very strong and very sweet, and of that curious reddish-brown colour which indicates the presence of tinned milk. When they were left to themselves again to drink it Kitty sat up, flexing her newly-bandaged arm, took an experimental sip, and gave the cup a look of incredulous distaste.

"I know," said Dominic apologetically. "I don't like it with sugar, either, but you're supposed to need it after this caper. It puts back the energy you've lost, or something."

"I don't feel as if I've lost any," admitted Kitty with some surprise, and looked thoughtfully at her bandage. "I'm still not sure what they've got in that bottle," she said darkly. "Wouldn't you have thought it would be beer?" She caught his lost look, and made haste to explain, even more bafflingly: "Well, after all, that's what I live on."

He was staring at her helplessly, more at sea than ever.
He hoped he was misunderstanding her, but how could
he be sure? He knew nothing about her, except that she
was the most charming and disturbing thing that had
ever happened to him. And there *was* her performance
that evening at the Boat Club dance.

"Oh, I don't mean it's actually my staple diet," she
said quickly. "I just meant it's what I *live* on—it's what
pays the bills, you know. I ought to have told you, I'm
Kitty Norris. If that means anything? No good reason
why it should," she hurried on reassuringly. "I'm just
Norris's Beers, that's all I meant." She said it in a
resigned voice, as though she was explaining away some
odd but not tragic native deformity to which she had
long become accustomed, but which might disconcert a
stranger.

"Oh, yes, of course," said Dominic, at once relieved
and mortified. What must she think of him for almost
taking her literally? And he ought to have known.
Katherine Norris the beer heiress was in and out of the
local news headlines regularly, he must surely have seen
her photograph occasionally. It couldn't have done her
justice, though, or he wouldn't have failed to recognise
her. Her name was prominent on about a third of the
pub signs in the county, all those, in fact, which weren't
the monopoly of Armiger's Ales. And hadn't she been
going to marry old Armiger's son at one time? Dominic
groped in his memory, but local society engagements and
weddings did not figure among the events he was in the
habit of filing, and he couldn't remember what was supposed to have happened to break off the merger. It was
enough to be grateful for the fact, no need to account for

it. "I should have realised," he said. "My name's Dominic Felse."

"Cheers, Dominic!" She drank to him in the acrid, sugary tea. "Did you know this used to be a bottle of stout once? I mean they used to give the victims stout to restore them afterwards. Old man Shelley told me so. I'm being done, Dominic, that's what."

"Norris's stout?" asked Dominic, venturing timidly on a joke. It had a generous success; she threw back her head and laughed.

"Too true! I'm being done two ways," she said indignantly as she swung her feet to the floor and shook down her sleeve over the already slipping bandage.

It was nearly at an end, he thought as he followed her out. The transport had arrived and was disgorging its load of volunteers on the forecourt; the evening had closed in as it does in late September, with swiftly falling darkness and sudden clear cold. She would get into the Karmann-Ghia and wave her hand at him warmly but thoughtlessly, and drive away, and he would walk alone to the bus stop and go home. And who knew if he would ever see her again?

"Where can I take you?" she said cheerfully, sliding across from the driving-seat to open the other door.

He hesitated for a moment, worrying whether he ought to accept, whether he wasn't being a nuisance to her, and longing to accept even if he was. "Thanks awfully," he said with a gulp, "but I'm only going to the bus station, it's just a step."

"Straight?" said Kitty, poker-faced. "That where you spend your nights?"

"I mean I've only got to catch a bus from there."

" Come on, get in," said Kitty, " and tell me where you live, or I shall think you don't like my car. Ever driven in one of these? "

He was inside, sitting shoulder to shoulder with her, their sleeves brushing; the plastic hide upholstery might have been floating golden clouds under him, clouds of glory. The girl was bliss enough, the car was almost too much for him. Kitty started the engine and began to back towards the shrubberies to turn, for the transport had cramped her style a little. The bushes made a smoky dimness behind her, stirring against the gathering darkness. She switched on her reversing light to make sure how much room she had, and justified all Dominic's heady pride and delight in her by bringing the car round in one, slithering expertly past the tail of the transport at an impetuous speed, and shooting the gateway like a racing ace. They passed everything along Howard Road, and slowed at the traffic lights.

" You still haven't told me where I'm to take you," said Kitty.

There was nothing left for him to do but capitulate and tell her where he lived, which he did in a daze of delight.

" Comerford, that's hardly far enough to get going properly. Let's go the long way round." She signalled her intention of turning right, and positioned herself beautifully to let the following car pass her on the near side. The driver leaned out and shouted something as he passed, gesticulating towards the rear wheels of the Karmann-Ghia. Dominic, who hadn't understood, bristled on Kitty's behalf, but Kitty, who had, swore and grinned and waved a hand in hasty acknowledgment.

" Damn ! " she said, switching off her reversing light. " I'm *always* doing that. Next time I'm going to get a self-cancelling one. Don't you tell your father on me, will you? I do *try* to remember. It isn't even that I've got such a bad memory, really, it's just certain things about a car that trip me up every time. That damned reversing light, and then the petrol. I wouldn't like to tell you how many times I've run out of petrol inside a year."

" You haven't got a petrol gauge, have you? " he asked, searching the dashboard for it in vain.

" No, it's a reserve tank. I thought it would be better, because when you have to switch over you know you've got exactly a gallon, and that's fair warning."

" And is it better? " asked Dominic curiously.

" Yes and no. It works on long journeys, because then I don't know how far it will be between filling stations, so I make a point of stopping at the very first one after the switch-over, and filling up. But when I'm just driving round town, shopping or something, I kick her over and think, oh, I've still got a gallon, I needn't worry, plenty of time, pumps all round me. And then I clean forget about it, and run dry in the middle of the High Street, or half-way up the lane to the golf links. I never learn," said Kitty ruefully. " But when I had a petrol gauge on the old car I never remembered to look at it in time, so what's the use? It's just me. Dizzy, that's what."

" You drive awfully well," said Dominic, reaching for the nearest handful of comfort he could offer her. That self-derisive note in her voice, at once comic and sad, had already begun to fit itself into a hitherto undiscovered place in his heart like a key into a secret door.

" No, do you mean that? Honestly? "

" Yes, of course. You must know you drive well."

" Ah! " said Kitty. " I still like to hear it said. Like the car, too? "

It was one subject at least on which he could be eloquent, doubly so because it was Kitty's car. They talked knowledgeably about sports models all the way to Comerford, and when she pulled up at his own door in the village the return to his ordinary world and the shadow of his familiar routine startled him like a sudden blow. Those few minutes of utter freedom and ease with her were the end of it as well as the beginning. He had to be thankful for a small miracle that wouldn't drop in his lap a second time. He climbed out slowly, chilled by the fall back into time and place, and stood awkwardly by the door on her side of the car, struggling for something to say that shouldn't shame him by letting down the whole experience into the trivial and commonplace.

" Thanks awfully for the lift home."

" Pleasure! " said Kitty, smiling at him. " Thanks for the lift you gave me, too. I can't think of anyone I'd rather shed my blood with."

" Are you sure you feel all right? " was all he found to say.

An end of muslin was protruding from Kitty's sleeve; she pulled it experimentally, and it came away in a twisted string, shedding a scrap of lint on the seat beside her. They both laughed immoderately.

" I feel fine," said Kitty. " Maybe I had blood pressure before, and now I'm cured."

An instant's silence. The soft light from the net-curtained front window lay tenderly on the firm, full curves of her mouth, while her forehead and eyes were in shadow. How soft that mouth was, and yet how decided, with its closely folded lips and deep, resolute corners, how ribald and vulnerable and sad. The core of molten joy in Dominic's heart burned into exquisite anguish, just watching the slow deepening of her valedictory smile.

" Well, thanks—and good-bye! "

" See you at the next blood-letting," said Kitty cheerfully, and drove away with a flutter of her fingers to her brow, something between a wave and a salute, leaving him standing gazing after her and holding his breath until the blood pounded thunderously in his ears, and the pain in his middle was as sharp and radical as toothache.

But she saw him again earlier than she had foretold, and in very different circumstances; and the blood in question on that occasion, which was neither his blood nor hers, had already been let in considerable quantities.

CHAPTER II

THE LATEST of Alfred Armiger's long chain of super-pubs, The Jolly Barmaid, opened its doors for business at the end of that September. It stood on a " B " road, half a mile from Comerford and perhaps a mile and a quarter from Comerbourne; not an advantageous position at first sight, but old Armiger knew what he was doing where making money was concerned, and few people seriously doubted that he would make the place pay.

Those who knew the beer baron best were already wondering if he had any inside information about the long-discussed by-pass, and whether it wouldn't, when it eventually materialised, turn out to be unrolling its profitable asphalt just outside the walls of the new hotel. It was seven months now since he'd bought the place and turned loose on it all the resources of his army of builders, designers and decorators, and everyone came along on the night of the gala opening to have a look at the results.

Detective-Sergeant George Felse of the County C.I.D. wandered in off-duty out of pure curiosity. He had often admired the decrepit stone-mullioned house and regretted its steady mouldering into a picturesque and uneconomic slum. Two old ladies had been living in it then, and like so many ancient sisters they had died within days of each other, leaving the place unoccupied for almost a year before their distant heir decided to sell and cut his losses. There was nothing else to be done with a place of such a size and in such a state; the only question had been whether he would ever find a buyer. But he had; he'd found Alfred Armiger, the smartest man on a bargain in three or four counties.

It still made no sense to George, even when he pushed open the new and resplendent Tudor door and walked into a hall all elaborate panelling and black oak beams, carved settles and copper-coloured glass witchballs. He estimated that ten thousand at least must have been sunk in the restoration, and he couldn't see how Armiger was ever going to get it back, short of shifting the place bodily on to the main road, which was liable to tax even his formidable powers. Even if he could continue to fill it as he'd apparently filled it to-night, which was very doubtful, it would still cost him more to run, with the staff he'd need here, than he'd make out of it.

It was certainly lively enough to-night. In the crowded public bar on the left, lantern-lit and period down to the fire-dogs in the hearth, George recognised most of the Bohemian population of Comerbourne, more especially the young ones. Ragged beards and mohair sweaters gave the place the texture of goats and something of their pungent smell. In the two small lounge-bars on the right the eighteenth century had been allowed a toe-hold, and there were some nice brocade chairs and some comfortable couches, and a fair number of the more sober county posteriors were occupying them. The dining-room seemed to be doing a considerable trade, too, to judge by the numbers of white-coated waiters who were running backwards and forwards for drinks to the saloon bar. Most of them seemed to be strangers to the district, probably newly recruited for this house. He saw only one whom he knew, old Bennie from the White Horse in Comerbourne, no doubt transplanted here for his local knowledge. It would pay to have someone about the place who knew all the celebrities, and all the nuisances, too.

They were a mixed bag in the saloon bar, neither big shots nor Bohemians. The big room had been virtually rebuilt, and Tudorised with a monstrously heavy hand. The ceiling beams were too low and too obtrusive, and hung with far too motley an array of polished copper, much of it shamelessly new. Armiger always knew exactly what he wanted, and if he couldn't get it in period he'd have it manufactured specially, even if it involved some surprising anachronisms. But at least the customers were genuine enough here, farmers, tradesmen, travellers, local cottagers and workmen, and scattered among them the occasional county elder who still preferred this kind of company.

George inched his way patiently to the bar and ordered a pint of mild, and a blonde with a topknot like the Prince of Wales's feathers and long pink finger-nails set the pot in front of him and informed him with a condescending smile that to-night everything was on the house, with Mr. Armiger's compliments. Hence the crowd, he thought, though the evening was yet youngish, and no doubt hundreds more would get wind of the party before closing-time. When drinks were free George stopped at one, indeed if he'd known he would probably have deferred satisfying his curiosity until another night, but he was here now. And the spectacle was undoubtedly interesting. More than half the members of the Borough Council were somewhere in the house, and a good sprinkling of the more widely scattered County Council, too. Armiger crooked his finger and people came running, but how many of them out of any love for him? You wouldn't need the fingers of both hands to count 'em, thought George, one would be enough.

He was carrying his pint pot to the most retired corner he could see when a heavy hand thumped him on the shoulder and a voice resonant and confident as brass, but tuned as truly as brass, too, bellowed in his ear: " Well, well, my boy, is this an honour or a warning? "

Speak of the devil, and his bat-wings rustle behind you.

" Don't worry," said George, turning to grin over his shoulder at the man who had bought him the beer.

" I'm off duty. Thirst brought me in on you. Thanks for this, I wasn't expecting it. Cheers! "

Armiger had a whisky in his other hand; he hoisted it to George and downed it in one quick swig. Not a tall man, hardly medium height, but built like a bull, shoulder-heavy, neckless, with a large head perpetually lowered for the charge. He ran head-down at business, at life, at his enthusiasms, at his rivalries, at everyone who got in his way and everything that acquired a temporary or permanent significance for his pocket or his self-esteem. He was dark, with thinning hair brushed across his sun-tanned scalp, and the short black moustache that bristled from his upper lip quivered with charged energy like antennae. His bluish chin and brick-red cheeks gave him a gaudy brilliance no matter how conservatively he dressed. Maybe he'd consumed a fair quantity of his own wares, or maybe he was merely high on his pride and delight in his new toy, and his ebullient hopes for it. Come to think of it, it was very improbable that he ever got tight on liquor, he'd been in command of it and manipulated his fellow-men by means of it too long to be susceptible to it himself at this late stage. He glittered with excitement and self-satisfaction; the bright, shrewd eyes were dancing.

" Well, how do you like my little place? Have I made a good job of it? "

" Terrific," said George reverently. " Do you think it's really going to pay for transferring the licence out of the town? Looks to me a costly house to run."

" You know me, boy, I never throw money away without being sure it'll come back and bring its relations along. Don't you worry, I'll make it pay."

He slapped George on the back again with a knowing grin, and was off through the crowd head-down, big shoulders swinging, distributing a word here and a hand-shake there, and radiating waves of energy that washed outward through the assembly and vibrated up the panelled walls to clang against the copper overhead. Self-made and made in a big way, Alfred Armiger; many a lesser mortal had been bowled over in that head-down charge to success. Some of the casualties were here to-night; more than one of the looks that followed his triumphal progress through his Tudor halls would have killed if it could.

" He's in high fettle," said a voice in George's ear. " Always is when he's been walking on other people's faces." Barney Wilson of the architect's department slid into the settle beside him, and spread lean elbows on the table; a long, saturnine young man with a dis-illusioned eye. " Don't take too much notice of me," he said with a wry smile, catching George's curious glance, " I'm prejudiced. I once had hopes of taking this place over myself, pulling down the rubbishy part of it and making the rest over into a house for my family. I still grudge it to him. What does he need with another hotel? He has more than he can keep count of already."

" Biggish job for a private man, restoring this place, the state it was in," suggested George, eyeing him thoughtfully.

" Biggish, yes, but I could have done the necessary minimum and moved Nell and the kids in, and taken my own time over the rest. And the way sales trends are running these days, a place this size and in that sort of state was the only kind of place I had a chance of getting. Everybody wants a modern, easy-to-run semi or bungalow, they fetch fantastic prices everywhere, but these bigger properties are going for next to nothing. You can't run 'em without servants, or so everyone supposes, and they cost the earth to maintain. But the maintenance would have just been my job to me, and Nell was raised on a Welsh farm, she knows all about managing a lot of house-room with a minimum of effort. Oh, we thought we were in. I'd even started drawing plans for my conversion, believe it or not, I was that confident. What a hope! The minute I clapped eyes on his man at the auction I knew we'd had it. If it hadn't been for him we could have got the place for the reserve, nobody else wanted it." He gazed glumly into his beer and sighed. " But no, he had to snatch it from under our noses and turn it into this monstrosity. You can expect anything of a man who'd turn The Joyful Woman into The Jolly Barmaid! "

" Is that what it used to be called? " asked George, surprised and impressed. " I never heard that."

" I'm well up in the history of this house, believe me. I read it up from the archives when I thought we were going to live in it. It was a pub, for centuries before it was used as a private house, and that was the sign— The Joyful Woman. Lovely, isn't it? Goes right back to about 1600. And before that it was a private house again, and before that, until the Dissolution, it was a grange of Charnock Priory. But now it's The Jolly Barmaid, and that's that."

" Business is business, I suppose," said George sententiously.

" Business be damned! He's willing to run this place

at a loss rather than let his son have any part of it, that's
the beginning and the end of it."

" Was his son going to have some part of it? "

" He was coming in with me. We put together all we
could raise between us to bid for it. We were going to
convert the barn into a studio for him and Jean, and Nell
and I and the kids were going to have the house. You
know the barn? It's right across the yard there, beyond
where he's laid out the car-park. It's stone, built to last
for ever. It would have made an ideal studio flat. But
somehow his loving father got to know about it, and he
thought a few thousands well spent to spite his son."

The Armiger family quarrel was no news to George, or
indeed to any native of the Comerbourne district. It was
natural enough that Armiger, self-made, ambitious and
bursting with energy as he was, should intend his only
son to follow him in the business, and marry another beer
heiress who would nearly double his empire. Natural
enough also, perhaps, that the boy should react strongly
against his father's plans and his father's personality, and
decline to be a beer baron. The story was that Leslie
wanted to paint, and most probably the rift would have
been inevitable, even if he hadn't clinched his fate by
getting engaged to a humble clerk from the brewery
offices instead of falling in with his father's arrangements
for him. Variations on the theme were many and fantastic from this point on; what was certain was that
Leslie had been pitched out of the house without a penny,
and the girl had either left or been sacked, and they had
married at a registry office as soon as they could. Once
married they had dropped out of sight, their news-value
exhausted. What was news was that Armiger should

still be pursuing them so malevolently that he grudged them even a home.

" There must have been a limit to what he was prepared to throw away in a cause like that," suggested George mildly. " He likes his money, does Armiger."

Wilson shook his head decidedly. " We went to our limit, and he was still as fresh as a daisy. Maybe he does love his money, but he's got plenty of it, and he loves his own way even more."

" Still, Leslie shouldn't have any difficulty in getting credit, with his expectations——"

" He hasn't any expectations. He hasn't got a father. This is final. And believe me, the news went round fast. They know their Armiger. Nobody's going to be willing to lend money to Leslie, don't think it. He has the thousand or so he got from his mother, and what he can earn, that's all. And can you think of anyone round these parts who's going to ally himself willingly with somebody on whom Armiger's declared total war? "

George couldn't. It wasn't just the money and power that would frighten them off, it was the sheer force of that ruthless personality. There are people only heroes would tackle, and heroes are few and far between. " What's young Leslie doing? " asked George. Come to think of it, that made young Leslie a hero; and starting heavily handicapped, too.

" Working as packer and porter and general dog's-body at Malden's, for about eight pounds a week," said Wilson bitterly. " He's never been trained to earn his living, poor devil, and painting isn't going to pay the milkman. And a baby on the way, too, so Jean will have to give up her job soon."

Armiger had erupted into the saloon bar again, sweeping newcomers towards the free drinks, dispensing hospitality in the grand manner. They followed the compulsive passage of the cannon-ball head through the crowd, their eyes guardedly thoughtful. He seemed to have a party with him now, he was busy seating them in a far corner of the big room.

" Parents usually come round in the end, however awkward they may be," said George without too much conviction.

" Parents, yes. Monoliths, no. Leslie never had but one parent, and she died nearly three years ago, or she might have ventured to stick up for him when the crash came. Not that she ever had much influence, of course, poor soul."

Wilson was craning to see past undulating shoulders to the group in the far corner, and the passage of a waiter with a loaded tray had just opened a clear corridor to the spot. Others were equally interested in the spectacle. A woman's voice said dispassionately: " Vulgar little monster! " and a man's voice, less dispassionate, murmured: "So that *was* Kitty's red bus I saw in the car-park. I thought there couldn't be two like it round here."

There were three people with Armiger. The man was everything that Armiger was not, and valuable to him for that very reason; George was familiar with the contrast and all its implications. Into houses where Armiger's bouncing aggression would not have been welcomed Raymond Shelley's tall grey elegance and gentle manners entered without comment; where negotiations required a delicacy of touch which Armiger would have disdained

C

to possess, he employed Shelley's graces to do his work for him. Nominally Shelley was his legal adviser, permanently retained by the firm; actually he was his other face, displayed or concealed according to circumstances. Middle-aged, quiet, kind, not particularly energetic or particularly effective in himself, but he supplied what Armiger needed, and in return Armiger supplied him with what he most needed, which was money. He was also Kitty Norris's trustee, having been for years a close friend of her father. And there was Kitty by his side now, in a full-skirted black dress that made her look even younger than her twenty-two years, with an iridescent scarf round her shoulders and a half of bitter in her hand. So that, thought George, admiring the clear profile pale against the subdued rosy lights, is the girl who gave our Dom a lift home the other night. And all Dom could talk about was the car! How simple life is when you're as young as that!

The third person was a handsome, resigned-looking, quiet, capable woman of forty-five, in a black suit, who was just fitting a cigarette into a short black holder. The movements of her long hands were graceful and strong, so was her body under the severely-tailored cloth. She let the men talk. Intelligent, illusionless eyes swept from face to face without noticeable emotion; only when she looked at Kitty she smiled briefly and meaningly, owning a contact with her which set the men at a slight distance. Women as efficient as Ruth Hamilton and as deeply in the business secrets of their employers frequently entertain a faint contempt for the temples they sustain on their shoulders and the gods they serve.

" His secretary," said a man's voice in an audible

whisper somewhere behind them. " Has been for twenty years. They say she does more than type his letters."

That was no new rumour, either, George had heard it bandied about for at least ten of the twenty years. The only surprising thing about it was to hear it mentioned at all; it had been taken for granted, whether believed or discounted, for so long that there was no point in trying to squeeze a drop of sensation out of it now. Nor was anyone ever likely to know for certain whether it was true or not. The legend had been more or less inevitable, in any case, for Miss Hamilton had virtually run Armiger's household as well as his office ever since his wife's long, dragging illness began, and that was a good many years ago.

Wilson emptied his pint and pushed the tankard away from him. " Jean is quite a girl. But sometimes I wonder how Leslie ever managed to see her in the first place, with Miss Norris around. Not that I think he made any mistake, mind you. Still—look at her! "

George had been thinking much the same thing, though he did not know Jean Armiger. Young men frequently reject even the most dazzling of girls, he reflected, when thrust at them too aggressively by their fathers, and if Armiger's mind was once made up he would certainly tackle this enterprise as he did every other, head-down and bellowing. Still—look at her!

She was the last person at whom he did turn and look when he left the saloon bar at about ten o'clock. She hadn't moved, she'd hardly spoken; she sat nursing the other half, but only playing with it, and though Armiger had vanished on one of his skirmishes and Miss Hamilton seemed to be gathering up her bag and gloves and preparing to leave, Kitty sat still; so still that the sparkles in the glittering scarf were motionless, crumbs of light arrested in mid-air. Then the swing-door closed gently on the grave oval of her face, and George settled the collar of his coat and strolled across the hall towards the chill of the September night.

Old Bennie Blocksidge, a lean, tough little gnome, was crossing the hall with an empty tray, all the copper witch-balls repeating his bald pink dome as he passed beneath them. He stopped to exchange a word with George, jerking his head in the direction of the side door which led out to the courtyard.

" He's in high feather to-night, Mr. Felse. No holding him."

" He " could be no one but Armiger. " I noticed he's vanished," said George. " Why, what's he got up his sleeve now? I should think he'd had triumph enough for one night."

" He's just gone off with a bottle of champagne under his arm, any road up, off to show off his new ballroom to some bloke or other. That's the old barn what was, off across the yard there. Wanted to open it this week, he did, but they've only just finished the decorations. Sets great store by it, and so he ought, it's cost him a packet."

So that was what was to become of young Leslie's studio. George stepped aside to allow free passage to two people who had just followed him out of the saloon bar, and watched Miss Hamilton and Raymond Shelley cross the hall together and go out through the swing-doors and the nail-studded outer portals which stood open on the night; and in a few moments he heard a

car start up in the car-park, and roll out gently on to the
road, and caught a glimpse of Shelley's Austin as it swept
round and headed for Comerbourne.

" Told us not to disturb him, neither," said Bennie,
sniffing. " Says he'll be back when he's good and ready.
Ordered his car for ten, and here it is turned ten, and he
says, 'tell him he can damn' well wait till I'm ready,
if it's midnight.' Clayton's sitting out there in the
Bentley cursing like a trooper, but what's the good?
There's never no doing anything with him. If you
like your job you just go with him, nothing else you can
do."

" And you do like your job, Bennie? "

" Me? " said Bennie with a grin and a shrug. " I'm
used to it, I go with the stream. There's worse bosses
than him, if you just go along with him and don't worry.
These youngsters, they fret too much."

" Well, let's hope he soon drinks his champagne and
lets Clayton take him home."

" It was a big 'un, a magnum. He thinks in magnums."

" He does indeed! " said George. The Jolly Barmaid
was a classic example of Armiger's inflated habits of
mind. " Good night, Bennie! "

" Good night, Mr. Felse."

George walked home into Comerford, and gave his
wife and son a brief account of his evening's entertainment.

" Your girl-friend was there, Dom," he said, glancing
mischievously at Dominic, who was in his homework
corner still bent over a book, though it was a late start
rather than an exaggerated sense of duty that had kept
him at it until this hour. He slapped the Anglepoise lamp

away from him and quickly switched it off, to hide the
fierce blush that surged up into his cheeks, and assuming
his protective colouring with the dexterity of a cornered
animal, said eagerly: " No, was she? Did you see the
car? Isn't it a beauty? "

" I wasn't looking at the car."

"Gosh, can you beat it! No soul!" said Dominic disgustedly, for once removing himself to bed without
having to be driven. He had told his parents about
coming home in the Karmann-Ghia because he was
experienced enough to know that even if they had not
witnessed his arrival themselves, someone among the
neighbours was sure to have done so, and to retail the
information over pegging out the washing or giving the
lawn its last autumn mowing. Better and safer to give
them an edited version himself, and the car made wonderful cover; but if his father was going to spring nasty
little surprises like that sudden dig to-night, Dominic was
going to have to stay in dark corners, or keep his back
turned on his family.

Bunty Felse awoke just after midnight from her first
light doze with a curious question on her mind, and
stroked George into wakefulness with the gentle ruth-
lessness wives employ instead of open brutality.

" George," she said as he grunted a sleepy protest into
her red hair, " do you remember that singer girl at
Weston-super-Mare last summer? The one who dragged
Dom into her act, the way they do? "

" Mmm! " said George, dazed by this seeming
irrelevance. " What about her, for goodness' sake? "

" He noticed *her* all right, didn't he? "

" Couldn't very well miss her," admitted George,

" she was round his neck. How on earth did she get him
up there? Some trick—I don't remember. I know I
blushed for him."

" Yes, *you* did," said Bunty significantly. " *He* didn't.
He bragged about it for days, the little ass. He said she
was a dish."

" That's all those paperbacks he reads."

" No, I think it's pop records. The point is, apparently
this Norris girl really is a dish. But he never said so.
Why? "

" No accounting for tastes," mumbled George. " Maybe he doesn't think she is a dish."

" Why shouldn't he? Everybody else does. *You* do,"
said Bunty, and was drifting off to sleep again, still
worrying over the discrepancy, when the telephone beside
their bed rang.

" Damn and blast! " said George, sitting up in bed
wide awake and reaching for the instrument. " *Now*
what's up? "

The telephone bleated in a quavering voice which at
first he hardly recognised for Bennie Blocksidge's. " Mr.
Felse? " it wailed. " Oh, Mr. Felse, I dunno if I'm doing
right, but I'd sooner it was you, and you're the nearest,
and being as you were here to-night it's you I called. We
got bad trouble here, Mr. Felse. It's the guv'nor, Mr.
Armiger. He never come back. Past closing-time, and
he never come, and eleven, and half past eleven, and
the lights still on in there. And Mr. Calverley got
worried, and one thing and another, even if he did
say not to disturb him, they went to see was he all
right——"

" Make it short," said George, groping for his slippers.

"What's happened? I'm on my way, but what's happened? Make it three words, not three hundred."

"He's dead," said Bennie, making it two. "There in the barn, all by himself, stone dead and blood all over."

CHAPTER III

THE MOMENT of truth had overtaken Armiger in the middle of an expanse of new flooring almost big enough for a bull-ring, and of a colour not so far from that of fine sand. He lay in the full glare of his brand-new lights, sprawled on his face with arms and legs tossed loosely about him, his right cheek flattened against the glossy parquet. If you stooped to look carefully the thick profile in its bold, bright colouring still showed clear and undamaged; but the exposed back of his head was crumpled and indented, welling dark blood that oozed up out of the splintered cavities and spilled sluggishly over into the puddle gathering on the floor, where the crimson of blood and the thin clarity of wine met and intermingled in long, feathery fronds of pink.

All round his head and shoulders blood and champagne had spattered to a distance of two or three feet, but not so lavishly as old Bennie had made out, you could easily approach him between the splashes, at least from the back, from which position, George thought, squatting over the body, this ferocious damage had been done. Any enemy of Alfred Armiger's might well prefer not to face him when he hit out at him at last. The neck of the magnum lay in the pink ferns of the pool, close to the shattered head, and slivers of glass glittered on the bull shoulders; two yards away the rest of the bottle lay on its side, a thin dotted line of blood marking where it had rolled when it broke at last.

Well at least, thought George grimly, we're spared the classic hesitation between accident, suicide and murder; the one most easily associated with Armiger was the one that overtook him, and nobody's ever going to argue about it.

He had called his headquarters in Comerbourne before he left home, called them again after his first check-up on the scene, and turned everyone else out of the ball-room until the van should arrive. He had the place to himself for a quarter of an hour at the most. For Armiger he felt as yet nothing but a sense of shock and incredulity that so much demoniac energy could be so abruptly wiped out of existence. The blob of black in the acres of pallor looked like a squashed fly on a window-pane.

He stood back carefully, avoiding the splashes of blood, and looked round the room. No sense of reality informed this scene, it was a stage set, lavish and vulgar, the curtain rising on a run-of-the-mill thriller. The barn, pretty clearly, had once been the hall of the older house. Its proportions were noble, and its hammer-beam roof had been beautiful until Armiger got at it. His impact had been devastating; the hammer-beams and posts, the principals and curved braces and purlins had all been gilded, and the squares of common rafters between the gold had been painted a glaring glossy white, while from the centre beam depended four spidery modern electric chandeliers. The concentration of reflected light was merciless. All round the upper part of the walls he had built a gallery, with a dais for the band at one end, and a glass and chromium bar at the other, a double staircase curving up to it from the dancing floor with an incongruous Baroque swirl. Beneath the gallery the walls were lined with semi-circular alcoves fitted with seats, in every alcove an arched niche with a white plaster dancer; Empire, this part of it, if it could be said to have a style at all. Small tables nestled in the curves of the balustrade all the way round the gallery. The walls were white and gold and a glitter of mirrors. The palais crowd, thought George, dazed, will love it. Poor Leslie Armiger, he'd never see his beautiful bare, spacious studio home again. He'd never have been able to afford to heat it properly, in any case, it would have been Arctic in winter.

So much for the setting in general. Of notable disarrangements in this vacant and immaculate order there were only two, apart from the body itself. One of the plaster statuettes, from the alcove on the right of the door, lay smashed at the foot of the wall. There was no apparent reason for it, it was a good fifty feet from where Armiger lay, and apart from the broken shards there was no sign of any struggle, no trace even of a passing foot. The other detail struck a curiously ironical note. Someone, almost certainly Armiger himself, had fetched two champagne glasses from the bar and set them out on the small table nearest to the gilded dais at the top of the staircase. Evidently he had had no forewarning, he had still been in high feather, still bent on celebrating; but he had never got as far as opening the magnum.

George paced out thoughtfully the few yards between the sprawling feet in their hand-made shoes, and the foot of the staircase. No marks on the high gloss of the floor.

He eyed the broken magnum; there was not much doubt it was the instrument which had killed Armiger. It was slimed with his blood right to the gold foil on the cork, and no artificial aids were necessary to see clearly the traces of his hair and skin round the rim of the base.

George cast one last look round the glaring white ballroom, and went out to the three men who waited nervously for him in the courtyard.

" Which of you actually found him? "

" Clayton and I went in together," said Calverley.

There was a sort of generic resemblance in all the men Armiger chose as managers for his houses, and it struck George for the first time why; they were all like Armiger. He singled out people of his own physical and mental type, and what could be more logical? This Calverley was youngish, thick-set but athletic, like an ex-rugby-player run very slightly to flesh; moustached, self-confident, tough as fibre-glass. Not at his debonair best just now, understandably; the face made for beaming good-fellowship was strained and greyly pale, and the quick eyes alert for profit and trouble alike were trained on trouble now, and saw it as something more personal than he cared for. He'd even gone to meet trouble half-way, it seemed, by arming himself with a companion. People whose daily lives were spent in Armiger's vicinity soon learned to be careful.

" What time would that be? " They'd know, to the minute; they'd been watching the clock for him over an hour, waiting to get him off the premises and call it a day.

" About four or five minutes after midnight," said Calverley, licking his lips. It was not yet one o'clock.

" We gave him until midnight, that's how I know. We'd been waiting for him ever since closing-time, but he'd said he didn't want to be disturbed, so—well, we waited. But from half past eleven we began to wonder if everything was all right, and we said we'd give him until twelve, and then go in. And we did. When it struck we left the snug at once, and came straight over here."

" All the lights were on like that? You touched nothing? Was the door open or closed? "

" Closed." Clayton fumbled a cigarette out of the pocket of his tight uniform jacket, and struck a match to light it. A lean, wiry, undatable man, probably about thirty-five, would look much the same at sixty; flat sandy hair brushed straight back from a narrow forehead, intelligent, hard eyes that fixed George unblinkingly and didn't mind the light. And his hands were as steady as stone. " I was first in, I handled the door. Yes, the lights were on. We never touched a thing once we'd seen him. We only went near enough to see he was a goner. Then I run back to the house to tell Bennie to call the police, and Mr. Calverley waited by the door."

" Had anyone seen Mr. Armiger since he came over here? " George looked at old Bennie, who was shivering in the background.

" Not that I know of, Mr. Felse. Nobody from the house has been across here. He never showed up after he took the champagne off the ice and walked off with it. I saw him go out of the side door. You know, Mr. Felse, you just come into the hall then yourself."

" I know," said George. " Any idea who this fellow was, the one to whom he wanted to show the ballroom? You didn't see him? "

" No, he wasn't with him when I saw him go out."

" He made quite a point of not wanting to be disturbed? "

" Well—— " Bennie hesitated. " Mr. Armiger was in the habit of laying off very exact, if you know what I mean. It wa'n't nothing out of the way this time."

" Can you remember his exact words? Try. I'm interested in this appointment he had."

" Well, I says to him, ' Mr. Clayton's 'ere with the car.' And he says: 'Then he can damn' well wait until I'm ready, if it's midnight. I'm just going over to show a young pal of mine my ballroom, he'll be right interested, he says, to see what you can do with a place like that, given the money and the enterprise—and I don't want anybody butting in on us,' he says, 'I'll be back when I'm good and ready, not before.' And then he goes."

" But he didn't sound upset or angry about it? " The words might have indicated otherwise in another man, but this was how Armiger habitually dealt with his troops.

" Oh, no, Mr. Felse, he was on top of the world. Well, like he was all the evening, sir, you saw him yourself."

" Odd he didn't mention a name."

" With that much money," said Clayton in his flat, cool voice, " he could afford to be odd."

" He was laughing like a drain," said Bennie. " When he said that about showing off the ballroom he was fair hugging himself."

" Somebody must have seen this other fellow," said George. " We shall want to talk to all the rest of the staff, but I take it all those who don't live on the premises

have gone home long ago." That would be the first
job, once the body was handed over to the surgeon.
" Any of the waiters living in, besides Ben? "

" Two," said Calverley, " and two girls. They're all
up, I thought they might be needed, though I don't
suppose they know anything. My wife's waiting up,
too."

" Good, we'll let her get to bed as soon as we can."
He pricked his ears, catching the expected note of the
cars turning in from the road. " That's them. Go and
switch the corner light on for them, Bennie, will you?
And then I think you three might join the rest of the
household inside."

They withdrew thankfully; he felt the release of a
quivering tension that made their first steps almost as
nervous as leaps. Then the ambulance wagon came
ponderously round into the yard, and Detective-Super-
intendent Duckett's car impatiently shepherding it, and
the machinery of the County C.I.D. flowed into the
case of Alfred Armiger and took possession of it. It was
a mark of the compulsive power of the deceased that the
head of the C.I.D. had climbed out of his bed and come
down in person at one o'clock in the morning. Only the
murder of his own Chief Constable could have caused
him greater consternation. He stood over the body,
hunched in his greatcoat against the chill of the small
hours and the hint of frost in the air, and scowled down
at the deformed head which would never plan mergers
or mischief again.

" This is a hell of a business, George. I tell you, my
boy, when you came on the line and told me, I thought
you'd gone daft or I had."

" I felt much the same," said George. " But there's not much mistake about it, is there? "

Death, like its victim, had never been more positive. Superintendent Duckett viewed the setting, the body and the instrument, and said nothing until the doctor was kneeling over his subject, delicately handling the misshapen skull. Then he asked briefly, growling out of his collar: " How many blows? "

" Several. Can't be sure yet, but six or seven at least. The last few possibly after he was already dead. Somebody meant business." The doctor was youngish, ex-army, tough as teak, and loved his job. He handled Alfred Armiger with fascinated affection; nobody had cherished him like that while he was still alive.

" And I always thought it would be apoplexy," said Duckett, " if it ever happened to him at all. How long's he been dead? "

" Say half past eleven at the latest, might be earlier. Tell you better later on, but you won't be far out if you consider, say, ten-fifteen to eleven-thirty as the operative period. And most of these blows were struck while he was lying right here, and I'd say lying still."

" The first one put him out, in fact, and then whoever it was battered away at him like a lunatic to make sure he never came round again."

" Not like a lunatic, no. Too concentrated and accurate. He was on target every time. But you could call them frenzied blows—they went on long after there was any need."

" So it seems. Didn't stop till the bottle broke. Marvel it didn't break sooner, but glass plays queer tricks. George, on the details of this we sit, but firmly," said

Duckett heavily. " Dead, yes, of head injuries if we have
to go that far, but keep the rest under wraps for the
time being. I'll issue a statement myself, refer the boys
to me. And warn off those fellows who found him. We
don't want this released until I see my way ahead."

" Very good," said George. " I don't think they'll
be wanting to talk about it, they're too close to it for
comfort. Can you make anything of that broken
statuette? "

Duckett approached and stared at it, glumly frowning,
then picked up its nearest neighbour, a couple locked
in a tango death-grip. He grunted with surprise at its
lightness, and turned it upside down to stare with disgust into its thin shell. " Sham as the rest of the set-up."
He put it back in its place and thumped the wall beneath
it experimentally, but light as it was it sat sturdily on
its broad base, and never even rocked. " Wouldn't fall
even if you crashed into the wall beside it, you'd have
to knock the thing off bodily. No trace of anything else
in the wreckage, nothing was thrown. No scratched
paint. And anyhow, if it fell it would fall slightly out-
wards from the foot of the wall, this is right in the angle
of the wall. May be dead irrelevant, may not. Get a
record of it, Loder, while you're about it. Not a hope of
getting any prints off it, surface is too rough, but I
suppose Johnson may as well try." The photographer,
circling Armiger's body, murmured absorbed acquies-
cence, and went on shooting.

" And the champagne glasses," said George.

" I saw them. You know whose prints will be on those,
don't you? Be a miracle if there are any others, unless
it's the maid's who dried them and stacked them away

here when they were unpacked. Still, we'll see. Door, of course, Johnson, all the possible surfaces, baluster of that staircase. And that disgusting mess." He indicated the magnum with a flick of his foot. " His own liquor turned traitor in the end."

" Whoever was holding the neck of that," said George, " must have been pretty well smeared. Blood all over it, right to the cork. His shoes and trousers may be spattered, too, though maybe not so obviously as to attract attention. I figure he was standing this side. He took care not to step in it. Not a trace between these marginal splashes and the door."

" Well," said Duckett, stirring discontentedly, " give me all you've got."

George gave it, including his own accidental contact with Bennie during the evening.

" And those other two? What account have they given of their moves from ten o'clock on? "

" Clayton was sitting in the car out front when I left, which would be several minutes after ten. He says he moved the car into the yard about twenty past, as he saw no sign of Armiger coming back, and he was in the pub until closing-time, had one pint of mild, and that's all. From half past ten until nearly eleven he hung around by the car. Still no boss. Then Calverley asked him to come into his own sitting-room, and he was there with Calverley and Mrs. Calverley all the time from then on. All three vouch for that. Bennie was clearing up in the bars with the other waiters, and keeping an eye open for Armiger returning, so that he could give Clayton the item. Around half past eleven Calverley and Clayton began to think they ought to investigate.

D

They're all used to doing what Armiger says and making
no fuss about it, but they'd also be blamed if anything
came unstuck and they didn't deduce it by telepathy
and come running, so whatever they did was pretty sure
to be wrong, it was only a question of which was wronger,
to butt in on him when he didn't want them or to be
missing when he did. I won't say they were worried
about him, but they were getting worried about their
own positions with relation to him. Come midnight, they
said to each other, better risk it. And they walked in
solidly together and found him like this. The only
period they don't cover for each other is approximately
half past ten to eleven, but I fancy you'll find the indoor
staff can account for Calverley for most of that time, too.
Clayton could have moved around outside without being
observed. I haven't had time to see the others yet, but
they're waiting for me."

"So many more mouths to shut," said Duckett.
"Those three will have spread the load by now."

"You know, I doubt it. Don't forget, this place only
opened to-night, and all the staff except Bennie Blocksidge seem to have been brought into the district from
all over. None of them knows the others yet. And when
this drops on a bunch of strangers it's just as likely to
shut their mouths as open them. After all, somebody
killed him, it might be the bloke sitting next to you."

"Get on to 'em, anyhow. When we finish here and
take him away I'm leaving you holding it, George. Ring
me early, and I'll send you a relief."

"I'll stay with it all day," said George firmly, "if it's
all the same to you." He wanted to be sure of an undis-
turbed night rather than an uneasy and solitary sleep

during the day. " Want me to contact Armiger's solicitors, or will you do that? "

" *Cui bono ?*" said Duckett absently. " I'll get on to them myself. You make what you can of the bunch here, and I'll send Grocott to help you with the day staff when they come in, and the list of people who were in the pub last night."

George left them still busy with cameras and flashes, and went to interview the frightened maids and waiters and the pretty, bleached blonde who was Mrs. Calverley. He got as little from them as he had expected, but deduced from the frozen silence in which he found them that they had justified his forecast by withdrawing into themselves rather than sharing their fears. Laboriously he put together an account of Armiger's movements during the last hour or two of his life. Shortly before ten, according to Mrs. Calverley, one of the waiters, a young man named Turner who lodged in Comerford, had come into the saloon bar and relayed some message to Mr. Armiger, who had excused himself to his friends and followed him out. A couple of minutes later he had returned, gone straight to his party and had a word with them, and then gone out again. It appeared that this must have been when the anonymous young pal arrived to see him, for what he did next was to bounce into the servery by the dining-room, help himself to a magnum of champagne, and make off in the direction of the side door, bumping into Bennie and giving him his orders with regard to Clayton and the car on the way. No one had again seen him alive.

By the time George had done with the last of them it was almost daylight, and the ambulance had long since taken the dead man away, though Johnson was still in possession of the ballroom, indefatigably combing every hospitable surface for prints. George took himself home for a bath and breakfast and a brief and troubled conference with Bunty, and then took himself off again before Dominic should come scurrying downstairs and begin to ask questions.

He called at the house where the waiter lodged, and found him sitting in his room poring over the day's runners, half-dressed and not yet shaven. Turner was a Londoner, pale with the city pallor on which summer has no influence, thin and sharp-eyed and dubious of Comerford already. He wouldn't last long, he'd be off back to town. Meantime he might well be detached about all the people involved in this case, since he knew none of them. He wasn't worried about being visited by the police, only puzzled and intrigued.

Yes, he said, some time before ten, maybe five minutes or so, he couldn't be exact, he'd been passing through the hall and a young man had walked in at the door and buttonholed him, and asked for Mr. Armiger. Didn't give a name, just said ask Mr. Armiger if he can spare a few minutes, say it's important and I won't keep him long. And he'd delivered the message, and thought no more about it, and Mr. Armiger had gone out to his visitor, who had waited in the hall for him. That was the last Turner had seen of either of them, because he'd been back in the dining-room after that. Did he know the young man? He knew nobody here, he'd only just come. Could he describe him? Well, there was nothing special about him. Young fellow about twenty-five or twenty-six. Dark overcoat and a grey suit. No hat.

Tallish but not tall, clean-shaven, brown hair, nothing particular to notice about him. But he'd know him again if he saw him. Or a photograph? Well, probably, but you can't always tell with photographs. He could try. Why, anyhow? What did they want him for? What had happened?

George told him, in the shortest and most startling words he could find, watching the cigarette that dangled from a colourless lip. The ash didn't even fall, but at least Turner's eyes opened fully for the first time, staring at George with a curiosity and excitement in which he could see no trace of fear or even wariness. The unmistakable tint of pleasure was there. Nothing against the boss, you understand, but after all, he'd hardly clapped eyes on him a couple of times, and it isn't every day you get up this close to a murder.

" Go on! " he said, gleaming. " Well, I'll be damned! " And so he might, but not, thought George, for anything to do with Armiger's death. " You reckon it was this fellow I saw who done it? "

" It's merely one line of inquiry," said George dryly. " What I'm trying to do is to fill in all the details of the evening, that's all. What time did you leave the job last night? "

" About twenty to eleven." The thought that he might have to account for himself had not shaken his confidence in the slightest. " I got back here before eleven, the old girl'll tell you the same. What's more, one of the other blokes walked back with me, name of Stokes, you'll find him just up the street here, Mrs. Lewis's." He pushed the paper aside, not even the runners could win back his attention now. " Can you beat it! " he said, and whistled long and softly. " And they think they've got all the life down home! "

George went down the dingy stairs turning over in his mind the irony of this last comment, and betting himself, though without relish because he was on a virtual certainty, that Turner would be in for work before his time that day, if never again.

The news hadn't got out yet, or at least it was not yet public property, for there was no crowd dawdling hopefully about The Jolly Barmaid when George returned to its bright new doors. He put in a call to Duckett, outlined his moves up to date, and the little information he had gleaned from them, and settled down to compile, with Bennie Blocksidge's help, a list of people who had been present at the gala opening on the previous evening. There would be no opening hours to-day, that was out of the question with the emperor dead; and once half past ten arrived and the first customer was brought up short against a closed door and a laconic notice, the secret wouldn't be a secret long.

By the time their list was as complete as their combined memories could make it, Grocott and Price were on the premises and waiting for orders. George unloaded the more promising of the routine calls on to them, and went to telephone Duckett again. By this time even solicitors should be working, and " *Cui bono?* " was still one of the leading questions. Had Armiger really cut off his son completely, or had he only threatened him and left him to stew a while in his own juice? Not in the hope of bringing him to heel, since marriage can't be sloughed off as easily as all that even to satisfy an Armiger; but perhaps merely out of spleen, to punish him for his rebellion with a taste of poverty, before taking him back chastened and amenable.

And plus an ex-clerk wife who would be a constant reminder of a defeat to her unloving father-in-law? No, it wasn't easy to imagine it, after all. George turned a thumb down as he dialled Duckett's number. About a hundred to one Leslie didn't figure in the will, unless in some peculiarly hurtful and humiliating way. And Armiger's wife was some years dead, and he had no other child. So somebody was due for a windfall. He wouldn't disseminate his empire, living or dead. Nor was it really conceivable that he would have neglected to make a revised will, or even postponed it for a period of reflection. He had never reflected, but always charged, and this time would be no exception.

" I talked to old Hartley," said Duckett. " The terms of the will won't be much help to us at first glance, but they're interesting, very interesting. Seems he had his old will destroyed and dictated the terms of a new one the very day he threw his son out. The boy isn't so much as mentioned. Might as well be dead, apparently, to his father."

" I've been betting myself," said George, " that he wouldn't let his pile be divided up. Right? "

" Right. He was a born amasser, he didn't want things to disintegrate after he was gone, either. There's a long list of minor legacies to staff, not one of 'em interesting to us, you wouldn't consider killing a mouse for the amounts he considered a due reward for service. Mind you, he paid good wages living, I don't think it's meanness, it's just this empire-building tendency of his. But the residue of his property, after payment

of these flea-bites, is left to—did I hear you make a
guess? "

" You did not," said George. " My mind's a blank.
He didn't, by any chance, think of the possibility of
grandchildren, and leave it in trust for them? "

" Not a hope. The whole dynasty is cancelled, he's
making a new and surprising start. The name is Katherine
Norris, George. And what, if anything, do you make of
that? "

CHAPTER IV

AND WHAT *did* George make of it? Just plain spite?
A reaction towards Kitty Norris simply because Leslie
had veered off from her and married someone else?
A way of hitting Leslie as hard as possible by so pointedly
deflecting his expectations into the lap of the girl he
wouldn't marry? Not a gesture of consolation to Kitty,
Armiger wasn't quite as clumsy as that, surely, even
when he was angry. Or was there more to it than met
the eye? Plainly this represented a move to amalgamate
Armiger's Ales and Norris's Beers and vest the lot in
Kitty after his death; but might it not be intended
primarily as a move in a game which was to be played
with Armiger very much alive and in shrewd command
of his forces? Kitty would be welcome to the show after
he was dead, provided he ran it while he was alive. His
naming her as his heiress might well be an earnest of
good faith designed to bring off a deal which had so far
eluded him, and the deal could only be the acquisition

of Norris's to add to his own barony here and now. After all, with Leslie out of the picture Armiger was making no sacrifice in declaring his intention of leaving everything he had to Kitty, since he had no other close relatives, and he couldn't take his fortune with him. He had to dispose of it somehow; how better than by buying a present gain with it, while he was here to enjoy it?

Supposing there existed a tentative proposition for a merger, thought George, and Miss Norris's manager was holding off—as he understandably might, for once the two firms were joined there wasn't much doubt who would turn out to be the boss—wouldn't such a disposition for the future strengthen Armiger's hand considerably? What had he to lose, in any case? If he failed to get what he wanted this will was as easily revoked as the previous one. It was at least worth a try. What Armiger wanted he usually got, hence the ferocity and finality of his reaction on the one occasion when he failed in his aims.

George got out his car and sat behind the wheel, and thought out his next move without haste. A rum set-up, when you came to think of it, old Norris making Armiger's right-hand man trustee for his daughter, but the three men had been fairly close friends, and nobody had ever questioned Shelley's integrity; it seemed to work well enough in practice. He didn't know whether the trust was wound up now that the girl was of age, or not. There were a lot of relevant things he didn't know, and on the face of it he had very little right so far to inquire into them. There was only one person he had a perfect right to see about Kitty Norris's movements and affairs, and that was Kitty Norris. She had been at The Jolly

Barmaid last night, she had been with Armiger, he had spoken to her, among others, just before he went off happily to display his latest garish toy; and sooner or later George would have to see her. It might as well be sooner, he decided, and started the car.

Kitty had a flat in Comerbourne, not far from the main shopping centre, but tucked away in a quiet street in the lee of the parish church, and therefore clear of the business traffic which made the town bedlam all through the day. Even there, however, parking was a problem, and George had to take his Morris a good way past the house in order to find a vacant space into which he could insert it. He was lucky, the red Karmann-Ghia was there at the kerb, so Kitty was in. It was nearly noon when she opened the door to him, in a sweater and skirt and a pair of flat, childish sandals, and gazed at him for a moment with nothing in her eyes but patient bewilderment, waiting for him to state his business.

" My name is Felse," said George. " I'm a police officer, Miss Norris." The bewilderment vanished so promptly, she stepped back from the doorway so instantly, that he knew she knew. " You've heard already about Mr. Armiger? "

" Mr. Shelley telephoned me," she said. " Come in, Mr. Felse."

She was looking at him, he noticed, with a certain grave curiosity which he thought was not all for his office but partly for himself, and he was human enough and male enough to be flattered and disarmed by her attention. Some people cannot look directly at you in conversation even when they have nothing to hide; Kitty, he thought, would look straight at you even if she had a guilty secret to hide, because it was the way she was made, and she wouldn't be able to help it.

" I'm making investigations into Mr. Armiger's death, and there are points on which I think you may be able to help me, if you will. I promise not to keep you very long."

" I wasn't doing anything," she said, leading him into a big, pastel-coloured room, lofty and unexpectedly sun-lit, for she lived on the fourth floor, and the buildings opposite were lower, and showed her only their roofs. " Please sit down, Mr. Felse. May I get you a drink? " She turned and looked at him with a small, wry smile. " It sounds like a Raymond Chandler gambit, doesn't it? But I was just going to have a sherry, actually. And after all, you're not a private eye, are you? "

" More of a public one," said George. It wasn't going as he'd expected, but he was content to let it wander; it might arrive somewhere very interesting if he let well alone.

" I hope you like it dry," said Kitty deprecatingly. " It's all I've got." The hand that proffered the glass was not quite steady, he saw, but there was every excuse for that tremor.

" Thanks, I do. I'm afraid it must have been a great shock to you, Miss Norris—Mr. Armiger's death."

" Yes," she said in a low voice, and sat down directly in front of him and looked straight at him, just as he'd for-seen she would have to do. " Mr. Shelley and Miss Hamilton both rang up to tell me," she said. " I didn't want to believe it. You know what I mean. He was so alive. Whether you liked him or not, whether you approved of him or not, there he was, and you couldn't imagine the world without him. And there were things about him that were admirable, you know. He was brave. He came up with nothing, and he took on the world to get where he got. And even when he had so much he wasn't afraid. People often learn to be afraid when they have a lot to lose, but he was never afraid of anything. And he could be generous, too, sometimes. And good fun. If you were a child he wasn't afraid or ashamed to play with you like a child—even though there was really nothing childish left in him. I suppose it was because children made good playthings for him, because we were satisfied with lots of action, and never made difficulties of principle for him like grown-ups do. It was very easy to get on with him then. And very hard afterwards." She looked down into her glass, and for the first time George saw, as Dominic had seen, the essential sadness of her face, and like Dominic was dumbfounded and engaged by it, inextricably caught into the mystery of her loneliness and withdrawal.

She moved, he thought, as though her course was set, and her own volition had nothing to do with it, having aligned itself long ago with some other influence which was disposing of her. Not Armiger's influence, or she could not have talked of him like that. Perhaps not any man's, only a tide of events in which she felt herself to be caught, and which she had to trust because she had no alternative.

"We're all imperfect," said George, trying to speak as simply as she had done, and hoping he didn't sound as sententious to her as he did to himself. "I think he'd like what you've just said of him."

"There was a great deal that I had against him," she

said, choosing her words with scrupulous care. "That's why I want to be fair to him. If there's anything I can tell you, of course I will."

"You were with him last night, at least for part of the evening. Towards ten o'clock, so I understand from one of the waiters, someone asked Mr. Armiger to spare him a few minutes, and Mr. Armiger went out to speak to him. He then came back and spoke to you and the other people at his table, before leaving again. Is that right?"

"I didn't look at the time," she said, "but I expect that's accurate enough. Yes, he came back to us and said would we excuse him for a quarter of an hour or so, he had to see someone, but he'd be right back, and he hoped we'd wait for him."

"That's all he said? He didn't mention a name, or anything like that?"

"No, that's all he said. And he went, and then Ruth said she had to get back, because she was expecting a call from her sister in London about a quarter to eleven, she'd promised she'd be in at that time. That's Miss Hamilton, you know, Mr. Armiger's secretary. And as Mr. Shelley had brought her he had to leave, too, so I was on my own. I thought at first I would wait, and then I didn't, after all. I was tired, I thought I'd have an early night. I think it must have been just after a quarter past ten when I left, but maybe someone else might know. The car gets quite a lot of attention," said Kitty without a trace of irony in her voice or her face, "someone may have seen me drive off."

Someone had; Clayton had, as he chafed and cursed in his boss's Bentley in front of The Jolly Barmaid, five minutes or so before he resigned himself to a long wait

and moved the car into the courtyard. He had watched
her drive out from the car-park and pull out to the right
on her way to Comerbourne; and devoted car-enthusiast
though he was, it was doubtful if he had been looking at
the Karmann-Ghia.

" I see," said George. " So you'd be home by soon
after half past ten, I suppose."

" Oh, before, I expect. It only takes me ten minutes,
even counting putting the car away. Oh, God! " said
Kitty, recollecting herself too late, as usual. " I shouldn't
be telling you that, should I? "

" I'm incapable of working it out without a pencil and
paper," George reassured her, smiling. But even when
she made you laugh there was something about this girl
that had you damn' near crying, and for no good reason.
She wasn't heartbroken about Armiger, she'd stated her
position with reference to him punctiliously; shocked she
might well be, but that wasn't what had got into even
her smile, even the sweet, rueful clowning that came
naturally to her.

" May I ask you some personal questions about your
affairs, Miss Norris? They'll seem to you quite irrelevant,
but I think if you care to answer them you may be
helping me."

" Go ahead," said Kitty. " But if it's business it's
odds on I won't even know the answers."

" I understand that your father left his estate in trust
for you, dying as he did when you were quite a child.
Can you tell me if that trust terminated when you came
of age? "

" I know the answer to that one," she said, mildly
astonished, " and it did. I can do whatever damn-fool

thing I like with my money now, they can only advise
me. Actually it all goes on just the same as before, but
that's the legal position."

" So if a merger was proposed between Armiger's and
Norris's it would be entirely up to you to decide whether
you wanted to go through with it? "

" Yes," she said, so quietly that he knew she had
heard the further question he had not asked. " He did
want that," she said, " you're quite right. He's been
working at it for some time. The people at our place
weren't very keen, but he was like the goat in that silly
song, and I dare say he'd have busted the dam in the
end. But nothing had happened yet, and now it doesn't
arise any more."

" And what did you want to do? "

" I didn't want to do anything. I wanted not to know
about it, I wanted to be somewhere else, and not to have
to think about it at all. I'd have been glad to give it to
him and get rid of it, myself, but after all, people work
there, a lot of people, and it means more to them than it
does to me. One ought not to own something that
matters more to other people. If I knew how to set about
it, or could persuade Ray Shelley to understand what I
wanted, I'd like to give it to *them*."

George had a sense of having been drawn into a tide
which was carrying him helplessly off course, and yet
must inevitably sweep him, in its own erratic channel,
towards the sea of truth. He certainly wasn't navigating.
Neither, perhaps, was she, but she swam as to the manner
born with this whirling current, its overwhelming simplicity and directness her natural element. She meant
every word she said now, there was no doubt of that, and

she expected him to accept it as honestly; and confound
the girl, that was exactly what he was doing.

Trying to get his feet on to solid earth again, he said:
" This idea of uniting the two firms wasn't a new one,
was it? Forgive me if I'm entering on delicate ground,
but the general impression is that Mr. Armiger had the
same end in mind earlier, and meant to achieve it in a
different way, by a direct link between the two families."

" Yes, he wanted Leslie to marry me," she said, so
simply that he felt ashamed of his own verbosity. She
looked up over her empty glass, and he saw deep into
the wide-set eyes that were like the coppery purple velvet
of butterfly wings. You looked down and down into
them, and saw her clearly within the crystal tower of
herself, but so far away from you that there was no hope
of ever reaching her. " But it was his idea, not ours.
You can't make these things for other people. He ought
to have known that. There never was any engagement
between Leslie and me."

A moment of silence, while she looked steadily at him
and her cheeks paled a little. He had one more question
to ask her, but he let it ride until he had risen to take his
leave, and then, turning back as if something relatively
unimportant had occurred to him, he asked mildly:
" Do you happen to know the terms of Mr. Armiger's
will? "

" No," she said quickly, and her head came up with
a sudden wild movement, the velvet eyes enormous and
eager upon his face. He saw hope flame up in her as
though someone had lighted a lamp; a word, and something like joy would kindle in the crystal tower of her
loneliness. What was it she wanted of him? Beyond the

relatively modest needs of her car and her wardrobe and this almost cloistral flat of hers, money seemed to mean very little to her. He had to go through with it now, because he had to know if what he had to tell her was what she wanted to know.

" He's left everything to you," said George.

The light in her was quenched on the instant, but that was the least of it. She stood staring at him open-mouthed, and the colour drained slowly from her face. Her knees gave under her, she reached a hand back to grope for the arm of a chair, and sat down dazedly, her fingers clenched together in her lap.

" Oh, *no!* " said Kitty in a gasping sigh that seemed to contain disappointment and consternation and rage inextricably mingled, and something else, too, a kind of desperation for which no effort of his imagination could account. " Oh, *God*, no! I hoped he'd never really done what he threatened—or if he had done it I hoped he'd taken it back. I mean about *Leslie*! He always swore he hadn't and wouldn't, but then even if he had he wouldn't have been able to admit it, you see. And now —Oh, *damn* him! " she said helplessly. " Why? There was no possible reason, the thing never arose. He knew I didn't need it, he knew I shouldn't want it. *Why?* "

" He had to leave it to someone," said George reasonably, " and he had a free choice what he did with his own, like everyone else. There's no need for you to feel responsible for someone else's deprivation, you know, it was none of your doing."

" No," she said dully, and let the monosyllable hang on the air as though she had meant to add something, and then could find no suitable words for what she wanted

E

to say. She got up again resignedly to see him out,
punctilious in accompanying him to the door, but all the
time with that lost look in her eyes. When the door had
closed between them he made three purposeful paces
away from it towards the stairs, and two long, silent ones
back again. She hadn't moved from the other side of the
door, she was leaning against the wall there, trying to
think, trying to get hold of herself. He heard her say
aloud, helplessly: " Oh, God, oh, God, oh, *God*! " in
childish reproach, as though she was appealing to an
unreasonable deity to see her point of view.

What had he done to her? What *was* it he'd done?
Granted she didn't want the money, granted she thought
it ought to have gone to Leslie, she needn't have received
the news as though it embodied some peculiarly insidious
attack upon her. He couldn't say he hadn't provoked
any interesting reactions, the trouble was he didn't know
how to make sense of them now he'd got them.

He went down the carpeted stairs displeased with himself, almost ashamed, not even trying to make the odd
pieces of jigsaw puzzle fit together, since they were so
few and so random that no two of them touched as yet;
and there, leaning negligently on the Morris, when he
reached it, was Dominic.

He was a little out of breath, having run all the way
to the car while George was coming down the last flight
of stairs; but George was too preoccupied with other
things to notice that. The bright inquisitive smile looked
all right, the " Hallo, Dad! " sounded all right, and
George didn't look closely.

" Hallo! " he said. " What are you doing here? "

It was the third time Dominic had skipped his school

lunch and made do with a snack in the town, in order to
have time to walk slowly up and down Church Lane in
the hope of catching a glimpse of Kitty. The telephone
directory had supplied her address, once she herself had
told him her name. He hadn't yet quite recovered from
the shock of strolling past the open door of the block and
seeing the unmistakable shape of his father slowly
descending the last turn of the stairs; and if it hadn't
been for the sudden inspiration the sight of the car had
given him, he would have been running still.

" I've been on an errand for Chuck," he said, mastering
his breathing with care. Chuck was the least offensive of
the several names by which his house-master was known
to the upper school.

" Here? " said George, divining an improbability even
where he had no reason to feel suspicious.

" To the rector," said Dominic firmly, jerking his
head towards the corner of the churchyard wall.
Blessedly the rector was a governor of the school and
chaplain to its cadet corps. " I saw the car and hung
around on the offchance. As it's getting round to half
past twelve I thought with a lot of luck you might buy
me a lunch."

On reflection George thought he might. Beer barons
may die, but the rest of the world still has to eat. " Get
in," he said resignedly, and took his offspring to a
restaurant not far from the school, so that there should
be no risk of his being late in the afternoon. " What about
Chuck? Can the answer wait? "

" No answer," said Dominic. " That's all right." The
odd thing was that he didn't feel as if he was lying at all;
it was quite simply unthinkable to let the truth be seen

or known, or even guessed at, though there was nothing
guilty or shameful about it. Privacy as an absolute need
was new to him. Ever since starting school at five years
old he'd lied occasionally in order to keep something
exclusively for himself, like most children, but without
ever reasoning about what he was doing, and only very
rarely, because his parents, and particularly his mother,
had always made it easy for him to confide in them
without feeling outraged. This was something different,
something so urgent and vital that he would have died
rather than have it uncovered. And yet he had to do
things which would expose him to the risk of discovery;
he had to, because what was his father doing there in
the block of flats where Kitty lived? What was he doing
there, the morning after old Armiger was killed, the
morning after Kitty'd been with him at The Jolly Barmaid? " Your girl-friend was there——" And now this
visit. They'd have to see everyone who'd been there, of
course, but why Kitty, so soon?

"You're on this murder case, aren't you? " he said,
trying to strike the right note of excited curiosity.
" Mummy told me this morning old Armiger was dead.
What a turn up! I never said anything to the fellows,
naturally, but it leaked in around break, with the milk.
It's all over the town now, they've had half a dozen
people third-degreed by this time, and one or two
arrested."

" They would," said George tranquilly. " The number
of people who can do this job better than I can, it's a
wonder I ever hold it down at all. Who's the favourite? "

A sprat to catch a mackerel was fair enough. Dominic
trailed his bait and hoped for a rise. " That chap Clayton.

I bet you didn't know he was under notice, did you? "

" The devil he is! " said George, wondering if Grocott had collected this bit of information yet, wondering, too, from which school theorist the item of news had come.

" Then you didn't know! Old Armiger's gardener's son is in our form. There was a blazing row three days ago over hours, Clayton pitched right in and said he wouldn't stand for being shoved around all hours of the day and night, and Armiger threw it up at him that he'd done time for larceny once and once for receiving a stolen car, and he was bloody lucky to have a job at all——"

" Language! " said George mechanically, drawing in to the kerb.

" Sorry; quoting. And then he fired him. Did you know he had a record? "

" Yes, we knew. A record ten years old. Not enough to hang him."

" It isn't capital murder," said Dominic.

" I hope you're not going to turn into a lawyer in the home," said George. " I was using a figure of speech."

He locked the car, and ushered his son before him into the dining-room of The Flying Horse. They found a table in a corner, and settled purposefully over the menu. Bad timing, thought Dominic, vexed. I shall have to come right out and ask.

" Are you on to anything yet? " The ardent face, the earnest eyes, these would pass muster with George; it was Dominic himself who suffered, making this enforced use of a travesty of something so real and so important to him. His father *was* wonderful, and he *did* feel a passionate partisan interest in any case his father was handling. But here he was putting on the appropriate face for his own ends, parodying his own adoration, and it caused him an almost physical pain when George grinned affectionately at him, and slapped him down only very gently.

"Just routine, Dom. We've hardly begun, there's a long way to go yet."

"Who was it you had to see in Church Lane? There aren't any suspects there, are there?"

After a moment of consideration George said calmly: "I'd been to see Miss Norris. Just as I told you, pure routine. I'm working my way through a whole list of people who were on the premises last night, that's all."

"And no real leads yet? I don't suppose *she* was able to tell you much, was she?"

"Practically nothing I didn't know already. Get on with your lunch and stop trying to pump me."

And that was all he was going to get, for all his careful manipulations. He tried once or twice more, but he knew it was no good. And maybe there was nothing more to extract, maybe this was literally all. But Dominic wasn't happy. How could he be, with murder passing so close to Kitty that its shadow came between her and the sun?

CHAPTER V

"Yes," said Jean Armiger, "I've heard the news. It's in the noon papers, you know. I've been expecting you."

She was a slender dark girl, with short black hair clustering closely round a bold, shapely head. Her face was short, broad and passionate, and her spirit was high. She couldn't be more than twenty-three or twenty-four. She stood squarely in the middle of her ugly, inconvenient furnished bed-sitting-room on the second floor of Mrs. Harkness's seedy house in a back street on the edge of town, facing George and the full light from the window, and scared of neither. The slight thickening of her body beneath the loose blue smock had robbed her of her quick-silver lightness and precision of movement, but its unmistakable qualities were there in every motion she made with her hands and head. For some reason, perhaps because Kitty had a way of dimming everyone else around her, George hadn't expected anyone as attractive as this, or as vivid. Jean, as Wilson had said, was quite a girl. It wasn't so difficult, after all, to see how Leslie Armiger might contrive to notice her existence, even in Kitty's presence. He had grown up on brotherly terms with Kitty.

" You'll understand, I'm sure, that we have routine inquiries to make. Were you at home last night, Mrs. Armiger? "

She curled a lip at the phrase, and cast one flying glance round the room he had dignified by the name. True, there was a cramped make-shift kitchenette out on the landing to be added to the amenities, and a shed in the garden where Leslie was allowed to keep his easel and canvasses and colours. But—home?

" Yes," she said, forbearing from elaborating on the glance, which had been eloquent enough. " All the evening."

" And your husband? "

" Yes, Leslie was here, too, except for a little while, he

went out about half past nine to post some letters and get a breath of air. He was in the stores packing orders all day yesterday, he needed some fresh air. But it was only for about half an hour."

" So he was home by ten? "

" I think it was a little before. Certainly by ten."

" And he didn't go out again? "

" No. You can check that with him, of course," she said disdainfully. At this very minute, if all had gone according to plan, Grocott would be asking Leslie Armiger the same questions, discreetly in the manager's office, at Malden's, so that the staff, no doubt already agog, shouldn't jump to the conclusion that he was due to be arrested any moment; but Jean didn't know that, of course. George wasn't even sure why he had taken the precaution of arranging these two interviews to take place simultaneously; he had no reason as yet to distrust this young couple rather than any other of the possible suspects, but he had learned to respect his hunches. And if they had no lies to tell he had done them no wrong.

" We shall do that, of course," he said disingenuously. " Tell me, Mrs. Armiger, have you had any contact with your father-in-law since your marriage? Ever seen him or spoken to him? "

" No, never," she said firmly, with a snap which said plainly that that was the way she had wanted it.

" Nor your husband, either? "

" He hasn't seen him. He did write to him once, only once, about a couple of months ago."

" Trying to effect a reconciliation? "

" Asking for help," said Jean, and bit off the consonant viciously and clenched her teeth on silence.

" With your consent? "

" *No!* "

She wasn't going to much trouble to hide her feelings, but she hadn't intended to spit that negative at him so bitterly. She turned her head away for a moment, biting her lip, but she wouldn't take it back or try to soften it now it was out.

" With what result? "

" With no result. He sent a contemptuous answer and refused to do anything for us." She had been grateful for that, it had salved the fierce pride Leslie had involuntarily injured by making the appeal.

" And there's been no further approach? "

" None as far as I know. But I'm sure none."

After some inward debate George told her the terms of Armiger's will; it seemed a justifiable line of inquiry. " Does that come as a surprise to you, Mrs. Armiger? "

" No," she said steadily. " Why should it? He had to leave his money to someone, and he had no relatives left that he hadn't quarrelled with."

" You didn't know of this plan of his to make Miss Norris his heiress? "

" All we knew was that Leslie was written off for good, so it no longer concerned us. His father had made that very plain."

She was turning the narrow wedding ring upon her finger, and George saw that it was loose. The cheek on which the dark hair curled so lustrously was thinner than it should have been, too, perhaps with too much fatigue and worry, carrying the child, running this oppressive, cramped apology for a home and working part-time to eke out the budget; or perhaps with some other strain that gnawed at her from within. Something terrifying and destroying had happened to her when Leslie caved in and wrote to his father, something he might never be able to undo. Thanks to that unrelenting old demon of a father of his, he had another chance to come up to her expectations, if he had it in him; but after that one slip he had to prove it, up to then probably she'd been serenely sure of him. And yet George could see Leslie's point of view, too. He must love his wife very much, or he wouldn't have burned his boats for her sake; and to see her fretting here, to think of his son spending the first months of his life here, was surely enough to bring him to heel, however reluctantly. You could even argue that his attitude was more responsible than hers. What was certain was that by that one well-meant gesture he'd come dangerously near to shaking his marriage to pieces.

"I won't trouble you any longer, Mrs. Armiger. Thank you for your help."

He rose, and she went with him to the door, silent, disdaining to add anything or ask anything. Or hide anything? No, she would do that, if she had to. Maybe he'd soon know whether she was already hiding something.

The stairs were dark and narrow, the house smelled of oilcloth, stale air and furniture polish. Mrs. Harkness's frigid gentility would never stand many visits from the police, even in plain clothes. George had already observed that no telephone wires approached the house, and that there was a telephone box only fifty yards away at the corner of the road. He drove away in the opposite direction, but turning left at the next by-road came round the block and parked under the trees within sight of the bright red cage, and sat watching it for a quarter of an hour, twenty minutes, twenty-five; but Jean Armiger didn't come.

That pleased him; he had liked her, and he wanted her on the level, and though he had suffered some reverses in the past he had never yet learned to be sufficiently wary of the optimism with which he viewed the motives and actions of those people who made an instant good impression upon him. However, he went through the motions of scepticism; he wouldn't commit himself to believing absolutely in her until he'd called Grocott, who was back in the office by now waiting for the telephone to ring.

The call tended to confirm his view that Jean was honest, and her testimony reliable. Young Leslie, called discreetly into conference from his dusty warehouse behind the big shop in Duke Street, had told a story which tallied at all points with his wife's. Instead of going straight back after posting his letters he'd gone for a walk round by the park. He hadn't been away quite half an hour, because he was certain the church clock hadn't struck ten when he let himself into the house again. All very simple and entirely probable, and there had certainly been no contact between husband and wife. Yet the result, perversely, was to make George turn and take another look at his dispositions; and there was still room for doubt. As Jean had so unwisely revealed that she knew, Duckett's bald statement was in the noon papers. Armiger had been found dead last night on the premises of The Jolly Barmaid with severe head injuries; foul play was, by implication, taken for granted, though Duckett had avoided committing himself. That was

enough to alert both the dispossessed son and his fiercely
loyal wife; guilty or innocent, they would know they
must shortly account for their movements on that evening,
guilty or innocent they might find themselves without a
surety except each other, and make haste to co-ordinate
the details of their story before the questions were asked.
There'd been time for a telephone call between the
appearance of the early editions on the streets and
George's two-thirty deadline. Depressed, George searched
for the vindicating detail which should justify him in
throwing this doubt overboard, but he couldn't find one.
Given the intelligence Jean certainly did not lack, there
could have been collusion.

" How did he look?"

" Not too bad. A bit shocked, naturally, but he didn't
pretend they'd been on good terms, or that he was
terribly cut up. Even if he was, actually, he wouldn't
let you see it. A very reserved chap, and a bit on the
defensive, too."

" Scared? "

" I wouldn't say scared. But he's well aware that he's
in a spot to attract, shall we say, the unwelcome attentions
of the nosy public as well as ours. He's no fool, and he
knows his affairs are common property. Knows his
strongest card is that he had nothing to gain by killing
his dad, too."

" Did he take pains to call your attention to the fact? "

" You underestimate him," said Grocott with a short
laugh. " He's giving us credit for seeing that much ourselves. He just seemed to me to be leaning back on it
for reassurance every time the going looked a bit rough."

" How does he get on with the drivers and warehouse-

men? " asked George curiously. Such little communities
don't always take kindly to young men of superior education and manners accidentally dropped among them,
especially if the alien tends to keep himself to himself.

" Surprisingly well. They seem to like him, call him
Les, and let him mull in with them or keep quiet according to how he feels. Main thing is, I think, that there's
nothing phoney about him. He doesn't try to be hail-
fellow-well-met or drop his accent and pick up theirs.
They'd soon freeze him out if he did, but he's a lot too
sensible for that. Or too proud. Either way it's worked
out to his advantage."

The picture that emerged, thought George as he walked
back to his car, was an attractive one, but he had to
beware of being disarmed by that into writing off Leslie
Armiger as innocent. Money is not the only motive for
killing. There on one side was the heiress, already so
wealthy that the money motive was no motive at all, and
on the other side this young couple, very poor indeed
but with nothing whatever to gain by Armiger's death.
He was of some potential value to them still so long as
he remained alive, since in time he might have relented
and taken them into favour after all. Especially with a
grandson or granddaughter on the way. On the other
hand, those who knew him best had said that he was
extremely unlikely to change his attitude—and anyone
can let fly in a rage, even with nothing to gain by it but
the satisfaction of an overwhelming impulse of hatred
and a burning sense of injury.

And there were others who didn't love him, besides his
own son. Clayton, that quiet tough in uniform, had
turned out to be under notice, and Armiger had apparently

tossed his prison record in his teeth when they fell out, and told him he was " bloody lucky to have a job at all." Had that been merely a shaft at random, or meant to suggest to him that Armiger could, if he chose, make it practically impossible for him to find alternative employment anywhere in the Midland counties? People have been killed for reasons a good deal less substantial than that. And there was Barney Wilson, who had been done out of the home on which he'd set his heart, merely to satisfy Armiger's spite against his son. That way the injury might smart even more fiercely than if the blow had been aimed directly at him. And others, too, people who had done business with Armiger to their cost, people who had worked for him.

Sitting there in the car contemplating the width of the field wasn't going to get him anywhere. George hoisted himself out of a momentary drowsiness and drove to the head office of Armiger's Ales, which was housed in a modern concrete and chromium building on a terrace above the cutting of the river. The main brewery was down behind the railway yards, in the smoke and grime of old Comerbourne, but the headquarters staff had broad lawns and flowering trees spread out before their windows, and tennis courts, and a fine new car-park for their, on the whole, fine new cars. Miss Hamilton's Riley was the only old one among them, but of such enormous dignity and lavish length that it added distinction to the whole collection.

She drove it well, too, George had often seen her at the wheel and admired her invariable calm and competence. As often as not there would be two or three callow teen-age boys in the car with her when she was seen

about at week-ends in summer, recruits from the down-
town youth club she helped the probation officer to run.
Maybe love of that beautifully-kept old Riley had been
the saving of one or two potential delinquents within the
past few years.

Raymond Shelley was just crossing the entrance hall
when George appeared. He halted at once, obviously
prepared to turn back.

" Do you want to see me? I was just on my way out,
but if you want me, of course——" He had his brief-
case under his arm and his silver-grey hat in his hand;
the long, clear-featured face looked tired and anxious,
and there was a nervous twitch in his cheek, but his
manners would never fall short of the immaculate, nor
his expression fail of its usual aristocratic benevolence.
" One of your men was in this morning, so I rather
assumed you'd done with us for to-day. I was going out
to see Miss Norris. But I can easily telephone and put
it off for an hour or two."

" Please don't," said George. " I'll talk to Miss Hamilton, if she's free. You go ahead with whatever you were
planning to do."

" You're sure? Naturally if there's anything further I
can do to help I'll be only too pleased. I'll bring you to
Ruth's room, at least." He reached a long, thin hand
to the polished balustrade of the staircase and led the
way. " We have already accounted for ourselves, of
course," he said with a wry smile.

" I happened to see you leave the premises with Miss
Hamilton last night," said George, returning the smile.
" I was in the hall when you left."

" Good, that puts us in a very strong position. I wish

all the other problems were going to be as easily resolved," said Shelley wretchedly. " This is a beastly business, Mr. Felse."

" Murder usually is, Mr. Shelley."

The word pulled him up motionless for a moment. " Is that absolutely certain, that it's murder? The official statement leaves the issue open, and your man this morning was very discreet. Well——" He had resumed his climb, and turned right in the broad panelled corridor on the first floor. " I won't pretend I'm surprised, every-thing pointed that way. At the moment I can't realise what's happened. I can think and understand, but nothing registers yet. It's going to take a long time to get used to his not being here."

" I can appreciate that," said George. " You've worked with him a good many years. Known him, per-haps, better than anyone, you and Miss Hamilton. You're going to miss him."

" Yes." He let the monosyllable stand alone, making no claims for his affection; if anything, he himself sounded a little surprised at the nature of the gap Alfred Armiger had left in his life. He tapped on the secretary's door, and put his head into the room. "A visitor for you, Ruth," he said, and went away and left them together.

She rose from behind her desk, a tall, quiet woman in office black which had suddenly become mourning black, her smooth dark hair parted in the middle and coiled on the back of her neck. Twenty years she'd been in Armiger's service. There wasn't much she didn't know about him and his family, and maybe to understand all is to forgive a good deal, at any rate. Her calm was as admirable as ever, but her face bore the marks of shock and strain. He saw her fine black brows contract at sight of him, in a reflex of distress and reluctance, but she made him welcome none the less, and sat down opposite him in front of her desk, instead of withdrawing behind it, to mark her abdication from her official status.

" I've come to you as the person who can best help me to understand the family set-up here," said George directly. " Anything connected with Mr. Armiger's circle and affairs may be of vital importance now, I know you realise that. As one who is in a position to be fair to both of them, will you tell me the facts about Mr. Armiger's quarrel with his son? "

She set an open box of cigarettes and a heavy glass ash-tray on the edge of the desk midway between them, and allowed herself a moment for thought before she answered. He had time to take in the character of the room, which from long association had taken on her strong, austere colouring. The small black wall-clock with its clear, business-like face and good design was of her choosing, so were the elegant desk fittings. And there were two large framed photographs on the wall, and one smaller one in a stand-up frame on the desk, all of groups of boys from the probation officer's club. Two of the pictures she herself had probably taken at some summer camp; the third showed half a dozen boys grouped round her at a party on the club premises. She looked entirely at home among them, firm and commanding still, but flatteringly handsome and feminine, guaranteed to make any unstable sixteen-year-old feel six inches taller every time she allowed him to light her cigarette or embrace her in a foxtrot. Waste of an able woman, thought George,

F

twenty years running nothing more personal than this office; she ought to have had a couple of promising boys of her own to worry about, instead of picking up the casualties after the kind of wastrel family that has a dozen and neglects the lot.

"There were faults on both sides," she said at last, a little tritely after so much thought. She felt the inadequacy herself, and smiled. "But in reality Mr. Armiger himself was responsible for all of them. I'm sure I needn't tell you that he was a most difficult man, whether as an employer or a parent. It wasn't wilful, he simply could not see another person's point of view. He was honestly convinced that everything and everybody ought to revolve about him and do what he expected of them. As a child Leslie was dreadfully spoiled. He could have anything he wanted provided it didn't cross his father's will, and while he was a child of course there wasn't any real clash. Every accomplishment such as his painting, everything he shone at, every superior possession, only flattered his father. And he was never punished for anything unless it annoyed his father, you see. After Mrs. Armiger began to be an invalid and kept to her room they asked me to move into the house. Mr. Armiger used to spend more of his time at home then, and manage a good deal of his business from there, before this place was completed. I won't say I didn't do my best to straighten up the accounts, the few years I was there, but it was a bit late to take Leslie in hand by then, the damage was done. Well, as soon as Leslie began to grow up and need a life of his own the clashes began, as you can imagine. They fought spasmodically for four or five years before the break came, and all the earlier fights Mr. Armiger naturally won.   All the effective weapons were on his side.   But when the issues at stake became more and more important it didn't work out that way any longer.   Leslie paints very well, he wanted to go in for it seriously, but his father wouldn't let him, he made him come into the offices here.   Everybody had to fall in with *his* plans. Leslie was supposed to marry Kitty Norris and go into beer in an even bigger way than his father.   And before they'd finished fighting out the battle about his painting, he'd met Jean and there was an even bigger row brewing up."

" He got to know her right here, in the offices? "

" At first, yes, and then they began seeing each other casually, not even secretly, and Mr. Armiger was furious. There was a terrible scene, and he ordered Leslie not to see her again, and laid down the law flat about what his future was to be, toe the line or go.   I don't think he meant it then, he was only trying to bring Leslie to heel, but this was the real issue at last, and it broke all the rules.   Leslie should have given in and promised to be a good boy.   Instead, he went right out and took Jean dancing and got himself engaged to her on the spot."

" Not the best possible prospect for a marriage," suggested George, " if he walked into it simply as a way of rebelling against his father."

" It wasn't that," she said, shaking her head decidedly. " All his father had done was make him realise what was at stake, how big it was and how very much he wanted it.   And as soon as he recognised it he grabbed it, like a sensible boy, and hung on to it, too, though the repercussions were hair-raising.   He walked right in here to his father's office the next day, and stood in front of his

desk, and just blurted out like a gunshot that he was
engaged. Maybe that's the only way he could get it out
at all. Mr. Armiger really thought, you know, even then,
that he could simply order him to break it off. When he
found he couldn't I expected a heart attack from pure
shock. Leslie dug his heels in and said no, no, no, and
went on saying no. He couldn't believe it was happening
to him. When he really grasped the idea, he threw them
out, and that time he did mean it. All right, he said, if
you want her, if she's worth that to you, take her. Take
her out of here now, this minute, and neither of you need
ever come back. And Leslie said O.K., that suited him,
and he went right downstairs and did just that, bundled
Jean into her hat and coat and walked out with her.
She stayed in her lodgings and he went to a hotel, and
they spent the time while they waited to get married
looking for somewhere to live. Leslie went to the house
just once more, to collect his things, but as far as I know
he never did see his father again. He couldn't find anything better for them than furnished rooms, and when it
came to getting a job, of course, he'd no qualifications
and no training. The only thing he'd taken seriously at
Oxford was his painting. He had to go to work more
or less as a labourer. I'm afraid he's collected all the
arrears of discipline he missed in one dose," she said
ruefully. " If he comes through it intact you can say he'll
be able to cope with anything else life may throw at
him."

" Would he ever have relented? " asked George.

" Mr. Armiger? No, never. Crossing his will was an
unforgivable blasphemy. I can imagine him as a senile
old man in the nineties, perhaps, turning sentimental and

wanting a reconciliation—but never while he had all his faculties."

" Did anyone try to reason with him at the time? " She smiled at that, rightly interpreting it as meaning in effect: did you?

" Yes, Ray Shelley broke his head against it for weeks, and Kitty did her best, too. She was very upset, she felt almost responsible. As for me, I know a rock when I see one. I didn't say a word. First because I knew it would be no good, and secondly because if by any chance he did have a sneaking wish to undo what he'd done, arguing with him would only have made him more mulish than ever."

" Did you by any chance see the letter Leslie wrote to his father two months ago? " asked George.

The level dark eyes searched his face. " Did Leslie tell you about that? "

" No, his wife did. I haven't yet seen Leslie."

Quietly she said: " Yes, I saw it. It wasn't at all an abject letter, in case you don't know what was in it. Rather stiff-necked, if anything, though of course it was a kind of capitulation to write at all. They'd obviously only just settled for certain that Jean was going to have a baby, and the poor boy was feeling his responsibilities badly, and I suspect feeling very inadequate. He told his father the child was coming, and appealed to him to help them at least to a roof of their own, since he'd robbed them of the one they'd hoped to have. I don't know if you know about that? "

" I know," said George. " Go on."

" Mr. Armiger made a very spiteful reply, acknowledging his son's appeal like a business letter, and repeating

that their relationship was at an end, and Leslie's family
responsibilities were now entirely his own affair. It was
deliberately worded to leave no hope of a reconciliation,
ever. He pretended he'd had no idea Leslie ever wanted
the barn, but then he ended by saying that since he was
interested in the place he was sending him a souvenir of
its purchase, and it was the last present they need ever
expect from him. As a would-be painter, he said, Leslie
might find it an appropriate gift. It was the old sign,
from the earlier days when the house used to be an
inn."

"The Joyful Woman," said George.

"Was that its name? I didn't know, but that accounts
for it. I saw it when Mr. Armiger brought it in for the
people downstairs to pack. It was a rather crude painting
of a woman laughing, a half-length. They found it in
the attics when the builders moved in on the house. It
was on a thick wooden panel, very dirty and damaged,
the usual kind of daub. One of the firm's cars took it
and dumped it at Leslie's landlady's house the day after
the letter was written."

Jean had said nothing about the gift, only about the
curt and final letter. But there might be nothing particular in that omission, since the gift was merely meant
to be insulting and to underline what the letter had to
say. This is all you need expect from me, living or dead,
and this is all you'll ever own of The Joyful Woman.
Make the best of it!

"Leslie didn't write or telephone again?"

"Never again as far as I know. But I should know if
he had."

And all day, thought George, I've been writing off a

certain possibility because I felt so sure that, firstly, if Leslie did go and ask for an interview Armiger wouldn't grant it, and secondly, if by any chance he did choose to see him it certainly wouldn't be to greet him with back-slapping heartiness, champagne and a preview of his appalling ballroom. But maybe, after all, that was exactly the way he might receive him, rubbing salt into the wounds, goading him with the shoddy miracles money could perform. On a night when triumph and success were in the air maybe this was much more his mark, not direct anger but this oblique and barbaric cruelty. " He'll be interested to see what can be done with a place like that, given plenty of money and enter-prise——" " He was fair hugging himself."

" Miss Hamilton, have you got a reasonably recent photograph of Leslie? "

She gave him a long, thoughtful look, as though she was considering whether he could need such a thing for any good purpose, and whether, in any case, denial could serve to do anything but delay the inevitable. Then she got up without a word, and went behind the desk, and brought out from one of the drawers a half-plate portrait, which she held out to him with a slight, grim smile shadowing the corners of her mouth. It had at some time been framed, for George saw how the light had darkened the pale ground slightly, and left untouched a half-inch border round the edges. More recently it had been torn across into two ragged pieces, and then care-fully mended again with gum and Sellotape. The torn edges had been matched as tenderly as possible, but the slash still made a savage scar across the young, alert, fastidious face.

George looked from the photograph to the woman behind the desk.

"Yes," she said. "I fished it out of his wastepaper basket and mended it and kept it. I don't quite know why. Leslie has never been particularly close to me, but I did see him grow up, and I didn't like to see the last traces of him just wiped out, like that. That may help you to understand what had happened between them." She added: "It's two years old, but it's the only one he happened to have here in the office. I'm pretty sure it wouldn't be any use looking for any of those he had at home."

George could imagine it. A much-photographed boy, too, most likely. He saw bonfires of cherubic babies, big-eyed toddlers, serious schoolboys, earnest athletes, self-conscious young men-about-town, Armiger's furnace fed for hours, like a Moloch, on images of his son.

"Thank you, Miss Hamilton. I'll see that you have it back," was all he said.

The face was still before his eyes as he went out to his car. Leslie Armiger was not visibly his father's son. Taller, with long, fine bones and not much flesh. Brown hair lighter than his father's curled pleasantly above a large forehead, and the eyes were straight and bright, with that slight wary wildness of young and high-mettled creatures. The same wonder and insecurity was in the long curves of his mouth, not so much irresolute as hyper-sensitive. No match for his father, you'd say on sight, if it came to a head-on clash either of wills or heads. But in spite of the ceremonial destruction of his image, young Leslie was still alive; the bull had pawed the ground and charged for the last time.

It was just four o'clock, and Dominic was walking up Hill Street on his way to the bus stop. Since he had to pass the main police station it was his habit to call in, on days when he hadn't biked to school, on the off-chance that George might be there with the car, and ready to go off duty; and sometimes he was lucky. To-day George picked him up at the corner and took him to the office with him while he filed his latest report; then they drove home together.

"One little call to make," said George, "and then we'll head for our tea. You won't mind waiting a minute for me? It won't take long."

"And then you've finished for the day?" Dominic's anxious eyes were searching his face surreptitiously, and trying to read the mind behind it. He would have liked to ask right out if anything positive had turned up, if Kitty was safely and irrevocably out of the affair; but how could he? They had had a family code for years in connection with George's work, governed by rules none the less sacred for being unformulated; and once already to-day he'd been warned off from infringing them. One did not ask. One was allowed to listen if information was volunteered, and to suggest if participation was invited, but never to ask; and a silence as inviolable as the confessional sealed in all that was said within the framework of a case. He contained the ache within him, and waited faithfully, but it hurt.

"Don't know yet, Dom, it'll depend on what I get here." He was turning into the empty parking-ground of The Jolly Barmaid. "If my man's here I shan't be five minutes, whatever the outcome may be."

But it did not take even five minutes, for Turner was

sitting in the curtained public bar, cigarette on lolling lip, devouring the racing results, and it needed only one good look at Leslie Armiger's photograph to satisfy him.

" That's him. That's the young bloke who come asking for Mr. Armiger. Stood on the doorstep to wait for him, but I saw him in a good light when he first come in. Different clothes, of course, but that's him all right, I'd know him anywhere."

" You'd swear to him? "

" Any time you like, mate. About five to ten he walked in, and Mr. Armiger come out to him, and that's the last I saw of 'em."

" Thank you," said George, " that's all I wanted to know."

He pocketed the photograph and went back to the car thinking grimly: Home by ten, were you, my lad! So you've solved the problem I've always wanted to get straightened out, how to be in two places at once. Now I wonder if you'll be willing to tell me how it's done?

CHAPTER VI

LESLIE ARMIGER was not a happy liar. There was almost as much relief as fright in his eyes as he looked from the photograph to George's face and back again. Jean came to his side, and he put his arm round her for a moment, with a curiously tentative gesture of protection, as though he had wanted to clasp her warmly, and either because of George's presence or his own predicament or her aloofness he could not.

" The best thing you can do now," said George sternly,
" is tell me everything. You see what happens when
you don't. You, too, Mrs. Armiger. Wouldn't it
have looked infinitely better if you'd told the truth in
the first place, rather than leave it to come out this
way? "

" Now wait a minute! " Leslie's sensitive nostrils were
quivering with nervous tension. " Jean had nothing to
do with this. She hasn't got a time sense, never did have.
She merely made one of her vague but confident guesses,
saying I was in by ten."

" And picked on a time and a few details that matched
your story word for word? That tale was compounded
beforehand, Mr. Armiger, and you know it as well as
I do."

" No, that isn't true. Jean simply made a mistake——"

" So you backed up her statement rather than embar-
rass her? Now, now, you can do better than that. Have
you forgotten that your statement and hers were made at
the very same moment, something like a mile apart?
My boy, you're positively inviting me to throw the book
at you."

" Oh, Christ! " said Leslie helplessly, dropping into a
chair. " I'm no good at this! "

" None at all, I'm glad you realise it. Now suppose
we just sit round the table like sensible people, and you
tell me the truth."

Jean had drawn back from them, hesitating for a
moment. She said quietly: " I'll make some coffee,"
and slipped out to the congested kitchenette on the landing; but George noticed that she left the door open.
Whatever her private dissatisfactions with her husband,

she would be back at his side instantly if the law showed
signs of getting tough with him.

"Now then, let's have it straight this time. What time
did you really come home?"

"It must have been about ten to eleven," said Leslie
sullenly. "I did go to that pub of his, and I did ask to
see him, but I give you my word Jean didn't know anything about it. All she did was get worried because of the
times, because there was three-quarters of an hour or
so unaccounted for. But I never told her where I'd
been."

George had no difficulty in believing that; it was
implied in every glance they cast at each other, every
hesitant movement they made towards each other, so
wincingly gentle and constrained. It was clear that they
knew how far apart they stood, and were frightened by
the gap that had opened between them. That fiery girl
now so silent and attentive outside the half-open door was
suffering agonies of doubt of her bargain. Had he, after
all, the guts to stand up to life? Was that disastrous appeal
to his father only a momentary lapse, or was it a symptom
of inherent weakness? George thought they had fought
some bitter battles, and frightened and hurt each other
badly; but now he was the enemy, and they stood
together in a solid alliance against him. He might very
well be doing them a favour just by being there.

"Then you'd better tell her now, hadn't you?" he
said firmly. "It'll come better from you than from anyone else. And she may be a good deal happier about
knowing than about not knowing."

"I suppose so." But he didn't sound convinced yet,
he was too puzzled and wretched to know which way to

turn. He swallowed the humiliation of being lectured, and began to talk.

"All right, I went out to post my letters, and then I kept going, and went straight to the pub and asked for my father. I didn't want to go in, I just stuck at the door until he came out to me. And I didn't happen to see anybody I knew—the waiter was a stranger—that's why, when this thing blew up this morning, I was fool enough to think I could just keep quiet about being there. But you mustn't blame Jean for trying to help me out."

"We won't bring your wife into it. Why did you go and ask for this interview? To make another appeal to him?"

"No," said Leslie grimly, "not again. I was through with asking him for anything. No, I went to get back from him something of mine that he'd taken—or if I couldn't get it back, at least to tell him what I thought of him." He was launched now, he would run. George sat back and listened without comment to the story of the first appeal, and the answer it had brought, the cruel and gloating gift of the old inn sign as a memento of Leslie's defeat and his father's victory. He gave no sign that he was hearing it for the second time that day.

"Well, then just two weeks ago something queer happened. He suddenly changed his mind. One evening after I got home old Ray Shelley turned up here positively shiny with good news. I knew he'd done his best for me at the time of the bust-up, he was always a kind soul, and he was as pleased as Punch with the message he had for me. He said my father'd thought better of what he'd done, come to the conclusion that though he'd still

finished with me it had been a dirty low-down trick to
needle me with that present of his. Said he now saw it
was a mean-spirited joke, and he withdrew it. But being
my father he couldn't come and admit it himself, he'd
given Shelley the job. He was to take back the sign, and
he'd brought me five hundred pounds in cash in its place,
as conscience money—not forgetting to repeat that this
was positively the last sub. we could look for. He said
he couldn't leave me to starve or sink into debt for want
of that much ready money, but from now on I'd have to
fend for myself."

Jean had brought in the coffee and dispensed it silently,
and because her husband in his absorption let it stand
untasted at his elbow she came behind him and touched
him very lightly on the arm to call his attention to it.
She could not have ventured contact with a complete
stranger more gingerly. He started and quivered at the
touch, and looked up at her with a flash of wary brown
eyes, at once hopeful and wretched. The shocks that
passed between them made the whole cluttered, badly lit
room vibrate like a bow-string.

"Go on," said George peremptorily. "What did you
say to his offer?"

"I refused it." He was taking heart now from the
very impetus of his own feelings, remembering his
injuries and recovering his anger. The guarded voice
warmed; there was even a note of Armiger's well-tuned
brazen music in it when he was roused. "I'd had it, I
was done with the whole affair, it could stay as it was.
It's a pity it was poor old Shelley who got the blast, after
all he'd tried to do for me, but there it was. So the old
boy went off very upset. He even tried to get me to accept

a loan out of his own pocket, but even if I'd have taken
it in any case, and I wouldn't, I couldn't from him.
I know him, even with all he makes he lives right up to
his income, sometimes over it. We tried to soothe him
down as well as we could, because, damn it, it wasn't
his fault. He said he hoped we wouldn't cut ourselves
off from him completely, couldn't he come down and
see us sometimes, he'd like to be sure we were all right,
and of course we said come any time, if he could bear
the place we'd be glad to see him. And we gave him all
the gen, because the old bag downstairs objects to having
to answer the door for our visitors, though she never
misses taking a good look at them, in case there's anything
fat in it to shoot over the garden fence to the other harpy
next door. She leaves the front door on the latch while
she's in, so that anyone who comes to see us can walk
right up. And we even told him where to find the key
of our room, in case he ever called a bit too early and
wanted to wait for us. I know," said Leslie, catching
George's faintly puzzled and inquiring eye. "You're
wondering if all this detail is really relevant. It's relevant,
all right! The day before yesterday, while we were both
out in the afternoon, somebody got into this room and
pinched my father's letter."

"The *letter*? The one accompanying the gift of the
sign? But why should anybody want to steal that?"

"If you can think of more than one explanation you're
a better man than I am. There *is* only one. Because my
father really wanted that sign back. That was why he
sent Shelley on his errand. He wanted it, and it was
even worth five hundred pounds to him to get it. And
when that attempt flopped his next move was to remove

the only proof that he ever gave it to me. Without that, its ownership would be a matter of his word against mine, and where do you think I'd be then? "

" That's not quite true, you know," said George reasonably. " Miss Hamilton typed that letter, she knows exactly what was in it, and has already told me all the facts about that gift. There would also be the testimony of the people who packed and delivered it to you. So it wouldn't have been a matter of your unsupported word."

Leslie laughed, with some bitterness but even more honest amusement. " Really, you don't know the kind of set-up he had with his staff, do you? Hammie may have been beautifully open with you now he's dead, but if he'd been still alive she'd have done and said whatever he wanted, she always did, it's the cardinal point in her terms of reference. She wouldn't have remembered anything that could make things awkward for him, don't you think it, and neither would the lads in the office, or the bloke who drove the van. Oh, no, *that* wouldn't complicate things for him. The letter was the only evidence in black and white. My father wanted that thing back, he was prepared to give five hundred to get it, and when that failed he started to clear the ground so he could claim the thing anyhow, even though I hadn't seen fit to part with it."

" Are you suggesting that Mr. Shelley was a party to this trick? "

" *No*! At least, not consciously. God, I don't know! I've never known how far he was aware of the uses Dad made of him. It went on all the time, whenever he needed a nice, benevolent front that would soften up the opposition. You must have seen them in action. *Can* you be totally unaware when you're being used as a cover man? For years and years? Maybe he shuts his eyes to it and hopes for the best, maybe he really doesn't see. Naturally he didn't simply go back and say: Easy, old boy, you just walk in, the door's on the latch, and they keep their key on top of the cupboard on the landing. Nothing like that. But he told him, all the same, consciously or unconsciously, because there's no other way he could have known. And he came, he or somebody else for him. *Somebody'd* been here, and the letter was gone."

" You didn't ask Mrs. Harkness if she'd seen the caller? She must have been in, or the street door would have been fastened."

" She was in, and I bet she knows who it was who called, but what's the good of asking her? She'd simply deny any interest in my visitors, and get on her high horse and turn nasty, because she knows damn' well I know she's always got her kitchen door ajar snooping and listening. I couldn't even begin to ask her."

" Yes, I see it would be easier for us to do it. Though probably no more effective. And then another question arises. I notice you haven't mentioned the sign itself. If he was removing the evidence of the gift, why not remove the gift at the same time? "

" He couldn't, it wasn't here. I got sort of interested in the thing. It's been overpainted so many times you can't tell what may not be underneath, and there's something about the shapes and proportions of the painting itself that isn't nineteenth century by a long chalk. It isn't that I think it's worth anything, not in money, but I should like to know something about its history, and see if there's something more interesting underneath the top layers. So I talked to Barney Wilson about it. He said how about that dealer who has the gallery in Abbey Place, the other side of town, he thought he'd be willing to have a look at the thing for us. So I got him to take the sign over to him for an opinion, and it's still with him now."

" When did you send it to him? Before the letter was abstracted, obviously. Was it also before Mr. Shelley came to see you? "

Leslie visibly counted days; colour had come back into his cheeks and something like excitement into his eyes. " Yes, by God, it was! Shelley was here on Thursday evening. Barney took the sign away with him in the van on Monday morning, three days before."

" Suggestive, you think? "

" Don't you? I'd had the thing six weeks, and Dad had shown no further interest in it. Then it's deposited with this dealer, and three days later Dad opens a campaign to recover it. Wouldn't you say there's a connection? "

" You think he got a direct tip from the dealer that it might be of value after all? "

" Well, I don't know that it need mean that, actually. It might be enough if it got to my father's ears that I'd asked for an opinion on it. If he thought he'd accidentally given me something valuable and turned the joke on himself it would just about kill him." He shied at his own choice of words, the sharp realisation of his position coming back upon him with a painful jolt.

" All right, leave it at that," said George equably. " The letter vanished. What then? "

" Well, then, last night, as I said, I suddenly set off to

tackle him about it, without saying a word to Jean.
I didn't want to go home to see him, and last night I
knew exactly where he'd be, and I suppose I was in the
mood to pick a fight, too, smouldering mad. Not that
mad, though," he amended with a wry grin, meeting
George's measuring eye. " I never touched him. I suppose I got there a bit before ten, and asked this waiter of
yours to ask him if he could spare a minute. I didn't
give a name because I thought if I did he wouldn't come,
but most likely he would have, anyhow, the way it turned
out. He came out bouncing and laughing when he saw
me, and banged me on the back as though I was the one
thing wanted to make his evening complete. He said
he'd just leave his friends a message and then he'd be
with me, and then he shoved me out of the side door and
said go on over and take a look at the barn now, see if
you recognise the old dump. Walk in, he said, the door's
unlocked, I was going over there in any case a bit later on.

" And I went on over, just as he said. I could guess
what he wanted with me over there, but I wanted
privacy for what I'd got to say to him, so it suited me, too.
You've seen the place, I take it, you know what he's
done to it. In a few minutes he came bounding in,
bursting with high spirits, with a magnum of champagne
under his arm. 'Well, what d'you think of your ideal
home now, boy,' he says. 'Doesn't it shake you?' But I
hadn't come to amuse him, and it was all rather water
off a duck's back. I let fly with what I had to say, told
him what I thought of his dirty tricks, and accused him
of stealing the letter. He just laughed in my face and
denied everything. ' You're crazy,' he said, ' why should I
want to steal my own letter?' I suppose I hadn't expected

any sort of satisfaction except just in getting the load off my own chest, so I unloaded. I told him what sort of lying, cheating devil he was, and swore I'd fight him to the last ditch, over the sign, over my career, over everything."

"And half an hour or so later he was dead," said George deliberately.

"I know, but I didn't touch him."

Jean moved her hand silently upon the table until it touched Leslie's hand; that was all, but the spark that passed between them quivered through every mass within the room.

"I didn't touch him," said Leslie again, with a softer and easier intonation. "He was running about the gallery there, getting out champagne glasses from the bar, and I said was he celebrating the final break, because this was it. And he said, 'this isn't for you, boy, I'm expecting better company. So I left.' I walked out and left him there fit and well. It couldn't have been half past ten, because only one or two cars had moved out, and there was no sign of turning-out time. I walked home, and I walked fast because I was still burning. By about ten to eleven I was home."

"Did you see anyone around when you left? Or on the way? Just to confirm your times?"

"Not that I noticed," said Leslie, paling. "I wasn't thinking about needing confirmation, or I'd have done something about it. I was inclined to fume off by myself, rather, the mood I was in."

"I can confirm the time when he got in," said Jean firmly, and the hand that had moved to touch her husband's now closed over it and gripped it tightly. "There's a chiming clock at the church just along the road. I heard it strike the three-quarter hour just two or three minutes before Leslie came in."

"Yes, well, there may be others who noticed him somewhere along the way, you know. We'll try to find them." Even so, Armiger could just as well have been left behind in his ballroom dead as living. According to the surgeon he might have died as early as ten-fifteen. "Mrs. Harkness didn't have to let you in, I suppose? You have your own key?"

"Yes. And she probably wouldn't hear me come in. She goes to bed early, and she sleeps at the back of the house." He was going to the opposite extreme now, producing all the possible unfavourable circumstances himself before they could be unearthed by others.

"Don't labour it," said George with a slight smile, getting up from his chair. "Others are having to account for themselves, too, you know. If you've done nothing wrong then you've nothing to hide and nothing to worry about. And if you'll let me advise you—hide nothing. And then stop worrying." He buttoned his coat, stifling a yawn. The coffee had helped, but what he needed now was sleep. "Meantime—you'll be here at our disposal, won't you?"

"I'll be here," said Leslie, slightly huskily because his throat was dry with returning fright.

The last George saw of them, as he looked back from the top of the stairs, was the two pale, unwavering faces, side by side and almost on a level, with wide, wary eyes staring after him; and the two hands gripped together between their bodies, clinging to each other as though they defied the world to tear them apart.

CHAPTER VII

"I'm inclined to believe him," said George, frowning over the litter of scribbled notes tucked under his coffee cup. "When his father told him to go across to the barn, he says the old man said: 'Walk in, the door's unlocked, I was going over there in any case a bit later on.' And then about the champagne, which put me off in the first place: 'This isn't for you, boy, I'm expecting better company.' That strikes me as sounding true, and fitting in with the facts. If the champagne had been all part of heaving his triumph in Leslie's face he'd had time to open it. But it wasn't opened. And the alternative seems much more probable. He was expecting someone, he was preparing a celebration, but it wasn't for Leslie. Leslie was just a pleasant interlude of devilment thrown in by sheer luck, to pass the time until the other person arrived. The real business of Armiger's evening was still to come. And if I'm right, then it was because of this other person, not because of Leslie, that he didn't want to be disturbed. Why should he care who heard him tormenting his son? He'd have enjoyed it all the better with an audience."

"Didn't you say Miss Norris told you he said he'd be only a quarter of an hour or so?" asked Bunty. "That makes his time schedule rather tight, doesn't it?"

"It does seem so. And as a matter of fact only she used that phrase. According to Miss Hamilton and Shelley he merely said he'd be back, and he hoped they'd

102

be able to wait.   Maybe her recollection isn't quite
accurate, maybe he was speaking rather loosely.   And
important meetings can take place in a quarter of an
hour, of course."

"Supposing Leslie did get back by ten to eleven,
would he have had time to be the murderer? He has no
car, there's no bus just then, it must be true that he
walked, and even walking fast it would take him fully
twenty minutes. So he must have left by half past ten
at latest."

When she was admitted into conference in this way
she used a level, quiet voice, careful to break no thread
of George's reasoning. Sometimes she put things into his
head, sometimes she showed him things that were already
there.

"Yes," said George, "there was time, though certainly
none to spare. The surgeon's report confirms that death
may have taken place any time between ten and eleven-
thirty."

"And it doesn't take long, of course," admitted
Bunty, "to bash somebody over the head with a bottle
and run for it."

"Well, it's not quite so simple as that. It wasn't just
one blow that killed him. Seems there were at least nine
blows struck, all at the back and left side of the head.
There are several fractures, and some splintering of the
bone. Then there's also a large abrasion on his right
temple and cheek, apparently from his fall when he was
first struck. That wouldn't have killed him, in any case,
he'd have been stunned but nothing worse. But at least
four of the other blows could have been fatal. It may
not take long to batter a man's head to pieces that way,

but it takes longer than just hitting out once and running. It must have been quick work if Leslie did it."

" Very messy work, too," said Bunty.

" Yes, we're not forgetting that. And Johnson's report isn't much help, except in establishing that somebody must have had some badly soiled gloves to dispose of after the event. No prints on bottle or glasses except Armiger's own, nothing to be got from that broken statuette, and all the prints lying at random about the room turn out to be Armiger's or else belonging to some of the decorators and electricians who were working on the place. Only one or two haven't yet been matched up. Clayton's prints are on the door handle, but nowhere else, and there are also some on the door we have to check up now with Leslie's." He shuffled the sheets of notes together, and reached for the toast. " Well, if the chief agrees I'm going to follow up this odd business of the inn sign. May as well see if there's anything to it."

Dominic was standing in the doorway of the room with his school-bag under his arm. He had been there for some time, waiting to be noticed, and unwilling to break into his father's concentration until he could catch his eye. The morning was bright, and the normality of everything wonderfully reassuring, and they had said not a word that could tend to cast a shadow on Kitty. Not that other people were expendable, of course, but he couldn't help being glad when Kitty slipped clean out of the discussion.

" Have I to bike to-day, Dad, or are you going in this morning? " he asked, seizing his opportunity.

" Yes, I'm going, I'll take you. Give me five minutes and I'm ready."

Dominic had hoped that he would be communicative on the ride, but he wasn't, he remained preoccupied, and nothing was said between them until they parted at the corner by the police station. It was still an effort not to ask questions, but since the inquiries seemed to be veering well away from Kitty it did not hurt him quite so much to contain his curiosity.

" Can I ride back with you this afternoon? I shall be a bit late myself, because it's rugger practice. Say quarter to five? "

" I hope to be free by then," agreed George. " You can call in and see, anyhow. I shall be here."

He watched his son shoulder his bag and stride away along the street. He was running to length these days, not so far off a man's height now, but still very slender. He was getting control of his inches, too, and learning to manage his hands and feet and all the other unco-ordinated parts of him. Give him a year, and he'd be downright elegant in movement. Odd how they do their growing-up by sudden leaps, so that however constantly and affectionately you watch them they still manage to transmute themselves while your back's turned, and con-front you every third month or so with another daunting stranger. Freckled and chestnut-haired and no beauty, apart, perhaps, from those eyes of his; but like his mother, whom he so engagingly resembled, he didn't need beauty. George found them both formidable enough as they were.

He went in to his conference with Superintendent Duckett assembling in his mind the details of his evening interview with Jean and Leslie Armiger. Duckett found them no less interesting than George had done, and en-

dorsed his proposition to follow up the curious affair of
the inn sign. The dreary, dogged search for blood-stained
clothing, the exhaustive interrogation of anyone and
everyone who had been present at the opening night of
The Jolly Barmaid, would go on all day and probably
for a good many more days into the bargain; but if
a promising side-track could shorten the journey, so much
the better for them all.

George telephoned County Buildings before he set out,
to check with Wilson.

" That's right," said Wilson amiably, " I offered to
pick up the thing for Leslie and take it over to Cranmer's
for him. Oh, yes, I think the chap's all right, knows his
stuff, and all that. He's had one or two good things in
since I've known the place. I don't know a thing about
this panel of Leslie's, no. I've seen it, of course, but
there's nothing exceptional about it on sight—except,
perhaps, the quality and solidity of the panel it's painted
on. I'd like to see the worm who could get his teeth in
that. No, I can't say I know Cranmer, except just from
looking round his place occasionally, and buying one or
two small things. He's been there a few years now.
Usual sort of antiquary, old and desiccated and hard as
nails."

The description fitted Mr. Cranmer very fairly, George
thought, when he entered the small gallery in Abbey
Place, and took stock of the person who hovered delicately
in the background, refraining from intercepting him
until he showed whether he wanted to gaze or do business.
The neighbourhood was a part of the old town, mainly
early Tudor, and the low black-beamed frontage of the
shop was beautiful. English black-and-white, in contrast

to some of its European kin, is so wonderfully disciplined, makes such a patterned harmony of a whole street, instead of a Gothic cadenza. The interior was also plain white beneath the enormous beams of the ceiling, and not cluttered. The man himself was of medium height, slightly stooped, grey of hair and complexion and clothing, and lean with an astringent leanness like that of roots and sinews and all that is most durable in nature. He wore thick-lensed glasses that made his eyes look enormous and incredibly blue. To approach him from the inoffensive side-view and be suddenly transfixed by that vast blue glare was electrifying.

The voice that went with the grey shape was old, prosaic and discreet; so discreet that until George identified himself as a police officer it produced no information whatever, and without even appearing to be wilfully stalling; as without any apparent volte-face it then became loquacious. Yes, he had the painting in question in his workshop, he understood that it had been the sign of an inn called The Joyful Woman. Yes, it might possibly turn out to be of some value, though questionably of very much.

" Several times clumsily overpainted, you know, and exposed to a great deal of weathering when in use as a sign, and therefore frequently touched up and varnished over, like most of its kind. But I have an idea—mind you, it is just an idea—that it may be based on an eighteenth-century portrait by a local artist named Cotsworth. You won't have heard of him, I dare say. Not important, but interesting, if it turns out to be his. Worth a few hundreds, perhaps, to a local collector." He trotted away into his back room to bring forth a foot-square framed canvas, the head of some long-dead worthy. "This is a Cotsworth," he said triumphantly. It seemed to George depressingly smug, clumsy and ugly, but he forebore from saying so.

"You've had the painting for about a fortnight, I understand. Are you making tests on it? Did young Mr. Armiger empower you to do that, or was he merely asking for an opinion first?"

"He asked for an opinion, but I should like, if he agrees, to try to uncover at least a corner of the older paint, and see if it confirms my guess. If it does, Mr. Felse, I may be prepared to offer Mr. Armiger as much as two hundred and fifty pounds for it myself."

"Very handsome, Mr. Cranmer. Did you inform Mr. Armiger senior, or anyone in his employ, that you had the painting here, and that it might conceivably be valuable?"

The two hundred and fifty pounds had struck the first really phoney note; if he was ready to mention such a sum he was thinking in terms of a thousand and upwards. And once that false quantity had jarred on George's senses this whole room began to seem as much a façade as the magnified blueness of the eyes.

"Certainly not," said the old man stiffly. "It came to me as the property of Mr. Armiger junior, through Mr. Wilson, and I wouldn't dream of communicating with anyone else about it. Except, of course, the police when they require me to co-operate." He made it a plaintive and dignified reproof, and George let him have it that way; but the fact remained that he had not been required to co-operate to the extent of naming a price, and there had been no need whatever for him to do so. Unless, of course, he wanted his offer to come back to the owner in this superlatively respectable fashion, relayed by the innocent police. It might not come off, but there was nothing lost in trying.

All very correct, thought George, halting for a moment outside to weigh up the three mediocre moderns in the low Henry VII windows; but then, he would be correct, and cautious too, now that Armiger's dead. The last thing he'd want would be to be involved. All the same, George suspected that Mr. Cranmer had indeed flashed the urgent warning to Armiger: look out, you're giving away something valuable. He probably didn't know that Armiger had gone as high as five hundred pounds in his attempt to recover it, or he wouldn't have stuck at two hundred and fifty himself, the discrepancy was too glaring to pass without comment. He hadn't, of course, actually made an offer, only hinted that he might be prepared to do so, but the implications were there. He would have collected a plump commission, no question of it, if he'd helped Armiger to get the better of Leslie, and acquired the great man's formidable patronage into the bargain. Now that that was knocked on the head, quite literally, he was going into the deal for himself. All that, thought George, strolling without haste back to his car, depends rather on whether Mr. Cranmer was acquainted with the painting's provenance; but since the thing came from young Armiger, and he evidently knows it to be the sign of The Joyful Woman, we may safely assume that he could guess Armiger had thrown it out as valueless, even if Wilson didn't tell him. And he probably did, he's a talkative soul, he confides easily.

The upshot, he decided, letting in the clutch, is that

young Leslie ought to take back that picture very firmly, resisting all offers to buy it from him, and take it to some absolutely immaculate authority for an opinion. And so I'll tell him, if he's in a listening mood, and if no unforeseen explosion blows him into gaol in the meantime.

He spent the rest of the morning in his office doing some of his arrears of paper work on the case, and the early afternoon with Duckett on a visit to the Chief Constable, who was anxious for quick results, partly because the case involved a family so well known in the Midlands, but chiefly because he wanted to get away from town for some shooting at the week-end. The visit comforted nobody, since the Chief Constable still thought of everybody and treated everybody as a classifiable item in a military hierarchy, and Duckett on an important case always became more and more laconic, until his gruffness amounted almost to dumb insolence.

" Waste of time! " snorted Duckett as he drove back towards Comerbourne at the solid, law-abiding pace which was also a symptom of his less amenable moods. " Never let that boy of yours go into the police force, George."

" He says he won't, anyhow," said George. " When it comes to the point he often seems to be on the side of the criminal."

" All his generation are anti-social," said Duckett disgustedly.

" No, it's just a natural sympathy with the hunted, I think, when the odds turn against them. Maybe a feeling that this society of ours makes its own criminals, too, and therefore deserves 'em." He wondered if he was pro-

jecting his own occasional qualms on to Dominic's
shoulders; better not look too closely in case he was. The
depression that sometimes followed a successful conviction
was bad enough, without being inhibited by doubts in
the thick of the hunt. " Never mind," he said placatingly,
" who knows if something won't have broken while we've
been away theorising? "

And when they turned the corner into Hill Street, and
saw the concreted apron frontage of the station alive with
staring, chattering people, it appeared that indeed something had. The station faced sidelong to the street on the
outer side of a wide curve, with a small garden and two
seats in front of its windows, and then the concreted
forecourt lined out into parking space for four cars. One
of the four spaces was now occupied by a flat two-wheeled
cart bearing a tin trunk, a small pile of old iron bolts and
oddments, a tumbled mound of old clothing and rags,
and a top-dressing of three small, silent, staring children.
A somewhat larger child in his father's cut-down trousers
and a steadily unravelling grey jersey held by the head a
shaggy, fat brown pony. A uniformed constable, with
the admirably detached, impervious solidity acquired
only after innumerable public embarrassments, sauntered
about between the door and the waiting family, gently
shooing the shifting crowd along if it became too stagnant,
and hypnotising it into pretending to an indifference as
monumental as his own.

" God! " said Duckett, as he parked his car. The constable permitted himself a fleeting grin on the side of his
face which was turned towards them and away from the
public view. " Has Grocott gone off his head and started
bringing in all the tickney lot? "

" No, sir, this one brought himself. Claims he has important information."

" So he got a load aboard before the pubs closed, and brought half the town along as well," Duckett diagnosed disgustedly, and eyed the composed and dignified children, who looked back at him calmly, as though they had no doubts at all as to who was the alien and the savage. They were not full-blooded gipsies, they had not the soft, mysterious Indian features, the melting eyes, the delicate bones, but something in a coarser grain, olive and wild and sinewy, with a bloom of dirt. " What are they? " said Duckett gruffly. " Lays? "

" No, sir, Creaveys."

" What's the difference? Nobody knows who's married to whom or which kids belong to which parents, anyhow. If you're a Creavey you are a Lay."

He stalked into the station, and pounded up three flights of stairs to his own office, with George at his heels. Grocott was at the door before he had time to be called.

" All right," said Duckett, " let's have it. That's Joe Creavey's pony, isn't it? "

Joe was the Creavey (or Lay) who was almost no trouble; an occasional blind when business in wool rags and old iron was booming, and just once, with ample provocation, a determined assault with an ash-plant on his wife, but no major sins were recorded against him. He fed his kids, minded his own business without unduly annoying other people about it, and was unmistakably a happy and well-adjusted man.

" Yes, sir. Joe's below with Lockyer. He came in just over an hour ago, saying he'd got important evidence in the Armiger case."

Joe was well known in the seedier outer districts of Comerbourne, where he made regular rounds with his pony-cart, collecting rags and scrap, and a good many residents automatically saved their cast-off clothes for him. It was worth making regular use of him, because he would take away for you all kinds of awkward and unmarketable rubbish on which the Cleansing Department tended to frown if it was put out for their attentions; though what he afterwards did with some of the items no one cared to inquire. On this particular morning he had been round the shabby-genteel corner of town which housed Mrs. Harkness, and in addition to collecting the contents of her rag-bag he had thoughtfully lifted the lid of her dustbin in case there should be anything salvageable there. People often put old shoes in dustbins, sometimes in a state which Joe regarded as merely part-worn. He didn't find shoes this time, he found gloves, and the gloves were aged but expensive leather gauntlets, with woven tapes stitched inside, lettered L.A. He took them instinctively, and only afterwards did he examine them closely, when he was pulled in at one of the suburban pubs and had his first pint inside him. It was then he found that the palm and the fingers of the right glove were stained and stiffened with something dark and crusted, and the left carried a few similar dark-brown stains here and there in its frayed leather. Joe knew who lodged with Mrs. Harkness, she was one of his regular clients; he knew what the initials L.A. stood for; and he knew, or was convinced that he knew, what had saturated and ruined those gloves, and why they were stuffed into the dustbin. He knew his duty, too; the police must be told. But his route to the station had

H

taken him through four more bars before it triumphantly delivered him, and if there was anyone left in Comerbourne who didn't yet know that Leslie Armiger had murdered his father and Joe Creavey had the proof of it, he must have been going about for the last couple of hours with his ears plugged.

"Blabbed it all over town, and pretty well brought a procession with him. He isn't exactly drunk—not by his standards—but well away. Do you want him? "

"No," said Duckett, "let him stew for a bit. I want the gloves, and I think I want young Armiger, too. If there's nothing in this, now's the time to talk to him, before we're sure there's nothing in it. But let's have a look at these first."

The gloves were produced, they lay on the desk with palms upturned, displaying the reddish-black, encrusted smears that certainly looked uncommonly like blood.

"Well, what do you think it is, George? "

"Creosote, for one thing," said George promptly, sniffing at the stiffened fingers, "but that doesn't say it's all creosote."

"No, traces of roofing paint, too. Johnson had better run them up to the lab., and we'll see."

"You're not thinking of keeping Joe overnight, are you? " asked Grocott.

"Eh? Keep him overnight? What, and dump all that tribe of kids into the receiving home when there's no need? The Children's Officer would murder me! All right, George, you be off and fetch the boy along."

George made the best of a job he never liked, approaching the manager's office discreetly without getting anyone to announce him, and making the summons sound as much like a request as he could; all the same, Leslie, coming up in haste from the warehouse, paled and froze at the sight of him. Once he had grasped the idea it wasn't so bad; colour came back into his face and a defiant hardness into his eyes, and he went out by George's side with a composed countenance and an easy stride, as though an old friend had called for him. They had to cross either the shop or the yard, and George hoped he was right in choosing the yard, where Leslie was better known and better understood.

Nobody was deceived, of course, they'd be muttering and wondering the rest of the day; but a van-driver caught Leslie's eye and cocked up a thumb at him and grinned, and one of the packers walked deliberately across their path so that he could offer a crumpled cigarette packet in passing. The boy looked harassed rather than cheered, but he smiled all the same, and accepted the offering; and with the first deep drag the pinched lines round his mouth relaxed. He sat beside George in the car, drawing deep, steadying breaths, and trying too hard to prepare himself.

" Mr. Felse," he said in a constrained voice, as George slowed at the traffic lights, " could you do something for me? I should be very grateful if you'd go and see my wife for me."

" You'll be seeing her yourself in an hour or so," said George equably. " Won't you? "

" Shall I? "

" That depends on what you've done, so only you know the answer."

" I hope you're right," said Leslie fervently. " I suppose you can't tell me what this is all about? "

"You suppose correctly. You'll soon know, but I won't anticipate. Now let me ask you the one question I somehow never asked you before. Did you kill him?"

"No," said Leslie without over-emphasis, almost gently.

"Then you'll be going home to your wife, and the worst that can happen is that you may be a little late. She'll forgive you for that, long before she forgives us for scaring you."

Leslie was so unreasonably soothed and calmed by this tone that he forgot to take offence at the assumption that he was scared. He walked into the police station briskly, wild to get to his fence and either fall or clear it; and suddenly finding himself without George, had to turn back and look for him. He had stopped to speak to a boy in a grammar school blazer who was standing in the hallway.

"My son," he explained as he hurried to overtake his charge. "He's still hoping—and so am I—that I'm going to be able to drive him home. I should be off duty by this time."

"Oh, now, look," said Leslie with a faint recovering gleam in his eye, "I should hate to keep you after hours, I can easily come some other time."

"That's the stuff!" George patted him approvingly on the shoulder. "You keep up that standard, and you'll be all right. Always provided you're telling us the truth, of course. Come on, three flights up, and I'm afraid the taxpayer doesn't provide us with a lift."

Dominic watched them climb to the first turn of the staircase and pass out of sight like that, his father's hand on the young man's shoulder. Was it possible that it was all over already? Leslie Armiger didn't look like a murderer. But then, what murderer ever does? But he *didn't*!

Dominic was convulsed by the secret, uneasy part of him that couldn't help identifying itself with those in trouble, those trapped by circumstances and cornered, however deservedly, by the orderly ranks of the law-abiding. He felt the demon in his own nature, and trembled, knowing there was no end to his potentialities. He had to let part at least of his sympathy go out to the hunted, because the quarry could so easily be himself. Infinitely more terrible, it could be somebody who mattered to him so desperately as to make him forget himself. It could be Kitty! And yet he wanted not to be glad that it should be the young man in the worn, expensive suit, with the strained smile and the apprehensive eyes.

The surge of relief in his heart outraged him, and drove him out from under the desk-sergeant's friendly but inquisitive eye into the impersonal pre-twilight of the September evening, to wait on one of the seats in the strip of garden.

So it was that he saw the red Karmann-Ghia swoop beautifully inward from the road to park beside the ragman's cart, and Kitty swing her long, slender legs out from the driver's door. His heart performed the terrifying manœuvre with which he was becoming familiar, turning over bodily in his breast and swelling until he thought it would burst his ribs.

She closed the door of the car with unaccustomed slowness and quietness, and walked uncertainly across the concrete towards the door; and as she came her steps slowed, until within a few yards of the step she halted altogether, her hands clasped tightly in front of her, in an agony of indecision. She looked to right and left as though searching for the courage to go forward; and she saw Dominic, motionless and silent in the corner of the wooden seat, clutching his school-bag convulsively against his side.

He couldn't believe, even when her eyes lit on him, that it would get him anything. He was just somebody she'd run into once, casually, and not expected to meet again. Probably she wouldn't even remember. But her eyes kindled marvellously, a pale smile blazed over her face for a moment, though it served only to illuminate the desperate anxiety that instantly drove it away again. She turned and came to him. He jumped to his feet, so shaken by the beating of his heart that he scarcely heard the first words she said to him.

" Dominic! I'm so glad to find you here! " He came out of a cloud of fulfilment and ecstasy to find himself sitting beside her, his hands clasped in hers, her great eyes a drowning violet darkness close before his face. She was saying for the second time, urgently, desperately: " Is Leslie in there? They were saying in the shops the police fetched him from Malden's. Is it true? Do you know if he's in there? "

" Yes," he said, stammering, " he came with my father. Only a few minutes ago." He was back on the earth, and the bump had hurt a little, but not much, because of her remembering his name, because of her turning to him so gladly. It wasn't as if he'd been expecting even that. And in any case he couldn't be bothered with such trivialities as his own disappointments, while she carried such terrible trouble in her face.

" Oh, God! " she said. " Is he under arrest? "

" I don't know. I don't think so—not yet——"

" Your father's in there, too? I'd rather it be him than any of the others. I've got to talk to him, Dominic. Now I've got to."

She released his hands with a vast sigh, and put back with a hopeless gesture the fall of smooth, pale hair that shadowed her forehead.

" I've got to tell him," she said in a tired, tranquil voice, " because if I don't they'll only put it on to poor Leslie, and hasn't enough happened to him already? I won't let them touch him." She lifted her head and looked into Dominic's eyes with the practical simplicity of a child confiding its sins, relieved to exchange even for punishment a burden too great to bear a moment longer. " I killed his father, you see."

CHAPTER VIII

DOMINIC TRIED to speak, and couldn't find his voice for a moment, and even when he did it tended to shift key unexpectedly, in the alarming and humiliating way he'd thought he was finished with; but Kitty didn't seem to notice.

" You mustn't say such things. Even if—if something happened that makes you feel to blame, that can't be true, and you shouldn't say it."

" But I did it, Dominic. I never meant to, but I did. He came to me, and he said: ' I'm just going to kick Leslie out of here once for all, and boy, shall I enjoy it.

And then I've got something to tell you. Not here, you come out to the barn, we can be quiet there. Give me fifteen minutes,' he said, ' to get rid of his lordship, and then come on over.' And I wasn't going to go, I'd made up my mind not to go. I got out the car and started to drive home, and then after all I didn't, I went round by the lane to the road behind the barn, and parked the car along under the trees by that little wood, and went into the courtyard by the back way. I thought if I begged him just once more he might give in and take Leslie back, and start acting decently to them. After all, he was his son. I couldn't get it into my head that it was really for keeps. People just don't act like that. Leslie wasn't there, only his father. He started telling me all his great plans for the future, all excited and pleased with himself, and he had a magnum of champagne and glasses set out on one of the tables. Oh, Dominic, if you knew how obscenely ridiculous it all was——"

His mouth ached with all the things he wanted to say to her and mustn't; his heart filled his chest so tightly that he could hardly breathe. " Kitty, I wish there was some way I could help you," he said huskily.

" You do help me, you are helping me, you're lovely to me. You keep right on looking at me as if I was a friend of yours, and you haven't moved away from me even an inch. But you will! "

" I won't! " he said in a gasp of protest. " Never! "

" No, perhaps you wouldn't ever, you're not the kind. Let me go on telling you, it makes it easier, and my God, I need rehearsing, this is going to be lousy on the night whatever I do."

He had her by the hands again, and this time the

initiative had been his, and the warm, strong fingers
clung to him gratefully, quivering a little.

"He'd had a brainwave," said Kitty in a half-suffocated
voice, laughing and raging. "If Leslie wouldn't have me
and join the businesses up, *he would*! He was going to
marry me himself! That's what the champagne and the
excitement was all about. He didn't even ask me, he
told me. He didn't even pretend to feel anything for me.
When he put his arms round me and wanted to kiss me
it wasn't even sexually revolting, it was just like signing
a merger. And I'd been trying to talk to him all the
while about Leslie, and he hadn't even heard me. I was
so mad, it was so mean and ludicrous and horrible, I was
out of my mind, I couldn't think of anything except
getting away. I just pushed him off like a demon. We
were by the table at the top of the stairs, where he'd put
the champagne and the glasses. I don't know how it
happened—he went backwards, and stepped off the edge
of the top stair, and went slipping and rolling and clawing
all the way down and crashed on the floor. I ran down
and past him to the door, I was terrified he'd get up and
try to stop me. I wasn't afraid of him, it wasn't that, it
was just that everything was so foul, I couldn't have
borne it if he'd tried to speak to me again. But he just
lay there on his face, and never moved. I didn't think
anything about it, I didn't stop to see how much he was
hurt, I just ran back to the car and left him lying there.
So you see, I killed him. And I've got to tell them.
I never meant to, it never even occurred to me until I
was in the car that he might be terribly hurt. But I did
it. And I can't let them go on thinking poor Leslie had
anything to do with it."

When she had finished she lifted her eyes and looked at him closely, already half sorry and half ashamed that she should be so weak as to unload this cruel and humiliating confidence upon a mere child, too old not to be damaged by it, and not yet old enough to be able to evaluate it justly. But it wasn't a child who was looking steadily at her, it was a man, a very young man, maybe, but unquestionably her elder at that moment. He kept firm hold of her hands when she would have drawn them away, and his eyes held hers when she would have averted them.

"Oh, God!" she said weakly. "I'm a heel to drag you into this."

"No, you did right, Kitty, really you did. I'll show you. That was all that happened? You're sure that was all? You pushed him and he fell down the stairs and knocked himself out. That was all?"

"Wasn't it enough? He was dead when they found him."

"Yes, he was dead. But you didn't kill him." He knew what he was about to do, and it was so terrible that it almost outweighed the sense of joy and completion that he felt at knowing her innocent, and being able to hold out the image of her in his two hands and show her how spotless it was. Never in his life before, not even as a small, nosy boy, had he betrayed a piece of information he possessed purely by virtue of being George's son. If he did it he was destroying something which had been a mainspring of his life, and the future that opened before him without it was lonely and frightening, involved enormous readjustments in his most intimate relationships, and self-searchings from which he instinctively

shrank. But already he was committed, and he would
not have turned back even if he could.

"Listen to me, Kitty. All that was published about
Mr. Armiger's death was that he died from head injuries.
But it wasn't just falling down the stairs that did it. It's
only because of my father's work that I know this, and
you mustn't tell anyone I told you. After he was lying
unconscious somebody took the champagne bottle and
battered his head in with it deliberately, hit him nine
times, and only stopped hitting him when the bottle
smashed. And *that* wasn't you! Was it? "

She whispered between parted lips, staring at him in a
stupor of horror and incredulity and relief: " *No*—no, I
didn't, I *couldn't*——"

" I know you couldn't, of course you couldn't. But
somebody did. So you see, Kitty, you didn't kill him at
all, you didn't do anything except push him away from
you and accidentally stun him. Somebody else came in
afterwards and battered him to death. So you see, there's
no need for you to tell them anything. You won't, will
you? There'll be nothing in this glove business, they won't
touch Leslie, you'll see. At least wait until we know."

She hadn't heard the half of that, she was still groping
after the release and freedom he was offering back to her.
The warm flush of colour into her face and hope into
her eyes overwhelmed him with a kind of proud humility
he had never experienced before.

" You mean it? You wouldn't just try to comfort me,
would you? Not with fairy stories? But you wouldn't!
Oh, Dominic, am I really not a murderess? You don't
know what it's been like since yesterday morning, since
they told me he was dead."

"Of course you're not. It's true what I've told you. So you won't tell them anything, will you?"

"Oh, yes," she said, "I must. Oh, Dominic, what should I have done without you? Don't you see, I don't even mind now, as long as I'm not—what I thought I was. I don't mind anything now. But I must tell them, because of Leslie. I can show them that he'd gone, and his father was still alive. I can prove he didn't kill him." She looked down at him, and was distressed by his consternation, but she knew what she had to do. "I've got this far and I'm not turning back now. I've had enough of concealing information. At least I can see that Leslie's safely out of it."

"But you can't," protested Dominic, catching at her wrist and dragging her down again beside him. "You can only prove he didn't kill him in the short time you were there. They might still think he came back. *Somebody* came. And don't you see, if you tell them what you've told me, they'll think you've left out the end, they'll think *you* stayed and finished him off."

"I don't see why you should say that," said Kitty, wide-eyed. "*You* don't think that, *you* believe me. Why shouldn't they?"

"Well, because their business is *not* to believe—and how can you prove it?"

"I can't," she agreed, paling a little. "But I can't turn back now, I couldn't bear to. You don't have to worry about me any more, the most wonderful thing anyone could have done for me is done already. *You* did it."

If she hadn't said that, if she hadn't suddenly touched his hot cheek so lightly and fleetingly with her fingertips, he might have been able to protest yet once again, perhaps even to persuade her. But her touch snatched the breath from his throat and the articulation from his tongue, and he couldn't say a word, he had to stand and watch, suffocating, mute and paralysed, as she turned to leave him; and when she looked back just once to say quickly: " Don't worry, I won't say a word about you," he almost burst into tears of frustration and rage because he lacked the power to shout at her that it wasn't about himself he was worrying, that he didn't care about himself, that only she mattered, and she was making a terrible mistake, that he couldn't bear it, that he loved her.

She was gone. The darkening doorway swallowed her, and it was in any case too late. He sat down again, huddled in the far corner of the seat, and wrestled with himself painfully until his mind cleared again, and presented to him the most appalling implication of the whole incident, producing it with cruel aplomb, like a magician palming an ace out of the pack. He had robbed her even of the defence of ignorance! He, and no one else. If she'd gone rushing in there as she'd wanted to, and poured out her story as she had to him, they'd have seen the glaring hole in it at once, just as surely as he had. They'd have questioned her about the weapon, about the injuries, and she wouldn't have known what they were talking about, and her manner and her bewilderment would have rung true past any mistaking. But now he'd told her. She couldn't pretend ignorance worth a damn, she'd be certain to betray her knowledge. And worse, she'd never tell them about his treachery, and explain how she got her information, because that would get him into trouble. One slip to warn them that she knew how that death had come about, and they'd be absolutely sure she was responsible for it. The details had never been published, only a handful of people knew them—and one other, the murderer. He'd as good as convicted her.

His manhood, so recently and intoxicatingly achieved, was crumpling badly, slipping out of his hold. He ought to get up and march in there after her and tell them honestly about his lapse, but he hadn't the courage, the very thought of it made him feel sick. It wasn't just for himself he was such a coward, it was his father's job, his whole career. C.I.D. officers ought not to discuss their cases in front of their families. They'd been the exceptional family, proud of their solidarity, disdaining to doubt their absolute mutual loyalty, over-riding conventional restrictions because they were so sure of one another. All this had made perfect sense while that solidarity remained unbreached, but now he'd broken it, and how did it look now? His father was compromised. He would have to own up, it was the only way he could even try to repair the harm he'd done to Kitty; but he'd have to do it in private, to his father alone. Maybe there'd be some grain of evidence that would extricate Kitty, and make it unnecessary for confession to go any farther. Supposing George felt he had to resign, supposing——

He longed for George to come and take him home, so that he could get the first awful plunge over. But when at last a step rang on the flags of the hallway and he jerked round in hope and dread to see who emerged, it was only Leslie Armiger, stepping lightly, buoyant with relief. He walked like a new man, for the old gloves he'd discarded after painting the garden shed where he kept

his materials had yielded a great many interesting sub-
stances, creosote, bituminous dressing, several kinds of
paint and lacquer, but not a trace of blood. As soon as
he'd seen them he'd laughed with relief; he could have
kicked himself for the imaginative agonies of anticipation
he'd inflicted on himself, all on account of these ancient
and blameless relics. His position now was actually
neither better nor worse than it had been before this
tea-cup storm blew up, but there was no doubt that the
recoil had raised his credit all round. Especially with
himself; this feeling of liberation was more than worth
the scare.

Detective-Sergeant Felse had been called away from
the interrogation to interview someone in his own room,
but Leslie didn't know who it was, or whether the caller
had anything to do with his father's death. He didn't
know, and he didn't care. He was on his way home to
Jean, still free and almost vindicated, and never again
would he scare as easily as that.

It was ten minutes more before George came out to
speak to his son, and then it was only to say tersely that
after all he wouldn't be able to leave for some time yet,
possibly several hours, and Dom had better get on home
by bus. He wasn't going to have an opportunity to
unburden himself here, that was obvious; his father
was gone again almost before he could open his stiff
lips to get out a word.

Miserably he took his dismissal and went home; there
was nothing else to be done. He countered Bunty's
queries with monosyllables, sat wretchedly over his tea
without appetite, and refuged in his corner with text-
books he couldn't even see for the anxiety that hung over

his eyes as palpable as fog. Bunty suspected a cold coming on, but he repelled her attempts to take his temperature so ill-humouredly that she revised her diagnosis. Something on his mind, she reflected with certainty, and it isn't me he wants, so it must be his father. Now what, I wonder, have those two been doing to each other?

It was twenty to ten before George came home. He looked tired and frayed and in no mood to be approached, but there was no help for it. Bunty fed him and allowed him to be quiet, though she knew by old signs that there was something on his mind, too, that would have to come out before long. It was without prompting that he leaned back wearily at last, and said in a voice entirely devoid of any pleasure or satisfaction: " Well, it's all over bar the shouting. We've just made an arrest in the Armiger case. We've charged Kitty Norris."

Bunty's exclamation was drowned by the shriek of Dominic's chair. He was on his feet, trembling.

" *No!* " he said faintly, and then, with the flat quietness of desperation: " Please, Dad, I've got to talk to you. It's about that. It's important." He looked imploringly at his mother, and his lips were quivering. " Mummy, do you mind awfully——"

" That's all right, darling," said Bunty, loading her tray methodically as though nothing out of the way was happening. " I'm going to wash up. You go ahead."

She made things sound so normal and calm, as she almost always did, that he longed to ask her to stay, but it couldn't be done that way, he had to have it out with George. She cleared the table, flicked Dominic's ear very lightly with the folded tablecloth as she went to put it away, and bore off the tray into the kitchen, closing the door firmly after her. They were left looking rather helplessly at each other, neither of them any longer able to doubt that this was a family crisis of the first magnitude. George flinched from it as much as Dominic did; he was tired and out of temper, and he knew it, and this luckless child was inviting trouble even their combined goodwill might not be able to avert.

What was the use of thinking how best to do it, when all that mattered was that it should be done?

"You know I was outside there this evening when Kitty Norris came to ask for you," said Dominic in the drained tones of despair. "I talked to her before you did. She told me all that tale about pushing Armiger down the stairs because he—he insulted her. But she told me she killed him. She didn't! You've got to believe me. All she did was go away and leave him there stunned. She said——"

"I don't know why it should be necessary for us to discuss it at all," said George, laboriously patient with him but desperately unwilling to go on hammering at an affair of which he'd already had about all he could take, "but if I'm supposed to humour you, I will. If she went away and left him there stunned, how did she know it was the champagne magnum that battered his head in? If she wasn't the one who killed him, if she was gone from the scene and somebody else came in and finished him off, how did she know how it was done? All that was ever made public was that he died of head injuries. So you tell me how she knew—how she *could* know and still be innocent?"

So they had tricked it out of her, questioned and cross-questioned and slipped in catch remarks until she gave

I

herself away. Dominic hated them all, even his father, but not so much as he hated himself for making such an appalling miscalculation. He should have known she'd still insist on going through with her confession, because Leslie must be safeguarded whatever happened to her, Leslie who wouldn't marry her, thank God, the stupid fool, Leslie with whom she was still so crazily, desolately in love that she couldn't see anyone else for him. Dominic sat down slowly and carefully at the table, braced his sweating palms upon its glossy surface before him, and said loudly and hoarsely: " She knew because I told her."

He was glad he'd sat down, however it diminished his dignity, he felt safer that way; his knees would never have held him up, standing. George had lurched forward in his chair and come heavily to his feet. He spread his hands upon the table and leaned over his son, and in spite of himself Dominic wilted. He wanted to close his eyes, but he wouldn't, because whatever was coming to him, he'd asked for it, he couldn't complain.

" You *what*? " said George.

" I told her. I told her because I thought then she wouldn't have to tell you about being there at all. She was going to tell you she'd killed him, and yet she didn't know anything about him being battered to death, she just thought he'd cracked his skull when he fell down the stairs. So I knew she hadn't, and how could I let her go on thinking she had? I had to tell her. I couldn't not tell her." Resolute in his desperation, he said with an altogether inaccurate suggestion of defiance: " I'd do the same again."

George said, after a blank and awful pause: " I've a good mind to tan the hide off you."

With all his sore heart Dominic almost wished he would, but with all his lively senses he knew he wouldn't. There was no getting out of things that way any more, the bolt-hole had been stopped at least two years now. Paying this debt was going to be a whole lot more complicated than that, a whole lot more long-drawn-out and painful. The compensations of being under juvenile discipline had never presented themselves to him before.

"I know," he said drearily, "but I had to do it. There wasn't anything else to do. And now I've made everything worse for her instead of better."

"Whether you've done that or not, you've certainly made it impossible for us to judge how far she's telling the truth. And you know what else you've done, don't you?" said George remorselessly.

Yes, he knew. He'd undermined the foundations of the house, and shaken the pillars that held up the roof. He wouldn't have believed himself that he could do such a thing; for a moment half of his heart was with George, astonished and reproachful, half of it with Kitty, injured and imprisoned. Between the two of them he wished he could die.

"I shall have to report this to the chief, of course," said George. "I blame myself more than you. There's nothing to be done but tell him that I've been consistently indiscreet. I'd no right to allow you such easy access to information in the first place, it was thoroughly unconstitutional behaviour, and I should have known better. It was unreasonable to expect that you could refrain for ever from shooting off your mouth, I suppose." But he had expected it; he'd been so sure of it, in fact, that it had never occurred to him to question

his discretion at all.   Only now that he'd lost that
absolute trust did Dominic know how to value it.

"I didn't do it lightly," he said, flinching.   "I never
have before."

"Once is all it takes.   I shall have to see Superintendent Duckett in the morning and take the responsibility for this myself.   That's putting it squarely where it
belongs."

"I'm sorry," said Dominic abjectly.   "Do you have
to?"

"Yes, I have to, in fairness to you as well as to Kitty.
If he asks for my resignation he'll be within his rights."
That was cruel, because he was virtually sure that Duckett,
things being as they were, the case as good as closed, and
this particular item of evidence now so much less vital
than Dominic supposed, would hardly even bother to
listen to him, and quite certainly be unable to muster
more than a token reprimand.   "In future, of course,"
he said, "I shall have to make sure I don't talk about a
case when you're within earshot.   I'll take good care this
doesn't happen again.   And you'll give me your word
here and now not to meddle in this affair any more.
You've done damage enough."

"I can't!   I *won't*!   I tell you Kitty didn't know until
I told her.   You've got to believe me.   Don't you see
there isn't really any evidence against her apart from
that?   Dad, you've got to let her go now, don't you see
that?   You've no right to hold her now that I've told
you about it.   She's innocent, and if you won't prove it,
I'll damn' well do it myself."

George had had more than enough.   He opened his
mouth to say something for which he would quite cer-

tainly have been sorry next moment, and which would
have cost Bunty days of patient, cunning negotiations to
put right again between them; and then the violent
young voice that was shouting at him cracked ominously,
and stopped him in his tracks, and he was saved. He
looked again, and more closely, at the pale, raging face
and the anguished eyes that didn't avoid his searching
stare, because the case was too desperate for considerations
of dignity to have any further validity.

Understanding hit George like a steam hammer.
Someone you're used to thinking of as a child, someone
who sounds like a hysterical boy, suddenly looks at you
with the profound, solemn, staggering grief of a man,
and knocks the breath out of you. It won't last, of
course, it isn't a constant yet, he'll be back and forth
between maturity and childishness a hundred times
before he loses the ability to commute. But it's the first
plain prophecy of things to come, and it's hit him deadly
hard. Oh, God, thought George, utterly dismayed, and
I teased him about her! How dim can you get about
your own kid?

Treading with wincing care, as though even a loud
noise might start them both jangling again like shaken
glasses, George went and sat down at the table opposite
his son. In a soft, reasonable voice he said: " All right,
boy, you owed me that. I haven't been fair to you.
This is the first time you ever let me down, and that's
not a bad record, all things considered. I don't really
think you did it lightly, I don't really under-value your
reasons. I don't blame you for not being willing to contract out. Probably in your place I should do exactly
the same as you've done. And since I'm the person who's

to blame for breaking all the rules in the first place, and I've been doing it for years, I may just as well do it just once more, and tell you how the case really stands now. It won't make you any happier," he said ruefully, " but it may settle your mind. Since Kitty Norris told us her story to-night we've been working hard at the details. We've questioned all the tenants of the block of flats where she lives, and we've found a couple on the ground floor who heard and saw her come in that night, not at half past ten, as she said at first, nor at ten past eleven, as she says now, but just after midnight. She declines to account for that missing time."

" They could be mistaken——" began Dominic strenuously.

" I didn't say she denied it, I said she wouldn't account for it." The voice was gentler and gentler. " And that's not all, Dom. We also brought in the clothes Kitty wore that night. I saw her, she had on a black silk dress with a full skirt, I didn't have any trouble picking it out. She had an Indian scarf, too, a shot red and blue gauze affair with gold embroidery. To tell you the one thing that fits in nowhere, since I'm telling you the things that do fit, only too well, the end of the scarf has a corner torn off, and we haven't been able to find a trace of it so far. The left side of the skirt of the dress has several smears along the hem, not easily visible because of the black colour, but enough to react to tests. They're blood. The same group as Armiger's. Her shoes I didn't notice, but we found them, by one spot of brown on the toe of the left one. That's blood, too, Dom. The same group. Armiger's group, but not Kitty's. We tested."

Dominic shut his eyes, but he couldn't stop seeing the

silver sandals glittering in her hands at the Boat Club. They wouldn't be the same shoes, but he couldn't stop seeing them.

" I'm sorry, old man," said George. He rose and drew away gingerly; the front view of Dominic was beginning to be too precarious, he moved considerately to the rear. The slender shoulders were braced and motionless. " It isn't the end of the world, or of the case, either," said George, " but it's no good pretending that the outlook's rosy, Dom. I had to tell you, in justice to you. Don't take it too much to heart."

He laid his hand for an instant on Dominic's shoulder, and let his knuckles scrub gently at the rigid cheek.

Dominic got up abruptly and steered a blind course for the door, and blundering past Bunty fled for the stairs. Bunty looked after him, looked at George, and hesitated whether to follow. It was George who said warningly: " No! " and shook his head at her. It couldn't be cured that way, either.

" Let him alone," said George. " He'll be all right, just let him alone."

CHAPTER IX

BY THE TIME he came down to breakfast next morning he had thought things out for himself, and arrived at a position from which he did not intend to be moved; that was implicit in the set of his jaw and the pallid resolution of his whole face, which seemed to have moved a long stage nearer to its mature form overnight. By his puffy eyelids and the blue hollows under his eyes thinking was what he'd been doing all through the hours of darkness when he should have been sleeping. He arrived at the breakfast table composed and quiet, greeted his parents punctiliously, to show there were no dangerous loose ends dangling, and made himself more mannishly attentive to Bunty than she had ever known him. Gravely she played up to him; having two men in the house was going to be interesting. She had no real complaints against George, but having a rival around wasn't going to do him any harm, and she was going to enjoy herself. If only it hadn't had to happen to him this way! She and George had spent the early hours of the morning in subdued and anxious colloquy over him, and it was difficult not to betray that they were watching him with equal anxiety now, intensely aware of every consciously restrained movement he made, even of the hesitations and selections that preceded every word he spoke.

"About last night, Dad," he said, embarking at last with a shivering plunge which he did his best to make look normal. "I've been thinking what I ought to do. I've thought over everything you said, and—and thanks for telling me. But there's one thing I know absolutely, and it's evidence to me even if it isn't to you—I mean you can't possibly *know* it as I do. When she talked to me Kitty *didn't know* how Mr. Armiger was killed. So she couldn't possibly be the person who killed him. I don't expect you to be sure of that, because you didn't see her and hear her, but I did, and I am sure. So all the other things you've found out against her can't really mean that she's guilty, there has to be some other explanation for them."

" We shall still be working on it," said George, " trying to fill up all the gaps. I told you, the case isn't closed yet."

" No. But you'll be trying to fill up the gaps with one idea in mind. The logical end of your gap-filling is a conviction, isn't it? "

George, moved partly by genuine bitterness and partly by a blind, brilliant instinct for the thing to say that would make them equals, asked with asperity: " Damn it, do you think I like this solution any better than you do? " He didn't even care, for the moment, whether Bunty caught the smarting note of personal resentment in that, provided it bolstered Dominic's developing ego.

The blue-ringed eyes shot one rapid, startled glance into his face and were hastily lowered again. They would be stealing measuring looks in his direction with increasing frequency from now on.

" Well, no, I suppose not," said Dominic cautiously. The tone suggested that he would have liked to linger inwardly over the implications, if there had not been something infinitely more urgent to be considered. " Only I start from what I know, and it makes the whole thing different for me. And so—well, maybe I might get somewhere different, and find out things that you wouldn't. You can see that I've got to try, anyhow."

" I can see you feel you have to," agreed George.

" You don't object? "

" Provided you don't impede us in any way, how can I object? But if you do happen on anything relevant, don't forget you have a duty to pass it on to the police."

" But I suppose that doesn't mean *you* have to tell *me* anything! "

The tone was so arrogant this time that George revised his ideas of the nursing this developing ego needed; it seemed, on the whole, to be doing very well for itself, and there was no sense in letting it get out of hand. " No," he said firmly.   " And after what happened yesterday that can hardly surprise you."

" O.K.," said Dominic, abashed and retreating several years. " Sorry! "

He rose from the table with a purposeful face, and marched out without saying a word about his intentions. It was Saturday, so at least he was saved from fretting barrenly over books he wouldn't even be able to see, and lectures that would be double-Dutch to him. Bunty followed him out into the garden, where he was grimly pumping up the tyres of his bicycle. She didn't ask any questions, she just said: " Good luck, lamb! " and kissed him; she thought she might justifiably go as far as that, it was what she'd always done and said when she was sending him out to face some dragonish ordeal like the eleven-plus examination or his first day at the grammar school. He recognised the rite, and dutifully raised his head from his labours to offer his mouth, as engagingly and as inattentively as at five years old; but instead of scrubbing off the kiss briskly with the back of his hand and leaning hard on the pump again, he straightened up and looked at her with the troubled eyes that didn't know from minute to minute whether to be a boy's or a man's. The first three ages of man were batting him back and forth among them like a shuttlecock.

" Thanks, Mummy! " he said gruffly, preserving the ritual.

She tucked a ten-shilling note into his pocket. "An advance against your expense account," she said.

For a moment he wasn't sure that he was being taken seriously enough. "I'm not kidding," he said sternly, scowling at her.

"I'm not kidding, either," said Bunty. "I don't know the girl, but you do, and if you say she didn't do it that goes a long way with me. Anything on the level I can do to help, you ask me. Right?"

"Right! Gosh, *thanks*, Mummy!"

It wasn't just for the ten shillings, which at first he'd suspected of being a bribe to him to cheer up, it wasn't even for the offer of help and support, it was for everything she'd implied about his relationship with Kitty: that it was adult, that it was real, that it had importance and validity, and was to be treated with respect. He experienced one of those moments of delighted love for his mother, of startling new discoveries in his exploration of her, which are among the unexpected compensations of growing up. And Bunty, who knew when to vanish, sailed hastily back into the house feeling almost as young as her son.

Flashes of pleasure and warmth, however, did nothing to solve the problem of Kitty, and the shadow and weight closed on him again more oppressively than ever as he straddled his bicycle and rode out of Comerford by the farm road that would bring him out close to The Jolly Barmaid. In the grassy verge by the cross-roads he put one foot to the ground and sat gazing at the house, thinking hard. People had almost given up standing about staring at the place by this time, the centre of attention had shifted now to wherever Kitty was likely

to be. The news was out, in morning papers and news
bulletins and by the ever-present grapevine that twined
across the back fences of the villages and burrowed its
roots into the foundations of the town. *Kitty Norris!* Can
you *believe* it?

The vulgar new sign in its convolutions of wrought-
iron gleamed at the edge of the road. The doors would
not be opened for business until after the funeral, for
which permission had been given at yesterday's adjourned
inquest. How it would have annoyed Armiger to have to
forgo a week-end's takings just because someone was dead.
The funeral, they said, would be on Monday, and Raymond Shelley was seeing to the arrangements, not Leslie
Armiger. The conventionally-minded, with magnificent
hypocrisy, were already beginning to censure Leslie for
want of filial feeling, and were quite certain in advance
that he wouldn't go to the funeral. Why in the world,
wondered Dominic, should he be expected to? He'd
been expressly dismissed from his position as a son, and
forbidden to feel filial; if he suffered any regrets for his
ex—or late—father it constituted a gesture of generosity
on his part, it wasn't in any way due from him. And
what did he feel now for Kitty, who had flown slap into
the net to make sure he should not be snared? He must
know by now. Everybody knew. Even when Dominic
rode past the first farm cottages the air felt heavy and
tremulous with the reverberations of the news, and two
women with their heads together over the fence could
only be retailing the rich imaginary details of Kitty's fall.

Dominic began to follow the course Kitty had taken
that night. Here she had halted before sweeping out in a
right-hand turn and heading for Comerbourne; it had

then been about a quarter past ten. Somewhere on her way she'd changed her mind and wished she'd stayed; somewhere before the next right-hand turn into the lane that wound its way to Wood's End, and there brought her into the rear farm road, the ridge-road from the back of The Jolly Barmaid, that followed the old contour track between the upland fields and the low, moist river meadows. Probably she'd driven this stage slowly and cautiously; she was a fast driver by inclination but not a reckless one, and at night the frequent bends and high hedges of the lane contained and shrouded even the beams of headlights.

Natural enough, when she changed her mind, to go round like this instead of turning and driving back along the high road; natural enough, that is, if she only made up her mind when the cross-roads came in sight, and what could be more likely? A cross-roads is an invitation to pause, to think again and confirm your direction. So she turned down here, saying to herself: I will, I'll have one more go at making him see reason.

A third of a mile or so, and the lane brought her to the next right-hand turn, under the signpost at Wood's End. Hardly a village, just a few farm cottages, the long drive of the farm, one tiny shop, and a telephone box. And from here to the right again, into the old road, and maybe just over a quarter of a mile to go to the tall boundary wall of The Jolly Barmaid. She had parked " along there under the trees by that little wood." When he reached the spot it was easy to see why, for the road broadened there into a wide stretch of trampled grass on the left, like an accidental lay-by under the hanging wood, and there she could get off the road. For by that time it must

have been nearly, if not quite, half past ten, closing
time at the pub, and though most of the customers would
be using the main road, there was always the possibility
that some of the countrymen would be leaving by this
way.

Dominic dismounted, and pushed his bike slowly the
last fifty yards or so from the place where she had parked
to the rear exit from the courtyard. It was not a gate
but a broad opening in the high wall, blocked with two
iron posts so that no cars could drive out that way. The
barn-ballroom was quite close, she had only to cross this
remote corner of the yard to the doorway and walk in.
And there Armiger had waited for her, full of his new
plan, entertaining no doubts of her complacency.

How long had it taken, what happened in there? Not
long, surely. She trying to get him to listen to her plea
for Leslie, he riding over everything with his great
schemes for the future, and convinced that she was with
him; like two people trying to convey to each other two
conflicting urgencies, without a word in common in any
language. If she had reached this place about half past
ten, or a little later, allowing for parking and locking the
car and perhaps for some final hesitation, Dominic
estimated that she must have taken flight well before
eleven. Armiger would never let the exposition of his
deal take him more than a quarter of an hour, he went
straight at things. There was a pretty good indication of
the times involved, too, in Kitty's declaration that she
had reached her flat by about ten past eleven; granted
that was discredited by the evidence of her neighbours,
yet it must be the time she had felt she ought to give, the
correct time to round off the version of her movements

which she wanted to have believed. Between ten and
five minutes to eleven she came running out of the ballroom and left Armiger lying at the foot of the staircase,
thought Dominic with certainty.

And then what? She would want only one thing, as
she herself had said, and that was to get away. Would
she drive on to the next turning and go right round The
Jolly Barmaid again to the main road? Or turn there
under the trees and drive back by the way she had come?
She'd turn, he decided, after only a moment's thought;
this way was quieter and also shorter. There was plenty of
room to turn under the trees. Almost certainly she headed
back towards Wood's End. And in fourteen or fifteen
minutes she should have been home. Why wasn't she?

He thought over and round it, and he was sure that
was the only point on which she had lied. And why?
There was an hour lost. Whatever she'd done with it,
he was quite certain she hadn't gone back and killed
Alfred Armiger, so why wouldn't she tell them what had
happened during that missing time? Because there was
someone else involved? Someone equally innocent,
whom she refused to harm?

Her whole desire had been to get away. If she hadn't
done it it was because she couldn't.

He had begun to push his bike back towards Wood's
End, trailing his toes in the fallen leaves under the trees.
He chose to walk because his mind was grinding over the
meagre facts so slowly that his feet had to keep the same
pace. Here she turned and drove back, and yet she
didn't get home to Comerbourne until after midnight.
She was going along here, probably fast, running away
from her sense of outrage and frustration and shame; and

somewhere along here fright fell on her, too, the dread
that she ought to have waited to make sure how badly
he was hurt; but by then it wouldn't stop or turn her,
it would only drive her on all the faster. So why didn't
she get home soon after eleven, as she should have done?

And then he knew why.

It was so simple and so silly that it had to be true.
He heard the busy low note of the engine cough and fail,
felt the power die away, and saw Kitty reach for the tap
with one impatient toe, to kick it over on to the reserve,
and then draw back furious and exasperated because it
was on the reserve already, and yet once again she'd done
her inimitable trick. Half the day she'd probably been
saying to herself cheerfully: " Plenty of time, I've got a
gallon, I'll call at Lowe's before I leave Comerbourne,
I'll look in at the filling station at Leah Green——"
making easy promises every time the necessity recurred
to her, until it didn't recur to her any more.

" I never learn. I run dry in the middle of the High
Street, or half-way up the lane to the golf links." He could
hear her voice now, and remember every word she had
said about her two blind spots. Nobody who didn't know
Kitty as he did, nobody who wasn't in her confidence as
he was, could ever have unearthed this simple explanation
for her lost hour. She just ran out of petrol! She was
always doing it; she'd told him so herself.

The next question was: Where did it happen? He
thought that over and decided that it must have been
somewhere close to The Jolly Barmaid and well away
from Comerbourne. If she had been near the town when
she ran dry she would simply have stopped a car on the
main road and begged the driver either to let her have

some juice or to call in at her garage and leave a message; to be immobilised on the main road near Comerbourne at around eleven o'clock would be innocent enough, just as good as being home by ten past eleven, and there wouldn't have been any missing hour, or any need for lies. But Kitty had lied, it was one of the main points against her. No, somewhere along here, somewhere unpleasantly close to the inn, she found herself stranded. And here she didn't want to stop a car and ask for help, she didn't want to have her garage man come out with petrol for her; she didn't want to call attention to her presence in any way, or let anyone know that she had been here.

Dominic was imagining her state of mind with so much passion that his own heart-beats quickened and his temples began to throb with panic. Every minute that passed must have driven her a little nearer to hysteria. Supposing Armiger was desperately hurt, and she'd run away and left him? Supposing, even, that he should die? Maybe she'd thought of going back to him, but she simply couldn't face it. She hadn't meant to do anything so dreadful, but it had happened and she was to blame. In that state of mind she would have only one instinctive idea, and that would be to hide the fact that she had ever been near the place after she left by the main road at a quarter past ten.

Supposing it happened somewhere here, he thought, walking slowly along the left-hand side of the old road, she'd be in a spot about getting the car as far as possible off the fairway, because it's rather narrow and winding. If I keep my eyes open I may be able to spot the place, because she'd have to try and run it almost into the

K

hedge, and I wonder if maybe her paint may not show some scratches, too?

He was almost within sight of the Wood's End cottages when he found one place at least where some vehicle had certainly been run as far as possible on to the bumpy grass verge, its near-side wheel-marks hugging the base of the hedge. There was no mistaking it; the crushing of the thick growth on the ground, the breaking of the overgrown shoots of the hedge, these were slight signs already partially erased by showers and winds and the passing of time, but the breakages were there to be seen if you looked for them, and the wheel-track was still evident. It might be Kitty, it might not, there was no way of knowing unless she chose to tell them.

However, supposing for the sake of the theory that this was where she ran dry, what would she do next? She would have to call on someone for help, and the obvious thing to do was to go to the telephone box at Wood's End, and from there ring up some private person, some-one she could trust absolutely. And the someone came in response to her appeal, and brought her petrol enough to get her home. But what had determined Kitty's silence was surely the fact that this simple act had now laid her benefactor open to a charge as an accessory after the fact in a murder case. If they convicted her they could charge her helper. Kitty wouldn't allow that; no word of hers was ever going to involve the friend who had come to her rescue. That was the kind of girl she was.

This long communion with himself had brought Dominic to the telephone box. He stood and looked at it for a moment, and then, without any clear idea of

what he hoped to find within, pulled open the door and
looked round the dusty interior. Absolutely impersonal,
a piece of the mundane machinery of modern living,
with the usual graffiti. He was letting the door swing to
when he caught an incongruous gleam of gold, and
pulled it hastily open again. Clinging in the hinge of
the door, shadowy as cobweb but for a few torn gilt
threads, a scrap of gauze hung like a crushed butterfly.

He put out a hand to pull it loose, and then checked
himself in the act, and did no more than smooth out the
delicate scrap tenderly with his fingertips until he could
distinguish the minute embroidered flowers of gold on
the almost impalpable silk. A corner of an Indian scarf,
shot dark blue and red, embroidered with gold thread;
the scarf Kitty had worn on the night of Armiger's death.
The one detail for which the police had no satisfactory
explanation, the bit that didn't fit in; but for Dominic it
fitted in miraculously.

He mustn't move it; he must let his father see it just
as it was. He shut himself into the box and dialled with
a hand trembling with excitement.

"This is Dominic Felse here. Can I speak to my
father, please? I know, but this is important, it's something to do with the case."

George was up to his neck in paper work, and impatient
of interruptions, but too sore from his recent mistakes to
take any new risks where Dominic was concerned. He
listened without any real expectations, and heard, in-
credulously: "I'm at the telephone box at Wood's End,
Dad. I've found the corner you said was torn from
Kitty's scarf."

"You've *what*?"

Dominic repeated his statement patiently. " It's caught on a rough place in the hinge of the door, she must have pulled it clear in a hurry and torn the corner clean off. I know, I *haven't* moved it. I'm keeping an eye on it until you come."

" How on earth did you come to walk straight to it? " asked George, humanly aggrieved.

" I used me natural genius. Come along and I'll tell you." He couldn't help the cocky note, but he wasn't really feeling elated; there was still too far to go, and too much at stake. He debated within himself, while he waited, how much he ought to tell his father, how much he was committed to telling. All that was really evidence was that scrap of silk, but it tended to consolidate his theories into something like facts, and perhaps he ought to confide everything. His accidental acquaintance with Kitty's idiosyncrasies in connection with cars, for instance, was evidence, too, and so was the shaved place along the hedge. In the end he told George the whole process of thought which had brought him to the telephone box, and was listened to with flattering attention. He added his initials to George's on the envelope in which George enclosed the shred of gauze, though he had a faint suspicion that that was a sop to his self-love.

" It all makes remarkable sense, as far as it goes," agreed George, inspecting the hedge. " We can check the car and see if it shows any traces. This chap's wings were well into the strong growth."

" I suppose," said Dominic, very carefully and quietly, " it wouldn't be possible for me to see Kitty, would it? "

" I'm afraid not, Dom. I'm pretty sure they wouldn't consider it. You'd need a solid reason like being her

legal adviser or a member of her family to get in to her
—yet, at any rate."

"Yes, I see. I didn't think I could, really. But you
could see her, couldn't you? You could ask her all my
questions for me, if you would—like where she ran out
of petrol, and whom she telephoned. I don't think she'll
tell you, of course, but she won't be expecting you to
know anything about it, and she may give something
away without meaning to. She isn't very good at telling
lies, really," said Dominic, suppressing the slight con-
striction in his throat. " She forgets and comes out with
a bit of the truth, without thinking. Only if she's lying
for somebody else she'll be twice as careful." He scrubbed
his toes along the deep grooves the wheels had left in the
soft grass under the hedge, and scowled down at his feet.
" I suppose you couldn't give her a message from me,
could you? Oh, nothing unconstitutional, I only meant
just to give her my regards—and maybe tell her I'm
doing what I can for her."

" I'll give her that message with pleasure," said George
gravely.

He didn't tell him that Kitty's car had yielded two
faint, minute smears of blood from the edge of the driving-
seat, obviously brushed there from the skirt of her dress,
or that the fine scratches on the near-side front wing had
already been preoccupying their minds for several hours.
It seemed ungenerous to keep these things back from
him, when he was making so notable a contribution, but
there was no choice about it. They'd agreed on their
terms of truce; Dominic wasn't expecting concessions.

George went to see Kitty that afternoon. Raymond
Shelley was just leaving her, his face worn and wretched,

his bulging brief-case hugged to him defensively as he passed George in the corridor, as though he had Kitty's life locked in it. It wasn't easy for them even to talk to each other now, they had become representative of the two sides, and communication was an effort.

"You realise, of course," said Shelley, "that her defence will be an absolute denial of the charge. Any competent doctor will be able to show that no woman could have been responsible for the attack, on physical grounds alone."

George said nothing to that. He had tentatively raised the same point, and Duckett had given him a derisive glare, and said: "Are you kidding? What, with a sitting target all laid out for her against a brand-new floor about as hard as ebony? A fairly lusty ten-year-old could have done it."

"I can't realise it, even yet," burst out Shelley, shaking his head helplessly. "Kitty! I've known her all her life, she couldn't wilfully hurt even an insect. It just can't be true, Felse, it simply can't. I can't forgive myself for leaving her alone that night. If I'd realised he had any such thing in his mind I could have stopped it."

Could he, wondered George, looking after him with sympathy as he flung nervously away. How much influence had he with Armiger, if it came to the point? What was it Leslie had called him?—a cover man. He was the one who was used; he was in his master's secrets only as far as Armiger chose to admit him for his own ends. No, Shelley would never have been effective in diverting the bull's rush, but if he'd tried he might have made one more casualty.

Kitty had survived the first anguish, the agonised tears

of helplessness and loneliness and shame that had scarified
his heart yesterday. Dominic, thank God, knew nothing
about that half-hour of collapse, and never would know.
Whatever his imagination inflicted upon him, it would
not be the reality George had seen and suffered. The first
thing to-day's Kitty did was to apologise for it, simply
and directly, without embarrassment. It was past, it
wouldn't happen again.

"I'm sorry I gave you such a bad time. I hadn't
expected it myself, I was shocked. It just shows, you
never know how you may react in a crisis. And I always
thought I had an equable temperament."

George said: "My son sent you his regards, and said
I was to tell you that he's doing what he can for you."

She lifted her head and smiled at him, with a smile
which he knew belonged by rights to Dominic. She looked
pale and drained, but all her distress had done to her
looks was to make her eyes look larger than ever, and the
vulnerable curves of her mouth more plaintive and tender.
She had on the same neutral-tinted sweater and skirt he
had seen her in at her flat, and a book was turned down
beside her; she looked like an over-earnest student surprised during the last week before a vital examination.

"Please thank him for me. He's almost the only one
who believes me when I say I didn't do it. Out of the
mouths of babes——" She shut her hands suddenly on
the air as if to snatch back the unforgivable indiscretion.
"No, don't tell him I said that. It isn't even true, and it
would hurt him. Just thank him for me, and give him
my love." At that she had taken a careful second look
before she ever let her lips shape the single significant

syllable, but she didn't take it back. The soft bow of her mouth folded firmly, and let it stand.

"We found the place where you pulled the car into the hedge when you ran out of petrol," said George in the same conversational tone. "Why didn't you tell us about that? You might have known we were sure to find it."

"*He* found it," said Kitty, and smiled again to herself, and that smile, too, was for Dominic. "What a boy!" she said. "Fancy remembering that! But even he could be wrong, you know. Now I'm not talking about that any more, it isn't a subject I like, and you can't make me. Come to think of it, there's absolutely nothing you people can do to me now. Except, perhaps, stop visiting me. I'd much rather see you than nobody. Poor old Ray looks so desperately sad he breaks my heart. And who else is likely to come near me?"

"You have hordes of friends, and you know it," said George, consenting to follow her disconcerting leaps.

"I *had*. The most popular deb. of her year, that was Kitty. Do you know how many eligible young men have wanted to marry me, since they knew Leslie was out of the market? Seven actually got as far as asking, and about five more were hovering pretty near the brink. And do you know how many have been to try and see me to-day, to show how much they loved me? One. And that was Leslie, the one who never pretended to." She laughed, and because Leslie had come it was a genuine, beautiful, even joyful laugh. Only then did George understand. Kitty had got something out of her disaster, after all.

"Did they let him in?"

" Oh, yes, he had a certain claim, you see, my victim's son, and brought up almost like a brother to me. He was sweet," said Kitty, looking down into her cupped hands and smiling with a brooding tenderness for which any man would have performed prodigies of love and loyalty. " And terribly upset." She didn't care who observed her personal sorrow or her personal rapture here; life had become so precarious as to be simple, there was no time for dissembling or being ashamed. " I believe he even feels responsible for me, simply because it was his father who got killed—as though he could help it. He feels almost as if it was he who got me into it. But I got myself into it—nobody else. You won't mistake that for a confession, will you? It isn't."

" And kept somebody else out of it," said George.

She turned her head and looked at him, not so abruptly that he could claim he had got a real reaction out of her, but at least so positively that he knew she was paying attention for once.

" The person you telephoned to come and help you out of your mess," said George. " We know you did, you left a bit of your scarf caught in the door of the telephone box at Wood's End. Did you think we shouldn't get wise to that call? You may as well tell us all about that interlude, you know, it's only a matter of time."

" I'm in no hurry," said Kitty, smiling, even teasing him, though the sadness that was in everything she did or said was in this perversity too.

" Who was it, Kitty? Better give us the name than have us give it to you."

" I don't even know what you're talking about. Look, I've thought of something," she said. " If I'm convicted, I can't inherit from my victim, can I? So what happens to the money? I never thought to ask poor old Ray, I was so busy stroking his hand and saying: There, there! Do *you* know? "

" I'm not sure. But I should think it would automatically go to the next-of-kin, unless there's some express veto on that in the will itself." He didn't know how much of this he could take, and still remember that he was a police officer, here on business. He wished he could think that she was doing it to him on purpose, to repay her own injuries, or out of bravado, to put them out of her mind, but he knew she wasn't. She was evading being questioned, but she asked her own questions because she wanted to know the answers.

" Good! " she said with a sigh of satisfaction. " Then at any rate Leslie and Jean won't have to worry any more, they'll be loaded. I suppose I ought to make a will, too."

George opened his mouth to answer her, and couldn't get out a word. She looked up, her isolation penetrated for a moment by the quality of his shocked silence, and searching for the reason in her own words, came up with the wrong answer.

" It's all right," she said quickly and kindly. " I didn't mean it like that. I know! Even if the worst comes to the worst, it isn't capital murder."

CHAPTER X

" THERE SHE IS," said Leslie, stepping back from the table " The Joyful Woman in person. I took your advice and fetched her back from Cranmer's yesterday. What do you think of her? "

If George had told the simple truth in answer to that it would have had to be: Not much! Propped against the wall to catch the light from the window, what there was of it on this dull Sunday morning, the wooden panel looked singularly unimpressive, its flesh-tints a sallow fawn-colour, its richer shades weathered and dirtied into mere variations on tobacco-brown. Not very big for an inn sign, about twenty by eighteen inches, and even within that measure the figure was not so bold as it could have been. Against a flat ground that might once have been deep green or blue but was now grained with resinous brown varnishes coat after coat, the woman was shown almost to the waist. At the base of the panel her hands were crossed under little maidenly breasts, swathed in a badly-painted muslin fichu. Her shoulders beneath the folds of muslin were braced back, her neck was long, and in its present incarnation shapeless, and inclined forward like a leaning flower-stem to balance the backward tilt of the head. In half-face, looking to the right, she raised her large bland forehead to the light and laughed; and in spite of the crudity of the flat masses of which she was built, and the want of moulding in the face, there was no doubt that this was the laughter of delight and not of amusement; she wasn't sharing it with an audience, it belonged to herself alone. Joyful was the just word for her.

" I know nothing about painting," said George truthfully, and taking care not to sound complacent about it. " Frankly, it's pretty ugly, isn't it? And a queer mixture. That frill round her neck, and those mounds of hair like wings, and the corkscrew curls at the sides, all look like touches of early Victorian realism. But her pose isn't Victorian—or realistic. More sort of hieratic—if I'm making any sense? "

" You're making quite remarkable sense. Which is it you find ugly, the mass or the detail? "

" The detail, I suppose. The mass balances—I mean the shape of her on the panel. The masses of paint are clumsy, but I suppose that's from years of over-painting by amateurs every time it got shabby."

" You know," said Leslie appreciatively, " you'd better be careful, or you're going to turn into an art critic." He had quite forgotten, in his excitement over this unimposing work of art, that his relationship with George had hitherto been one of mutual suspicion and potential antagonism. " That's exactly what's happened to her, and been happening for probably a couple of centuries. Every time she needed brightening up, some ham-fisted member of the family took a brush and some primary colours and simply filled in the various bits of her solidly, line to line, like a mosaic. And every now and again one of the artists got carried away and started putting in twiddly bits like the corkscrew curls—which, as you so justly remarked, don't belong. I'm betting they don't go below a couple of coats at all. But the shape, the way she fills the panel and stands poised, and leaves these rather beautiful forms round her—that's there from the beginning, and that's *good*. And I want her out of that coffin. I want to see what she was like once, before she went into the licensed trade, because I'm pretty sure there was a before. She hasn't always been an inn sign."

Jean, pausing for a moment on her way out to the landing kitchenette, stared intently at the laughing woman, and bit thoughtfully at the handle of the fork she was holding in her hand. "You know, she kind of reminds me of something, only I can never think what. Do you think she always laughed?"

"Yes, I think so, it's in the tilt of the head. But with luck we shall see, some day. I'm taking her to the chap who runs the university gallery this afternoon," explained Leslie contentedly. "I telephoned him yesterday—Brandon Lucas, I find I used to know his son at Oxford, so that broke the ice nicely—and he said yes, she sounded very interesting, and he'd like to have a look at her."

"Did you have any trouble getting it back from Cranmer?" asked George.

"No, no trouble. He wasn't very keen on parting, but I suppose he'd hardly be likely to commit himself to *too* urgent an interest, after your inquiries."

"Did he make you an offer?"

"Yes," said Leslie.

"How high did he go?"

Too late George felt the slight chill of constraint that had suddenly lowered the temperature in the room, and the tension that charged the air between husband and wife. He shouldn't have asked; money was something that had shadowed the whole of their short married life, the want of it, the injustice of its withdrawal, the indignity of stooping to ask for it.

" Six hundred pounds," said Jean, distinctly and bitterly, and made for the door.

Leslie's fingers pinched out his cigarette, suddenly trembling. " You didn't want to touch it when Dad offered five hundred," he said indignantly. " You said I did right to turn that down. What's so different about this offer? "

" It's a hundred more," she said flatly and coldly, " and it doesn't come from your father. It's straight money from a dealer, and it wouldn't burn me, and the things I could buy with it wouldn't be poisoned."

So that was it. When the offer was pushed up to so tempting a figure she had wanted him to take it. Perfectly logical and understandable. She was a breeding tigress, she wanted to line a nest for her young; not at any price, but at any price that didn't maim her pride. If her confidence in Leslie had been still unshaken she would have accepted his estimate of their best course, and gone along with him loyally, but that one disastrous move of his had ended the honeymoon once for all. Now he had to prove himself, he would never be taken on trust again, and his every act was to be scrutinised and judged mercilessly, not because she was greedy for herself, but because she was insatiable for her child. Looking round the shabby, congested room that was their home, George couldn't blame her for preferring to clutch at certain benefits to-day rather than speculate on riches to-morrow.

" And if I'd taken it, and then the thing had turned out to be worth ten times as much, you'd never have let me forget that, either," said Leslie, smarting. He flushed

at the petulant tone of his own voice, and to break off
the unseemly argument went forward and plucked the
panel from its place, his pleasure in it spoiled. He was
ashamed of having displayed their differences before
George, and probably so was she, for she said from the
doorway, without turning her head: " Well, it's no use
worrying now, in any case, it's done. We may be lucky
yet."

" Believe me, Mrs. Armiger," said George firmly, "if
Cranmer offered six hundred for it he was absolutely
certain of clearing a good deal more than that. He isn't
in business for fun. You hang on to it until you get a
really disinterested opinion."

He moved to Leslie's shoulder to take another look
at it. There was a queer ornament pinned between the
childish breasts, something that looked like an enormous
oval brooch with some embossed pattern on it. It rested
upright above the crossed hands, long, curved, inarticulate
hands pallid under the crazed vanish. " You've got some
definite idea of your own about this, haven't you? " he
asked curiously.

" Well, I have, but I don't dare believe it. It's too
staggering, I'd rather not talk about it until somebody else
has pronounced on it, somebody who knows a lot more
about these things than I do." He wrapped the panel
in an old dust-sheet and stacked it carefully in a corner.
" I'm sorry, I've been so full of her I can't think of much
else, but I'm sure you didn't come here to talk about *her*.
Is it something about Kitty? " His face was grave enough
at the thought of her, the vexation and the pleasure of
his own affairs both overshadowed.

" It is about her, as a matter of fact," said George.

" You paid her a visit yesterday morning, didn't you? "

" Yes, as soon as I could get away from the shop. I didn't even know she'd been arrested until I went to work. Why? It was all right, wasn't it? "

" Oh, quite. I was simply wondering if she'd been any more forthcoming with you than she was with us. There's an hour of her time, that night, from just after eleven until just after twelve, for which she refuses to account, and there's a possibility that her reasons for keeping quiet are concerned with some other person. My impression is that the best thing that could happen for her is that everything to do with her movements that night should come out."

" Guilty or innocent? "

" Guilty or innocent."

" From you," said Leslie after some thought, " I might accept that. But if you mean did she tell me anything yesterday morning that she wouldn't tell you in the afternoon, no, she didn't. Not a word about my father or that night. We didn't talk about it. We didn't talk a lot about anything. She just said she didn't do it, and I said I never thought she did. Which I suppose is a perfectly good reason for co-operating with you, now that I come to think of it."

" It is, if that's what you honestly believe. You were with her—how long? Half an hour or so? If you weren't talking, what were you doing all that time? "

" Most of that time," said Leslie, angry colour suddenly mantling over his shapely cheek-bones, " Kitty was crying, and I was trying to comfort her." He glared for a moment, but the flash of partisan indignation passed as quickly as it had flared up. " Oh, nothing shattering, just she needed to, and with me she could. She didn't tell me anything about your missing hour. And I suppose you know you're not the only one who's been asking me about it? Your boy came to see me yesterday."

"I didn't know, but I'm not surprised." Dominic had volunteered no information resulting from his inquiries in this direction, it seemed likely that he had acquired none. "We have a working arrangement," said George with a hollow smile. "Did he ask you this one? If Kitty was in a desperate hole and needed someone quickly, someone who wouldn't hesitate to come out to her late at night and get her out of trouble, to whom would she turn?"

"No, he didn't ask that exactly, but maybe we covered much the same ground another way. There was a time when I'd have said she'd come to me. We've been good friends, she was like my little sister most of the time we were growing up, but that ghastly scheme of my father's broke it all down. What could you expect? Kitty's odd, sweet and funny and candid, but very much alone, too. I'm very fond of her, and I think she was of me until Dad spoiled everything. I did say to her yesterday, why on earth didn't she call on me if she was in a spot, but all she said was something daffy about my not being on the telephone any more, as though that was any reason for locking me out of her life. Did you say something?"

George shook his head. "No, go on. If she wouldn't turn to you, then who would it be?"

"Well, of course she has fellows round her as thick as bees wherever she goes, and all that, but I can't imagine her going to any of them. I think it would be someone older, if she really needed someone. It would have been her aunt, the one who brought her up, of course, only she died a year or so ago. There's her manager—he's a nice old boy, and she's known him all her life—or Ray Shelley, he's her unofficial uncle, she always got on well with him, especially after he tried to stick up for me when the row burst. Someone like that. I'm not being much help? "

" You might be," said George.

" Don't get me wrong. It's Kitty I want to help, not you. No offence, you're only doing your job, I know. But I'm not a policeman, I'm just a friend of Kitty's."

" All right," said George, resigned to his exclusion from humankind, " that's understood. I suppose, by the way, that Dom made it quite clear where he stands? " He saw by the fleeting gleam of a smile in Leslie's eyes that indeed Dominic had, and that he had been welcomed accordingly.

He got as far as the door, and then turned back to say: " One more thing, you might like to know, we did find somebody who confirmed your timing that night. One of the colliers on late shift at the Warren happens to live at the bottom end of this road. He was coming off the miners' bus at the corner just as you turned in on your way home. That fixes the time pretty accurately at around a quarter to eleven, give or take a couple of minutes. So that's that. For what it's worth now."

" I see," said Leslie slowly. " Well, thanks for telling me, anyhow. It would have been worth a lot a couple of days ago. As you say, it doesn't seem to matter much now."

" It was only last night we got round to the idea of checking the miners' bus. If I'd known before I'd have told you. Well, good luck with your Joyful Woman this afternoon. How are you doing the trip? That's an awkward thing to tote around by bus. I could offer you transport, if you're in difficulties? "

" That's awfully kind of you, but we've got the use of Barney Wilson's van when he isn't using it himself. He lets me keep his spare key, so that I can fetch it if I want it. He stables it at the Department's depot just out on the main road, not having a garage at home, so it's nice and handy."

" Trusting chap," said George from the top of the stairs. " Most people would rather loan you their wives."

Well, he thought as he drove slowly and thoughtfully homewards, he hadn't come out of that encounter quite empty-handed, even if there were some annoying loose ends that didn't tie in anywhere. Chief among them was The Joyful Woman, that unpromising work of art, of such commonplace provenance and ungainly appearance, for which nonetheless a shrewd dealer was willing to pay six hundred pounds. Had she anything to do with Armiger's death, or had she not? She didn't fit in with the theory which had been devouring him ever since his visit to Kitty yesterday, but if she was going to turn out to be extremely valuable the possibility became worth considering.

Yet if money was the motive for this murder there was surely a greater prize to be considered than the few thousands which might be involved even in an important art find. Not the money Armiger had been playing for at the end of his life, but all the money he already had, the quarter of a million or so that young Leslie had always lightheartedly assumed would come to him. Had he

really resigned himself to doing without it? And even
if he had been on the point of coming to terms with his
new poverty, for want of the means to change it, what
would be his reaction if fate had suddenly presented him
with a wonderful, a unique opportunity of regaining his
fortune?

No doubt about it, Leslie had left The Jolly Barmaid
that night with no intention of doing anything more
reprehensible than walking home. That was what he
had meant to do, and that was what he had done; the
collier's evidence proved that quite conclusively. There
was no question of his having hung about outside and
witnessed Kitty's panic flight, and then returned to
finish the job she had accidentally begun. He had been
in Comerbourne at that moment, a mile and a quarter
away from the scene. If he had killed he had gone back
to kill, and the intent had been conceived as instan-
taneously as a flash of lightning—or, say, a cry for help.
A cry from Kitty.

George had arrived at this point when it dawned upon
him at last that he was thinking in terms which indicated
that he no longer entertained the slightest doubt of
Kitty's innocence. Whether that was Kitty's own doing
or Dominic's was something he couldn't determine. But
it didn't surprise him; he was only belatedly recognising
something which had been true for at least twenty-four
hours.

Not Kitty. Someone else. Someone to whom she had
telephoned from Wood's End? Supposing, for the sake
of the argument, that someone had found out from an
agitated Kitty that Armiger was lying unconscious in the
barn, and supposing that someone had, or abruptly dis-

covered at that moment, an overwhelming reason for wanting the job finished. There was Kitty all set up ready to take the blame, and herself alerting the murderer to his unique opportunity. A chance like that comes only once in a lifetime.

It was Kitty herself who had put the idea into George's head, without the slightest conception of the kind of seed she was sowing, merely clutching at a small satisfaction in her desolation of sadness: " If I'm convicted I can't inherit from my victim, can I? So what becomes of the money? " And again, reassured and consoled: " Good! Then Leslie and Jean won't have to worry any more, they'll be loaded."

The set-up, however accidental, was perfect. It didn't even involve the killer in conniving at Kitty's death, since, as she had said, this wasn't capital murder; but the division of murder into capital and simple murder did not affect the law that a murderer cannot inherit from his victim. Kitty convicted could forfeit her inheritance and still come out of prison at the end of her term a rich and comparatively young woman. With a quarter of a million at stake he might even have been able to persuade himself that he wasn't doing her such a terrible wrong. That much money can often drown out the voice of conscience only too effectively.

There had been, in fact, only two snags when George had set out to pay this unexpected Sunday morning visit. Leslie had no car he could have taken out that night to hurry back to the barn; and as he had so suggestively reported Kitty herself as reminding them, he wasn't on the telephone any more. He could be reached only during working hours, at the warehouse. Insurmountable obstacles both; except that one of them had already been surmounted, for it seemed he had the use of Barney Wilson's van whenever its owner didn't need it. The spare key was in his charge and the van was close at hand in the yard of the depot. Now if the other obstacle should prove equally illusory?

The thing had been getting more complicated by the hour, and yet George had felt all along that in reality the truth must be one single thread that passed through the tangle as straight as a ruled line, and only by accident formed part of this proliferated web of motives and feelings. And here it was, the clear thread, the convincing motive, the irresistible temptation. A man who has a quarter of a million in his sights can afford to turn down a mere six hundred pounds.

But—Leslie wasn't on the telephone.

CHAPTER XI

DOMINIC SOUGHT out his father on Sunday evening with a face so determined that it was plain he was bent on a serious conference. Bunty had gone to church; George wouldn't have minded having her sit in on their counsels, but in all probability Dominic would, considering that mothers should be shielded from too close consideration of such shocking things as murder. In his present mood of newly appreciated responsibility he probably blamed George for subjecting her to his confidences all these years.

" Dad, I've been thinking about this glove business,"

he began, squaring his elbows purposefully on the table
opposite George's chair.

" Yes? " said George. It was not the precise opening
he had expected, but it was apposite enough; there was
no getting away from the gloves.

" You know what I mean. Those gloves of Leslie's
were O.K., but somebody must have had some pretty
fouled-up gloves to dispose of after that night, mustn't
they? The bottle was plastered right to the cork. And
I could tell, the way you all pounced on even the possibility of those old painting gloves being the ones, that
that was what you were looking for and hoping for.
I mean, anything else the murderer had on *might* be
marked, but his gloves definitely *would*—and he definitely
was wearing gloves. That's right, isn't it? "

" That's right. So?"

" Well, you never did say, but was Kitty wearing
gloves that night? " He didn't ask it with any sense that
the answer was going to prove anything, he wasn't as
simple as that. But it was a necessary part of the develop-
ment of his ideas.

" Not indoors," said George at once. " But she could
very well have had some in the car. When she was dressed
up for the evening she'd probably wear them for driving."

" Yes—but you've never found any stained gloves
among her things." He didn't ask, he asserted, waiting
with sharp eyes levelled for a reaction, and whatever he
got satisfied him. " Well, bearing this glove question in
mind, I've been thinking exactly what happened that
evening. If I've got it right, she dashed out of the barn
to run home, and in a few hundred yards she ran out of
petrol. There she is in a panic, she thinks she's done

something dreadful, injured him badly, maybe even fatally, she's got to get away, she daren't call a garage or anything. She runs to the telephone box and calls up some friend she can trust, says where she is, says come and bring me some petrol, a can, or even a tube to siphon it, anything, just to get me home. Don't say a word to anyone, she says, and come quickly. I've done something terrible. And she blurts out all about it; she'd be in such a state she wouldn't be able to help it. Now suppose this person she calls has good reason to want Armiger dead. He might not ever have thought of doing anything about it until now, but now it suddenly strikes him, this is it, this is for me! There's Armiger knocked cold in the barn, a sitting target if only he stays out until I can get round there, and there's somebody else all lined up to take the blame. I don't say he's absolutely made up his mind to kill him, but it's just too good to miss having a closer look at the set-up. Obviously there are risks, he may only have been knocked out for a few minutes, he may be conscious by the time this fellow gets there, he may even have gone. But what is there lost if he is? If he's gone, that's it. If he's up off the floor and hugging his headache all you need do is fake concern, help him to his car, and go off and reassure Kitty. And if Armiger's still lying where Kitty left him, and still dead to the world—well, there you are, a chance in a million.

" So he goes all right, he goes like a shot off a shovel, not to Kitty but to the barn. And sure enough, there's Armiger still out cold, and the chance in a million has come off."

" Go on," said George quietly, studying the intent face that stared back at him across the table. However

hotly they both denied it, there must be something in this
likeness Bunty was always finding between them, especially
when they annoyed her.   It was like having a mirror
held up to his own mind.   Often enough before, when
the same interest had preoccupied them both, he had
found Dominic hard on his heels at every check, like an
echo; but now he was no longer sure who was the echo
and who the initiator.   " Go on, let's see what you can
do with the details."

" I can fit them in," said Dominic.   " All of them.
This fellow's all keyed up for action, but he hasn't really
believed in it until then.   No weapon, you see, no real
preparations.   That would be like tempting providence.
He's wearing gloves simply because he's been driving on
a coldish night.   Now he takes the chance that's really
been offered to him at last.   The minute he comes in at
the door and sees Armiger still lying there, he grabs at
the nearest weapon he sees—the plaster statuette from
the alcove just on the right of the door.   I heard you say
what they were like, and how surprisingly light and hollow
they turned out to be.   He snatches it up to brain Armiger
with that, but heaves it away again in disgust on the spot
because it's such a silly, light thing it couldn't brain a
mouse.   It smashes against the wall, and he rushes up
the stairs and grabs the bottle instead, and lets fly with
that again and again until it smashes, too.   And then
he comes to his senses with Armiger pretty obviously
dead, and he's got to get rid of the traces.   Especially the
gloves.   And quickly, that's the point.   Within a few
hundred yards of where he is he's got to jettison those
gloves.   Because, you see, he's got to go on to Kitty and
get her off the scene as he promised, otherwise whoever

doesn't connect him with it when the murder comes out, *she will*. The whole beauty of the set-up is that *nobody* shall know. He can afford to let the police find their own way to Kitty. He can't afford to leave her or her car where they are, and have her picked up in circumstances so tight that she'll have to come out with the whole story, and say: 'I called so-and-so to come and help me, and he swore he would, but he never came.' Because even if that didn't give her ideas, it would certainly give them to you people, wouldn't it? "

" We shouldn't be likely to miss the implications," agreed George.

" He may not actually have planned on forcing Kitty to take the blame. If the chips fell that way, there she was. But probably he hadn't anything against her, and rather preferred that she should get away with it, too— as long as he was all right, of course. Anyhow, he had to go through with the rescue part of it as though he'd rushed straight to her. This part in the barn can't have taken many minutes, he wasn't long delayed.   So he'd got to get rid of the gloves. He'd got to meet Kitty, talk to her, handle the petrol can. He couldn't afford to leave blood about in the wrong places, or let Kitty see it and take alarm. He daren't put the gloves in his pocket or anywhere in his own car, they'd be certain to leave marks. So you see, what it boils down to is that he'd got to jettison them or hide them somewhere *before he met Kitty*."

" You have thought it out, haven't you? " said George. " Go on, how does he get rid of them? "

" There's not too much scope and not too much time, is there? He hadn't time to go far from the road, he had

to stay out of sight of Kitty. He lets himself out of the
barn carefully, closing the door with his left hand, because
that glove wouldn't be so saturated, it might only be
splashed here and there. I don't think he'd leave the
gloves anywhere inside, even if there was a hiding-place,
because of the door handle. Better smears of blood on it
than fingerprints. Then he peels off the gloves, letting
them turn inside-out as he pulls them off, and probably
rolling the right one inside the left, to get the cleanest
outer surface he can. I've been over the ground, there's
a drain grid close to the back of the barn, that's tempting,
but too obvious, because unless there was a strong flow
of water going down, and there wasn't, gloves would
lodge under the grid, and anyhow it's the first place the
police would look——"

"The first place they did look. After the barn itself,
of course. Go on."

"Then there's just the road, the hedge-banks and
ditches, and the hanging wood opposite. Seems obvious,
but I should think it takes an awful lot of men an awful
long time to search the whole of a wood that size, or
even just the strip alongside the road—because he hadn't
time to go very far inside. And all the ground there is so
covered with generations of leaf-mould, they could hunt
and hunt, and still might miss what they were looking
for. Anyhow, that's what I should have done, rushed
up into the wood and shoved them somewhere down
among the mould. And then he goes on to Kitty's rescue,
arriving all steamed up and concerned for her, dumps
the petrol in her tank for her, and tells her to go home
and not worry, she's making a fuss about nothing, the
old fool's sure to be all right. And Kitty—you said she

was wearing a dress with a wide skirt—she's so relieved
to see him she keeps close to him all the time they're there
together, and her skirt brushes against his trouser legs,
where the blood's splashed—and a drop falls from his
sleeve on her shoe. In the dark there neither of them
would know. And that's it, all your evidence. Have I
missed anything out? "

George had to own that he had not; he had accounted
for everything.

" You're quite sure he must have killed Armiger before
he sent Kitty home, and not after? "

" Well, of course! He wouldn't stay unconscious for
ever. If this chap had gone first to Kitty I doubt if he'd
ever have had the impetus or the nerve left to go back
and look if opportunity was still waiting for him."

He had seemed utterly sure of himself until he came to
the end, but when George sat thoughtfully silent he
couldn't stand the strain. He'd poured out all his hopes
into that exposition, and he was trembling when it was
done. His eyes, covertly hanging upon George's face,
pleaded for a sign of encouragement, and the brief silence
unnerved him. If he'd only known it, George was still
staring into a mirror.

" Well, say something! " burst out Dominic, his voice
quaking with tension. " Damn you, you just *sit* there!
You don't care if they send Kitty to prison for life, as
long as you get a conviction. You don't care whether
she did it or not, that doesn't matter. You're not doing
anything! "

George, coming out of his abstraction with a start, took
his son by the scruff of the neck and shook him, gently
enough to permit them both to pretend that the gesture

was a playful one, hard enough to indicate that it wasn't. The flow stopped with a gasp; in any case the onslaught had shocked Dominic a good deal more than it had George.

"That's enough of that. You hold your horses, my boy."

"Well, I know, I'm sorry! But you *do* just sit there! Aren't you going to give me *anything* back for all that?"

"Yes, a thick ear," said George, "if you start needling me. If you'd been anywhere near that wood of yours since noon to-day you'd have found it about as full of policemen as it'll hold, all looking for your gloves—as they've been doing in various places, more or less intensively, ever since we were sure there must have been gloves involved. Maybe we're not as sure as you that they'll be in a logical place, but we're just as keen as you are to find them. We even have open minds, believe it or not, on such minor points as whether a few small smears of blood on the hem of a dress are really adequate—in the circumstances. You're not the only one who can connect, my lad. We'd even like to know *who* it was she called that night. You be working on that one, and let me know when you've got the answer."

He was aware, by the sharpness and intelligence of the silence that followed, that if he had not said too much he had been understood too well. Dominic resettled his collar with great dignity, studying his father intently from the ambush of a composed and inscrutable face.

So it's like that, said the bright, assuaged eyes. I *see*! *They* may be looking for the gloves to clinch their case, but *you*'re not, you're looking for them to break it. You don't believe she did it! What did I tell you? I knew you'd come round to my way of thinking in the end. He was understandably elated by the knowledge, comforted by not being alone any longer in his faith, but there was something else going on behind the carefully sustained calm of that freckled forehead, something less foreseeable and a good deal more disturbing. He was glad to have an ally, and yet he fixed upon him a look that was far from welcoming. He saw too much, recognised his own sickness with too sharp a sensitivity in someone else, and most penetratingly of all in his father. He'd longed for an ally, but he didn't want a rival.

" I am working on it," said Dominic deliberately. " What's more, I think I'm on to the answer." But he did not say that he was going to share it, with his father or anyone. Saint George had sighted another banner on the horizon. It was going to be a race for the dragon.

CHAPTER XII

ON MONDAY morning, about an hour before Alfred Armiger was escorted to the grave, against all predictions, by a grim-faced and sombre son, Kitty Norris made a formal appearance of about two minutes in court, and was remanded in custody for a week.

She sat quietly through the brief proceedings, without a smile or a live glance for anyone, even Raymond Shelley who appeared for her. Docilely she moved, stood, sat when she was told, like a child crushed by the burden of a strange place and unknown, powerful, capricious people. Her eyes, hollowed by the crying and the sleep-lessness which were both past now, had swallowed half her face. They looked from enemy to enemy all round her, not hoping for a gap in the ranks, but not actively afraid. She had surrendered herself to the current that was carrying her, and whatever blows it dealt her she accepted mutely, because there was no help for it. It was heart-breaking to look at her. At least, thought George, who had brought her to the court, Dominic was spared this.

In the few minutes she spent in court the news had gone round, and there was a crowd waiting to see her come out, and one lone cameraman who erupted in her face before George could shelter her. He ought to have known that Kitty Norris, whose clothes and cars and dates had always made news, couldn't escape the headlines even on this first unheralded appearance in her new role. For the first time the lovely, hapless face came back to life. She shrank back into George's arm, frightened and abashed, mistaking raw curiosity for purposeful malignance. He half lifted her into the car, but even then the eyes and the murmurs followed her, gaping alongside the windows as she was driven away.

" Why should they be like that? " asked Kitty, shivering. " What have I ever done to them? "

" They don't mean any harm, dear," said the matron comfortably, " they're just nosy. You get used to it."

There ought to be something better to say to her than that, thought George, suffering acutely from the brushing of her sleeve against his, and the agonising memory of her warmth on his heart; and yet this queer comfort did seem to calm her. She expected nothing from him, and

it was not upon his shoulder that she let her head rest
as she was taken back to prison.

" You'll have to brace up, you know, Kitty," he said
as he helped her out of the car, himself unaware until he
had said it that her name was there on his lips waiting
to slip out so betrayingly.

" Why? " said Kitty simply, looking through him into
a bleak distance.

" Because you owe it to yourself—and to your friends
who believe in you."

The cords of his throat tightened up, outraged that he
could ask them to give passage to such unprofessional
sentiments. And he told himself afterwards, nursing the
smart of being misunderstood, that he deserved no better
than he got. For Kitty smiled suddenly, affectionately,
shortening her range so that for a moment she really
seemed to see him. Then she said in a gentle voice: " Oh,
yes, I mustn't let Dominic down. You tell him I'm
coming out fighting when the bell goes. With him in my
corner, how can I lose? "

Well, thought George grimly as he drove back towards
the centre of Comerbourne, that's properly accounted
for me. The invisible man, that's all I am, an office, not
a person, and an inimical office at that. And it hurt.
He knew he was making a fool of himself, but that only
made the smart worse. Jealousy is always humiliating;
jealousy of your own young son is an indignity hardly
to be borne.

The very soreness of his own nerves, and the small,
nagging sense of guilt that frayed the edges of his consciousness, made him very affectionate and attentive to
Bunty, and that in itself was dangerous, for Bunty had

known him a long time, and was a highly intelligent woman in her artfully unpretentious way. But long familiarity had made George so unwary with her that even his occasional subtleties tended to be childishly innocent in their cunning. She loved him very much, and her security of tenure was unshakable.

After the long, fretting days with so little accomplished George would wake out of his first shallow, uneasy sleep to the ache of his own ineffectiveness, and reach for Bunty not as a consolation prize, but as the remedy for what ailed him; and she would open her arms and respond to him, half awake, even half awake knowing that she was called upon to be two women, and sure she could without extending herself be all the women George would ever want or need. It was mostly in the middle of the night that he confided with the greatest ease and benefit. It was in the early hours of Wednesday morning that he told her about his precariously based conviction that the person Kitty had called to her aid on the night of the crime was in all probability the murderer of Alfred Armiger.

" But wouldn't she have suspected as much herself, afterwards? " asked Bunty. " She wouldn't keep silent about it, surely, if she thought it over and came to that conclusion herself? No earthly reason why she should protect a murderer, even if he did bring her some petrol."

" Of course not, but naturally she must have called on some person she knew intimately and could trust absolutely. In real life nobody treats a murder investigation like an impersonal puzzle in a book, and suspects everyone who had an opportunity or a motive; to some extent

M

you're bound to go by what you know of them. There
are people it could be and people it couldn't be. Your
family, your friends, they're immune. This man was
immune. If you were in a hole, and you yelled to me for
help and I came, and afterwards there was a body
around to be accounted for, would it enter your head
that I might be the killer? "

" Never in a million years," said Bunty. " But there's
only one of you for me. I might look sideways at almost
anyone else."

" What, Dom, for instance? Or old Uncle Steve? "

She thought of her bumbling old sheep of a paternal
uncle and giggled. " Darling, don't be funny! That
sweet old fool! "

" Or Chris Duckett, say? "

" No, I see what you mean. The only people you'd
consider letting in on your scrape would be people you
couldn't possibly suspect of anything bad. But if someone
actually put it into your head afterwards, mightn't you
just begin to wonder? Have you put it to Kitty that
way? "

" I've put it every way I can think of." The words that
visited his lips when he thought of Kitty came spurting
out of him in breathless bursts of indignation and anxiety,
impossible to disguise however he muffled them by
nuzzling in Bunty's hair. He could never deceive Bunty
worth a damn, anyhow, he gave up trying. " All along
she's simply ignored questions about that telephone call.
She knows we know she did ring somebody. But still
she—no, she doesn't deny it, she just pretends not to
understand, or else she doesn't even pretend, she just sits
there and shuts her mouth and isn't with us any more.

I've tried, and Duckett's tried. Nobody can get anything out of her. Of course I've told her whoever she called may very well be the murderer. I've urged her, I've threatened her, I've bullied her—it's only made it worse. She's more determined than ever not to give him away."

"Because she doesn't believe he had anything to do with it," said Bunty.

"No, she doesn't believe it. There's no talking to her."

"So she thinks she'd only be shifting her own trouble on to someone else just as innocent."

"And that we'd be just as dead set on getting a conviction against him as we must have seemed to be against her," said George bitterly. Suddenly abjectly grateful for Bunty's presence and her oneness with him, that sturdily refused to be changed by any outer pressures or even by the helpless convulsions of his overburdened heart, he turned and wound his arms about her, burying his face in the warm hollow of her neck. She shifted her position gently to make him more comfortable, hugging him to her heart.

"And Chris Duckett still thinks she did it?"

He mumbled assent, too tired to free his mouth. The slight movement was like the beginning of a kiss; he turned it into one.

"So between the chief hell-bent on getting a conviction against her, and you just as hell-bent on getting one against someone she's certain is equally blameless, and who'd be equally helpless if she once dragged him into it, no wonder the poor girl's just giving up the fight and refusing to say a word."

George came out of ambush to protest indignantly that he wasn't hell-bent on any such thing, that nobody was trying to convict for the sake of a conviction, that there was a logical case for investigating X's movements very carefully. He outlined it, and in the quietness there in the small hours it sounded even more impressive than it had when Dominic had propounded it on Sunday evening, in terms that might have been conjured out of George's own mind as a direct challenge to him.

" If it's like that," said Bunty at last, " and she won't talk for you, why don't you turn somebody loose on her for whom she *will* talk? I don't know Kitty as you do ——" Her hand caressed George's cheek; he hoped she wasn't comforting him for the undignified pain of which she couldn't possibly know anything, but he was dreadfully afraid she was. "——But I can't help feeling that if you got Leslie Armiger to question her she might break down and tell everything. I may be wrong," said Bunty kindly, well aware that she was not wrong, " but they almost grew up together, and I gather they're fond of each other."

" But that's just what I can't do," said George.

" Why not? "

" Because *he's the one*! Because in spite of one snag I can't get round I'm almost sure it was Leslie." He felt her stiffen in disbelief, her fingers stilling in his hair. " I know! He isn't on the telephone! He remembered to remind me of that. I know, but look what he has to gain, he and nobody else." He poured out the whole of it, physically half asleep on her shoulder, but mentally, agonisingly wide awake, sensitive to every breath she drew, almost to every implication she was reading into his words.

"Still, I don't see how it could have been Leslie," said Bunty firmly when he had done.

"I know, I told you, I don't, either. No telephone—there's no getting past it."

"No, I didn't mean that. I meant I don't see how it could have been Leslie, because even if she could have called him, I'm pretty sure she wouldn't." She told him why. When she ended he was asleep, his mouth against her cheek. She kissed him, and he didn't wake up. "Poor old darling!" she said, and went to sleep embracing him.

But when he awoke before dawn he remembered everything she had told him, and sat up in bed abruptly. The whole thing to be re-thought from the beginning, a new cast to be made. He lay down again very softly, to avoid disturbing Bunty, and began to go over the ground yet again in his mind, inch by painful inch.

He came home that night late and on edge after a day of furious but so far unproductive activity, and it was no pleasure, the mood he was in, to have Dominic spring out of the living-room at him before he could so much as drop his brief-case and hang up his hat. The mirror had just presented him with the image of his forty-one-year-old face, fretted and drawn with tiredness, with straight brown hair greying at the temples, and he was afraid receding a little too, when there erupted into the glass, beside it the sixteen-year-old copy, fresh as new milk, just-formed, with lashes like ferns and a thatch as thick as gorse, a face as yet so young and unused that all the anxiety and trouble in the world couldn't take the springy freshness out of it. The contrast wasn't comforting; neither was the look Dominic fixed on him, waiting with held breath for the news he'd almost given up expecting.

" Sorry, boy," said George, " we haven't found them yet."

Dominic didn't move. The anxious eyes followed every motion with a hopeless concentration as George hung up his coat and made for the stairs. In his own mind he had given them until this evening; if they hadn't found the gloves by now it was no use relying on it that they ever would, no use waiting any longer for the turn of luck it didn't seem as if they were going to get. Luck's hand would have to be forced. When logs coming down a river jam, somebody has to set off a charge to release them and start them flowing again. Dominic did not particularly fancy himself as a charge of dynamite, but extreme measures were called for. And this time it was in any case impossible to confide in George, because the kind of shock tactics Dominic had in mind would not, and could not, be countenanced by the police. One word to George, and the whole thing would be knocked on the head. No, he had to do this alone, or if he had to ask for help it mustn't be from his father. And before he ventured he had to make sure he hadn't left any loopholes for want of sufficient briefing. There were still things he didn't know; by the terms of their toleration agreement he couldn't go to his father for them, but what he wanted to know Leslie Armiger could tell him.

" I'm going out, Mummy," said Dominic, following Bunty into the kitchen. It was already well past eight o'clock, and she was surprised, but she didn't ask him

where or why, she merely said: " All right, darling, don't
be too late." She was a nice mother, he was suddenly
moved to engulf her in a bear's hug before he fled, but
she was holding a hot iron, so he didn't do it. She hadn't
even said: "But you haven't finished your homework! "
though he hadn't. Any other mother would have been
all too liable to nag, the way he was skimping his work
these days.

He got out his bike and rode into Comerbourne, and
let himself into Mrs. Harkness's front garden by the low
iron gate. There was an outside bell for the Armigers,
but they didn't always hear it, you had to walk in at the
front door and climb the stairs and tap on the door of
their room.

Leslie was sitting over a pile of books at the table, in
his shirt-sleeves and a cloud of cigarette smoke. Dominic
might not be doing his homework, but Leslie was, with
dedicated concentration. He'd come down from Oxford
without a degree, having behaved there as his father had
fully intended him to behave, tossing his liberal allowance
about gaily, playing with zest, painting with passion,
cutting an engaging figure socially and working only just
enough to keep him out of trouble, and perhaps a little
over to appease his tutor after every grieved lecture,
purely out of liking for the old boy, and as a concession
to his conservative ideas of what universities were for.
That left him with a lot of leeway to make up now, when
marriage and responsibility had put a sharp end to his
prolonged adolescence.

" Oh, I'm sorry," said Dominic, dismayed. " I'd better
not butt in on you if you're working."

" No, come in, it's all right." Leslie closed his book

and pushed the whole pile aside, stretching his cramped shoulders. " I'm glad to have an excuse to stop. There's nothing new, is there? About Kitty? "

Dominic shook his head. " You haven't been to see her again, have you? "

" Not yet, it's no use asking too often, you know, they wouldn't let me. Is there something else I can help with? "

" Well, there is, as a matter of fact. You'll probably think it a funny thing to ask, but it's about this picture of yours. If you wouldn't mind telling me all that stuff about how somebody tried to get it back, I think it might help me. Because I've got a sort of theory, but I don't know enough about the details to know yet if it makes sense."

" You think The Joyful Woman may be mixed up in the business? " asked Leslie, studying him curiously through the haze of smoke. The queer thing about the kid was that there was nothing queer about him; tallish, pleasant-looking, reasonably extrovert, healthily certain of himself, taking himself a bit seriously at this stage, but then he'd be odd if he didn't. You could drop him among his kind in any public school, and he'd fall on his nice large feet and wriggle a place for himself on the spot. You could imagine him keeping well in the swim at whatever he touched, perhaps one notch ahead of average at games and two or three notches ahead at his books, with enough energy left over for a couple of reasonably intelligent hobbies, say climbing at one extreme and amateur theatricals at the other, and perhaps one amiable lunacy like an immoderate passion for fast motor-bikes or a weakness for blonde bits on the side.

Wonderfully ordinary, and yet here he was taking a pro-
prietorial hold on a murder case, and bringing all his
down-to-earth qualities to bear on a situation so un-
ordinary that the result was pure fantasy. For a moment
Leslie looked at him and couldn't believe he had his focus
right, the components tended so strongly to fall apart
into different dimensions. I suppose, he thought, in this
setting we all look a bit out of drawing; it's only his
being so young that makes it more marked in his case.

He sat down with him and told him the whole history
of The Joyful Woman over again from the beginning,
while Dominic followed with quick questions and hopeful
eyes. Jean came in half-way through the story and
brought him a mug of chocolate and some biscuits; she
had grown up with three young brothers, and was used
to feeding boys on principle at frequent intervals.

" So the idea is that this dealer, this Cranmer, had
dropped the hint to your father that the thing was
valuable." Warmth and eagerness had come back into
Dominic's eyes, and a calculating gleam; it was working
out as he'd thought it might. " But it was Mr. Shelley
who came to see you."

" On my father's behalf, of course."

" But why of course? You only know that because he
told you so. Look, suppose it happened this way. Cranmer sees some definite possibility in the picture, he
knows your father must have thrown it out as worthless,
and he knows it may be worth a great deal. He decides
it would pay him to keep in with your father, so he
telephones the office to warn him. But just by chance he
misses him. They put him on to Mr. Shelley, and he
tells him what he thinks, that his boss should think again,

he's giving away a small fortune. But instead of passing on the message Mr. Shelley does a bit of quick thinking. He's sure by then that you and your father are never likely to heal the breach, so you won't be comparing notes. And he sees a better use to make of this stroke of luck. You sit on it and keep quiet, he says to Cranmer, and you and I can do a deal and share the proceeds between us, never mind Armiger. And he comes to you with that story about your father having thought better of his mean joke, and sent him to offer you the five hundred pounds instead of the picture. You said he had the money in cash. Didn't that strike you as odd? "

" Not particularly. My father would think nothing of shuffling that much about in cash. But I agree it makes your version possible. I agree it might have seemed quite an easy way of getting hold of the sign too. But surely if the old boy had been in it for himself he wouldn't have dared to take it any farther after I turned him down? It was too risky."

" But if the stake was big enough? You refuse him, so he comes back and steals your father's letter, which is the only actual proof of ownership. He's banking on it that you won't touch your father in any way, having seen how you feel—not to take anything from him, not to see him, not to talk to him, but also surely not to make a public accusation against him over this business. He's betting you'll just write it off in disgust, and not do anything about it at all, because of course you're not going to be told the picture has any value, Cranmer will see to that end of it. Just commonplace rubbish! So you were supposed to think, what's the point, the joke will be on him, let him have it and much good may it do him!

The silly old fool jumped to conclusions just because it leaked out to him that we'd consulted a dealer, and now he's made himself just about as big an ass as he is a rogue, so let him hang the thing on the wall to remind him how he got too sharp and cut himself."

Carried away by his own eloquence, Dominic had lapsed into language which he suddenly realised might by conventional standards be thought offensive in the circumstances. Even if you thought about the dead like that you weren't supposed to say it, and even if Leslie had no reason whatever to love his late father he was supposed to observe certain rules and maintain certain attitudes. And you never know how conventional unconventional people may be just beneath the skin. He paled to the lips, and then flushed bright red to the hair. " I say, I'm sorry, I shouldn't be shooting off my mouth like this, it's terrible cheek. I really am sorry! I should have remembered he was your father, and all that——"

" That's all right," said Leslie with a rueful grin. " I might very well have taken it just like that. I probably should have, if I hadn't happened to reach my limit just about then. Don't mind calling my dad names, that's the last thing he'd have kicked about. One of the better things about him was that he didn't snivel about his virtue while he pulled off his sharp deals, he just slapped them down gleefully and said in effect: Go on, beat that! Carry on, you're doing all right."

" You really didn't mind? It was a hell of a cheek. But you see how important it could be if Shelley actually could have reasoned like that. There he is, sure you won't bother to claim the picture once Cranmer says your father's disputing its ownership, but just let the whole thing go, and put all the dirty work down to your father. So Shelley and Cranmer can quietly dispose of the goods and share the proceeds. And then suddenly out of the blue, when he's home after getting back from the pub that night, *Kitty rings him up*.

" You said he was one person she might very well turn to in her trouble. She blurts out everything to him, and asks him to come and get her away. She doesn't realise she's telling him anything very terrible when she says that you've been there in the barn with your father —because you know he told her it was you he was going out to see—but just think what it would mean to Shelley! The very thing he was sure wouldn't happen had happened. Instead of letting the whole thing drop you'd gone rushing off to your father, to pitch into him about the dirty trick he'd played you. Then of course he wouldn't know what you were talking about, and he'd say so, and the whole business would come out. And finish for Shelley! He'd been with your father—how many years? Just think what it would mean to him to be kicked out now and have to start afresh with your father against him, maybe even to be disgraced publicly and have a charge laid against him. But there's Kitty on the phone, babbling that she's pushed your father down the stairs and he's lying there in the barn unconscious. It's now or never if Shelley wants to shut down on the scandal for good, and keep hold of his share in the picture deal. So he tells Kitty yes, don't worry, just stay there, he's on his way. And he gets out the car and drives like hell back to the barn. And kills your father."

They were both gazing at him with wide and wary eyes, in wonder and doubt. Leslie said in a tight, quiet voice: " It could have happened, I suppose. It would certainly seem like the end of the world to him if Dad turned against him. And I'm not saying he wouldn't have gone the limit against him in the circumstances. He didn't mind a little sharp practice, he expected it and he could deal with it—but if there was a lot of money involved—— And then, his vanity would be desperately hurt if he found out that for once he hadn't been the smartest operator around."

" And when you pitched into him about pinching his own letter, he did deny all knowledge of it, didn't he? "

" He did," agreed Leslie dubiously, " but he could just as well have been lying like a trooper, I took it he was. Still, I suppose it could have happened like that."

Jean had sat silent and intent throughout this exchange, her eyes turning from one face to the other as they talked, her chin on her fists. She made a sudden movement of protest. " No, it couldn't," she said, " it didn't. I'm sorry, boys, there's just one thing wrong with it, but it makes it all wrong. Oh, I'm not saying it couldn't be Mr. Shelley who did it, but if so, it didn't happen like that."

They had both turned to stare at her. " Why not? " they asked together.

With the gentle reasonableness and absolute authority of a kindergarten teacher instructing her brighter charges, Jean told them.

CHAPTER XIII

OCTOBER CAME in cold and gusty, with squally days and ground frosts at night; the grass in front of the main offices of Armiger's Ales stopped growing and shrank into its winter sleep, and the leaves began suddenly to fall from the trees thicker than rain, until the pure, slender skeletons showed through the thinning, yellowing foliage against a blown and blustery sky. Inside, the full heating system was put into use for the first time that season. Ruth Hamilton, coming down the stairs at five o'clock on Thursday evening, listened to the moaning of the wind outside the long staircase window and hunched her shoulders. It was going to be a stormy night; the last fine spell had broken, and the last traces of summer had blown away in a day.

Old Charlcote, the pensioner who manned the janitor's desk in the hall, had come out of his cage and had his coat on already. Miss Hamilton was usually the last of the staff to leave, he often had occasion to curse her inflexible sense of duty, though never above his breath, she being the force she was in the affairs of the firm. He was just pulling on his home-knitted navy-blue mittens, the tail of one eye on the clock, the other on the stairs, and only a very small part of his attention indeed on the person who was doing his best to engage it. What on earth did a boy from the grammar school want here at this hour—or, for the matter of that, at any hour?

" What is it, Charlcote? " asked Miss Hamilton, sailing

authoritatively across the polished floor from the foot of
the stairs. " Is anything the matter? "

Why couldn't she have been just one minute later?
The kid would have been safely off the premises, and they
all could have gone home. Now that conscience of hers
would probably insist on probing into the last recesses of
whatever the little pest wanted, and he'd have to hang
about for an hour or more before he'd be able to lock
up and get out.

" Nothing we can do anything about, miss. This young
fellow was asking for Mr. Shelley, but he's left about
ten minutes ago. I don't suppose it's anything very
urgent."

The boy, gripping his school-bag very tightly under his
arm, said vehemently: " It *is* urgent. I did want awfully
to talk to him to-night. But I suppose if he's gone——"
The constrained voice faded out rather miserably. The
eyes, large and anxious and very bright, dwelt question-
ingly upon Miss Hamilton's face, and hoped for a sign
of encouragement. She thought she saw his lips quiver.
" It's difficult," he said. " I don't know what I ought
to do."

" I'm sorry, Mr. Shelley left a little early to-night. He
has a lot of work on his hands just now." She didn't go
into details; what could this child know about the case
that was preoccupying Ray Shelley's time and thought?
" I'm afraid you won't be able to contact him to-night,
I know he has an appointment, and they're liable to be
at work most of the evening." The appointment was with
counsel, and would include an interview with Kitty.
" Won't to-morrow do? He'll be in to-morrow."

" I shan't be able to skip school," explained the boy

with self-conscious dignity. " I should have been earlier,
to-night, only I had to stay for rugger practice. I did
hurry, I hoped I might be in time." He had certainly
hurried his shower, there were still traces of playing-fields
mud beneath his left ear and just along the hairline beneath
the thick chestnut thatch at his left temple. Miss Hamilton's shrewd eyes had not missed them; she knew quite
a lot about boys. There was something decidedly wrong
with this one, behind that composed, strained front of his;
it showed no less clearly than the tidemarks.

" Haven't I see you before somewhere? I'm sure I
ought to know you."

A pale smile relaxed the fixed lines of his face for a
moment. " We played your club a couple of times this
summer, I expect you saw me at tea. I bowl a bit—
spins, not awfully good. My name's Dominic Felse."

" Felse? Not the same Felse—isn't that right, the
detective-sergeant? "

" He's my father," said the boy, and clutched his bag
even more tightly, with a sudden contortion of nervous
muscles, as though he had shuddered. " It's something
about the case that I wanted to talk to Mr. Shelley
about."

" But your father surely wouldn't——"

" He doesn't know," said Dominic with a gulp. " It's
just an idea of my own that I thought I ought to put to
Mr. Shelley."

There was no doubt about it, some intense agitation
was shaking him, and if he received the slightest encouragement he would let go the tight hold he had on himself
and pour out whatever was on his mind. She was used
to receiving and respecting the confidences of boys, some

of them a great deal tougher propositions than this well-brought-up child. She cast a glance at the clock. Charlcote was looking significantly at it too. His time was his time, he had no intention of seeing anything pathetic in this nuisance of a boy, and he had been careful to block his ears against every word of this unnecessary conversation.

" Will I do? " she asked gently, and catching the eloquent roll of Charlcote's eyes heavenward in mute but profane appeal, suppressed a grim smile. " If I can help you, you're welcome to come in and talk to me."

The sharp jingle of the keys was like an expletive. " It's all right, Charlcote," she said, relenting. " You can just leave the outside door and go. I'll lock up when we come out, you needn't wait."

The old man had his coat buttoned and his cap in his hand before he could finish saying smugly: " It's my duty to lock up in person, miss, but of course if you care to give orders to the contrary——"

She wanted to say: " Get out, you silly old fool, before I call your bluff," but she didn't; he had ways of manipulating the heating system when he was aggrieved, or mismanaging the tea round, it was never worth while taking him on in a long-term engagement. " Consider it an order by all means," she said briskly, " and run off home to Mrs. Charlcote at once. I'll make sure we leave everything in order." And she took Dominic firmly by the arm and marched him towards the stairs. " Now, come along up to my room, we may as well be comfortable."

" May I really? You don't mind? " He let himself be led away gratefully; she felt him trembling a little with

N

relief and hope, though the trouble didn't leave his face. It was something that couldn't be so easily removed, but at least it could be investigated and possibly shared. She brought him to her own office and put him into the visitor's chair, and pulled up a straight chair to the same side of the desk with him, where she could watch his face and he wouldn't be able to evade her eyes. Not that he seemed to want to; he looked back at her earnestly and unhappily, and when she helped herself to a cigarette to give him time to assemble himself he leaped to take the matches from the stand and light it for her. Very mannish; except that his fingers were shaking so that she had to steady his hand with her own, and if the touch had been just a shade less impersonal she thought he would have burst into tears there and then.

" Sit down, child," she said firmly, " and tell me what's the matter. What is all this about? What is it you want with Mr. Shelley? "

" Well, you see, he's Miss Norris's solicitor, and I thought the best thing I could do was come to him. Something's happened," said Dominic, the words beginning to tumble over one another on his tongue, " something awful. I've just got to tell somebody, I don't know what to do. They've been looking everywhere— did you know?—for the gloves. The police, I mean. They've been looking for them ever since it happened. And now——"

" Gloves? " said Miss Hamilton blankly. " What gloves? "

" The murderer's gloves. They say whoever killed Mr. Armiger was wearing gloves, and they must have been badly stained, and they think they must have been hidden

or thrown away immediately after the murder. They've
been looking all over for them, to clinch their case. And
I've been looking for them, too, because," he said,
raising desperate eyes to her face, " I was absolutely
sure they wouldn't be Miss Norris's at all, if only I could
find them. I was sure she was innocent, I wanted to
prove it. And I have found them," he ended, his voice
trailing away into a dry whisper.

" Then that's all right, surely," she said in carefully
reasonable tones. " That's what you wanted, isn't it?
I suppose you've turned them over to your father, and
now everything will be all right. So what are you worrying
about? "

He had put down his school-bag beside him on the
floor. His hands, deprived of this anchor, gripped each
other tightly on his knees. He looked down at the locked
and rigid fingers, and his face worked.

" No, I haven't turned them in. I haven't said a word
to a soul. I don't want to, I can't bear to, and I don't
know what to do. I was so sure they'd be a *man's* gloves.
But they're not! They're a woman's—— They're
Kitty's! "

The knotted hands came apart with a frantic jerk,
because he wanted them to hide his face, which was no
longer under control. He lost his voice and his head,
and began to cry, in shamed little gulps and hiccups he
tried in vain to swallow. Miss Hamilton put down her
cigarette carefully in the ash-tray and took him by the
shoulders, shaking him first gently and then peremptorily.

" Now, this is silly. Come along, tell me about it.
Where did you find them? How did it happen that you
found them, if the police couldn't? "

" I shouldn't tell you," he got out between gulps, " I oughtn't to tell anyone. It just *happened*. If I told you— you'd have to tell lies, too."

" Oh, now, look, I'm trying to help you. If you don't tell me everything how can I judge the importance of these gloves? You may be quite mistaken about them, they may not be the ones at all. You may be fretting quite needlessly."

" They are the ones, I know they are. And they'll say— they'll say she——" He was trying to master the hiccups that were convulsing him, and to all her patient questions he could make no better answers than a few grotesque, incoherent sounds. It was quite useless to persist, he was half hysterical already. She released him and went into the small cloakroom which adjoined her office, and came back with a glass of water. She presented it to his lips with an authority there was no gainsaying, and he drank docilely, scarlet and tearful, still heaving with convulsions of subsiding frequency and violence. " There's blood on them," he gasped between spasms. " What am I going to *do*? "

She stood back and looked at him thoughtfully, while he knuckled angrily at his eyes and muffled his hiccups in a crumpled handkerchief.

" Is that what you were going to ask Mr. Shelley? "

He nodded miserably. " He's her solicitor, and—and I thought maybe I—I could just give them to him. I thought maybe he'd take the responsibility, because I —I——"

"You could destroy them," said Miss Hamilton deliberately, " if that's how you feel. Destroy them and forget all about it."

" No, I *couldn't*! How could I? Don't you see how I'm placed? My father—— I feel *awful*! He *trusts* me! " He struggled momentarily with an all too evident inclination to relapse into tears again. " But it's *Kitty*! "

Sixteen-year-olds miserably in love are a pathetic sight, and his situation, she saw, was indeed pitiable. Whatever his resolutions the issue was certain; he'd never be able to bear the burden for long, sooner or later out it would all come tumbling to his father. Meantime, someone had to lift the immediate load from him.

" Listen to me, Dominic," she said firmly. " You're quite sure in your own mind, aren't you, that Kitty didn't kill Mr. Armiger? "

Where, she was wondering, did Kitty manage to pick up this improbable adorer, and how on earth did they get on to Christian name terms? But Kitty had always been incalculable in her attachments.

" Then have the courage of your convictions. Don't say a word to Mr. Shelley. He's a legal man, it would be cruel to pass the buck to him of all people. You can give the gloves to me. I'm not a lawyer. I'm not afraid to back my own judgment."

Dominic's long lashes rolled back from large eyes gleaming with bewilderment and hope; he stared at her and was still.

" Law or no law," she said with determination, " I'm not prepared to help to send Kitty to prison for life, even if she did kill an unscrupulous old man in self-defence. And like you, I'm very far from convinced that she did. *I'll* take the responsibility. Let's consider that it was I who found them."

"Oh, would you?" he said eagerly. "If only you would, I should be so relieved."

"You needn't even know what I do with them. Give them to me and forget them. Forget you ever found them."

"Oh, I'd be so grateful! I haven't got them here, because I've just come straight from school, you see, and I couldn't risk carrying them about with me all day. The fellows can be awfully nosy, without meaning any harm, you know—and suppose somebody got hold of those? But I've got to come into Comerbourne again for my music lesson to-night, may I bring them to you then?"

"Yes, of course. I have to go to the club for part of the evening, though. Where does your music teacher live?"

He told her, brightening every moment now, his voice steady and mannish again. It was in Hedington Grove, a little cul-de-sac off Brook Street, near the edge of town. "I leave there at nine. I usually catch the twenty past nine bus home to Comerford."

"You needn't worry about the bus to-night," she said good-humouredly. "I shall be finished at the club by then, I'll pick you up at the corner of your teacher's road, on Brook Street, and drive you home. I'll be there at nine. Is that all right?"

"Fine, of course, if it isn't troubling you too much. You've been most awfully kind." He scrubbed once more at his eyes, quickly and shamefacedly, and smoothed nervous fingers through his hair. "I'm awfully sorry I was such an ass. But honestly I didn't know what to do."

" Feel better now? "

" *Much* better. Thanks *awfully*! "

" Well, now suppose you trot in there and wash your face. And then run off home and try not to worry. But don't say a word to anyone else," she warned, " or we should both be in the soup."

" I won't breathe a word to a soul," he promised fervently.

She shepherded him down the stairs again into the silent hallway, and out into the darkness, and switching off the last lights after them, locked the door. The boy was beginning to feel his feet again now, and to want to assert his precarious masculinity all the more because she had seen it so sadly shaken. He hurried ahead to open doors for her, and accompanied her punctiliously across the forecourt to the parking ground where the big old Riley waited.

" Can I drop you somewhere now? I could take you to the bus stop, if you're going home? "

" Thanks a lot, it's awfully kind of you, but I've got my bike here. I put it in the stand near the gate."

All the same, he came right to the car with her, opened the door with a flourish and closed it upon her carefully when she had settled herself in the driving-seat; and he didn't move away until she had fished her black kid gloves out of the dashboard compartment, pulled them on and started the car. Then he stepped back to give her room to turn, and lifted a hand to her with a self-conscious smile as she drove away.

When she was gone he awoke suddenly to the chill of the wind and ran like a greyhound for his bike. He rode back into the centre of the town as fast as he could go.

Some of the shops were already closing, and the dapple of reflected lights in the wet surface of the pavements blurred into a long, hazy ribbon of orange-yellow, the colour of autumn.

CHAPTER XIV

IT WAS ON Thursday evening that Professor Brandon Lucas, on his way to a week-end art school which did not particularly interest him but at which he had rashly consented to put in an appearance, made a sudden detour in his most capricious manner and called on Jean and Leslie Armiger. The visit could have been regarded as planned, since he had with him the notes and sketches relating to the sign of The Joyful Woman, but he had not admitted his intention even to himself until the miles between him and his boredom were shortening alarmingly, and his reluctance to arrive had become too marked to be ignored. Why get there in time for dinner? His previous experiences at Ellanswood College had led him to write off the food as both dull and insufficient, whereas there was a very decent little hotel in Comerbourne; and if the slight ground mist didn't provide a plausible excuse for lateness his errand to the Armigers could be pleaded as important, and even turned into a topic of conversation which might save him the trouble of listening to fatuities about art from others.

Being too short-sighted without his glasses to read the lettering on Leslie's bell, and too self-confident in any case to bother about such details, he startled the silent evening

street with a tattoo on Mrs. Harkness's knocker, and
brought out the lady herself; but he was equal even to
Mrs. Harkness, and made so profound an impression
upon her that Leslie's status with her went up several
notches on the strength of the call.

The professor climbed the stairs unannounced, to find
Leslie in his shirt-sleeves washing up at the little landing
sink, and the smell of coffee bubbling merrily from the
hot plate, and demonstrated his finesse by exclaiming in
delight that he'd come just in time, that the cooking at
The Flying Horse was splendid, but their coffee hadn't
come up to the rest. And having thus intimated that they
need not attempt to feed him, he sat down comfortably
and reassured them with equal dexterity that they were
not expected to try to entertain him.

" I'm on my way to a week-end course, as a matter of
fact. I mustn't stay long, but I thought I'd look in on
you with a progress report. That's a very interesting job
you've found me, my boy, very interesting indeed."

Leslie came in rolling down his sleeves, and produced
liqueur glasses and the carefully nursed end of the half-
bottle of cognac Barney Wilson had brought back from
his summer holiday in France. Jean had conjured up a
glass dish he hadn't known they possessed, and filled it
with extravagant chocolate biscuits which Leslie felt
certain would be the wrong thing to offer this unexpectedly Corinthian old buck of a professor, until he saw
how deftly and frequently they were being palmed. She
had also shed her old blue smock and appeared in a
honey-yellow blouse that made her hair look blue-black
and her skin as clear and cool as dew. Half an hour ago
they had been talking to each other with the cautious

forbearance of strangers in order not to quarrel, but whenever events demanded from her a gesture in support of her husband Jean would be there, ready and invincible.

" Is it going to turn out to be anything? I was afraid to touch it myself, but I could hardly keep my hands off it, all the same."

" You had definite ideas about it? "

" Well, rather indefinite, but very suggestive. Such as its possible date, and the genre it belongs to."

" Have you shown it to anyone else? "

" A dealer in the town here. He put forward some theory that it was originally a portrait by some local eighteenth-century painter called Cotsworth."

" Preposterous! " croaked Lucas with a bark of laughter, pointing his imperial at the ceiling like a dart.

" Well, not so much preposterous as crafty, actually, I think. Because he's offered as high as six hundred for it since."

" Has he, now! And you turned him down. Good boy! So you must have had an idea you were on to something much more important than a dauber like Cotsworth. As indeed I'm pretty sure you are. Mind you, the actual market value may not be very great, I'm not sure how much commercial interest such a discovery might arouse just at this moment. Ultimately it's likely to be considerable, when the full implications are realised."

Leslie was startled to discover that his hands were trembling with pure excitement. He didn't want to look at Jean, she would only think he was underlining the professor's vindication of his judgment; she would expect him not to miss an opportunity like that, not out of any meanness of spirit but out of his fundamental insecurity. And yet he was longing to exchange glances with her, and see if she was quivering as he was. There ought to be a spark still ready to pass between them, when they were on the verge of promised discoveries fabulous enough to excite this Olympian old man.

" Its possible date," said Lucas, harking back. " What did you conceive its possible date to be? "

If he wasn't actually teasing them he was doing something very like it, offering them marvels and then making them play guessing games for the prize. Well, thought Leslie, if he had to be tested he'd better put a good face on it, and say what he had to say with authority.

" Before fourteen hundred."

It sounded appallingly presumptuous when he'd said it, he would almost have liked to snatch it back, but now it was too late. He stuck out his chin and elaborated the audacity, refusing to hedge. " It seemed to me that the pose couldn't be later, or the hands—that want of articulation, the long curved fingers without joints. And then the backward-braced shoulders and head, and even something about the way the blocks of colour are filled in to make the dress. If we get all those layers of repainting off successfully I shall expect to see a kind of folded drapery you don't get as late as the fifteenth century."

" And the *genre*? You said you had ideas about that, too."

Leslie drew breath hard and risked a glance at Jean. Her eyes, wide and wondering, were on him; he didn't know whether she was with him or only marvelling at his cheek and expecting to see him shot down the next moment.

"I think she's local work," he said in a small voice, "because I think she's been kicking about here for centuries, never moving very far from where she was first put in position. And that wasn't on any pub. The only thing out of tradition is the laugh——"

"Yes," said Lucas, his eyes brightly thoughtful upon the young man's face, "the laugh. Don't let that worry you. The laugh is one of those things that happen to any tradition from time to time, the stroke of highly individual genius nobody had foreshadowed and nobody ventures to copy afterwards. And extraordinary experiences they can be, those inspired aberrations. Go on. Out of what tradition? You haven't reached the point yet."

Going softly for awe of his own imaginings, Leslie said: "That oval inset that looks like a brooch, that's what first made me think of it. In its original form it was that odd convention, a sort of X-ray plate into the metaphysical world. Wasn't it?"

"You tell me."

"It was then. It was an image of the child she's carrying. She's a Madonna of the Annunciation or the Visitation—something before the birth, anyhow——"

"Of the Magnificat, as it happens. You seem to have done very well without an adviser at all, my boy."

"I haven't dared even to think seriously about it before," owned Leslie with a shaky laugh. "You as good as hinted that I could go ahead with my wildest guesses and they wouldn't be too fantastic, or I wouldn't have ventured even now. Do you really mean that a piece of work like that has been lying about in attics and swinging in the wind in front of a pub ever since the fourteenth century?"

" More likely since about the latter half of the sixteenth. No doubt you know that the house from which the panel came was at one time a grange of Charnock Priory? And that the last prior retired there after the Dissolution? "

" Well, a friend of mine did dig out something of the kind from the archives, but until then I'm afraid I didn't know a thing about it."

" You didn't? You cheer me. Neither did I, but it seems it was so. What struck me about this panel of yours was its likeness in proportion and kind to one of the fragments in Charnock parish church. I don't know if you know the rector? A scholarly old fellow, quite knowledgeable about medieval art. Glass is his main line, but he knows the local illuminators and panel painters well, too, and he's spent a good many years of his life hunting for bits of the works of art that were disseminated from Charnock at the Dissolution. What's now the parish church is the truncated remains of the old priory church, of course, and such relics as he's been able to trace he's restored to their old places. This head of an angel with a scroll is all he has of what seems to have been a larger altar-piece, probably from the Lady Chapel."

" And you think we've found the lady? " asked Leslie, not meaning to be flippant, simply too excited to bear the tension of being entirely serious. An elevated eyebrow signalled momentary disapproval, but the knowing eye beneath it saw through him, and there was no reproof.

" I think it is a strong possibility. I went to see the rector. He has records which indicate that parts of the furnishings must have gone into retirement with the last prior, and some very interesting sketches and notes of his own, collected from many scattered sources. He holds that the angel with the scroll is the angel of the Magnificat, he has contemporary and later references to the painting which enable one to form a fairly detailed picture, and I'm bound to say there's every reason to feel hopeful that your panel is the Virgin from the same altar-piece. The master who painted it is not known by name, but various examples of his work have been identified, including some illuminations. One of them has an initial strongly resembling your Madonna."

" Including the laugh? " asked Jean in a low voice.

" Including the laugh. Altogether the evidence is so strong that I don't anticipate much difficulty in establishing the authenticity of your fragment. The rector has seen it. If I am cautiously prepared to pronounce it genuine, he is absolutely convinced. He had made a careful reconstruction from the various references of what the lost Madonna should be. It bore an unmistakable resemblance to your panel. He has since made another sketch from the panel in its present form and from his previous sources, to show what we should uncover."

He slapped his brief-case open on the table, and drew out a wad of documents and papers, spreading them out before him with a satisfied smile.

" I've brought you his notes and drawings to examine over the week-end, if you'd like to. And here is his latest sketch. There she is. As she was, and as she will be."

It was quite small, smaller than a quarto sheet of paper; they drew close together to look at it. The Joyful Woman had put off her muslin fichu and corkscrew curls and the Toby frills from round her wrists, and stood in all her early English simplicity and subtlety, draped in a blue

mantle over a saffron robe, all her hair drawn back
austerely under a white veil. She leaned back to balance
the burden she carried, clasping her body with those
hands feeble as lilies, and the symbolic image of the
unborn son stood upright in her crossed palms. She
looked up and laughed for joy. There was no one else in
the picture with her, there was no one else in the world;
she was complete and alone, herself a world.

Leslie felt Jean's stillness as acutely as if she had never
before been still. He moistened his lips, and asked what
would inevitably sound the wrong question at this
moment; but he had to know the answer. He had to
know what he was doing, or there was no virtue in it.

" Have you any idea how much she's likely to fetch
if I sell her? Always supposing we're right about her? "

" It's a matter of chance. But the master's work is
known and respected, and there are few examples,
possibly none to be compared with this. And there's a
local antiquarian interest to be reckoned with. I think,
putting it at the lowest, even if you sell quickly, you should
still realise probably between seven and eight thousand
pounds."

Desperately quiet now, their sleeves just touching, Jean
and Leslie stood looking at the promise of fortune.

" And the rector—would he be in the market? He
must want it terribly, if he's so sure——"

" He'd give his eyes for it, of course. You've stopped
him sleeping or eating since he's seen this. But he's
already appealing for twenty thousand to keep his poor
old rotting church together, there's no possibility whatever of earmarking any funds for buying Madonnas."

" Not even to bring them home," said Leslie. He

moved a little away from Jean because he wanted to see her face, but she kept it averted, looking at the little drawing. He wondered if she knew that she'd folded her own hands under her breasts upon the immemorial wonder, in the same ceremonially possessive gesture.

"Not even to bring them home. But there'll be other bidders. If you wait and collect enough publicity before you sell you may get double what I've suggested." Professor Lucas closed his brief-case and pushed back his chair. The boy was obviously in need of money, small blame to him for relishing it in advance.

"I can't afford to pay for all the work that will have to be done on the panel," said Leslie, his voice slightly shaky with the intensity of his resolution. "Would your laboratory be prepared to stand that, if I give the thing back to Charnock?"

Lucas straightened up to look at him intently, and came to his feet slowly. "My dear boy, you realise what you're saying?"

Yes, he realised, and he had to say it quickly and firmly and finally, so that there should be no possibility of withdrawing. Panic surged into his throat, trying to choke the words into incoherence. He was afraid to look at Jean now, he knew he'd done something she could never understand or forgive, but he'd had to do it, he couldn't have lived with himself if he'd let the moment go by.

"It isn't mine," he said, "only by the last of a long series of ugly accidents, and I don't like that. It ought to go back where it belongs. And it isn't because it's the church, either," he said almost angrily, in case he should be misconstrued. "I should feel the same if it was a secular thing and as fine as that. It was made for a certain place and purpose, and I'd rather it went back. Only it would be a bit rough if I gave it back to the rector and then he couldn't get the necessary work done on it for want of money."

" If you mean what you've just said that point needn't worry you. I would be prepared to undertake the work in our workshop, certainly. Indeed I should be very unwilling to let it go to anyone else. But you spend the week-end thinking it over, my boy," said the professor cheerfully, pounding him on the shoulder, " before you make up your mind to part with it. I'll leave all this stuff with you, better see how good our case is before you decide."

" I have decided, but I should like to read all this, of course. It isn't that I want to cut a figure," he said carefully, " though I shall probably enjoy that, too. But supposing I just took the highest offer and she went to America, or into some private collection here that does no good to anybody? I should never stop feeling mean about it. I want her to go back into her proper place, and if they can't pay for her they can't, and anyhow I have a sort of feeling they ought not to have to. Where she's going she'll belong to everybody who likes to look at her, and they'll see her the way they were meant to see her—or as near as we can get to it. Then I might really feel she's mine. I don't feel it now."

" I'm not trying to dissuade you, my boy, you don't have to out-argue me. I just don't want you to rush matters and then regret it. You make up your own mind and then do what you really want to do. Call me in a few days' time, will you, and we'll meet again, probably

o

at the gallery if you can make it. I shall have to go now."
He tucked his flattened brief-case under his arm. " Good
night, Mrs. Armiger! Thank you for the coffee, it was
excellent."

Jean came out of her daze to add her thanks and fare-
wells to those Leslie was already expressing. When
Leslie came back from seeing his visitor out she was
standing by the table, her face fixed in a grave, pale
wonderment, staring at the rector's sketch.

He closed the door gently behind him, waiting for her
to speak, or at least to look up at him, and when she did
neither he didn't know how to resolve the silence without
sounding abject or belligerent, either of which, in his
experience, would be fatal. The tension which strained
at his nerves she didn't seem to feel, she was so lost in her
own thoughts.

" I couldn't do anything else," he said helplessly,
aware of the defensive note but unable to exorcise it.

She started, and raised to his face eyes in which he
could read nothing, wide and dark and motionless, like
those of a woman in shock.

" It was mine," he said, despairingly abrupt, " I could
do what I saw fit with it."

" I know," she said mildly, and somewhere deep within
her uncommunicative eyes the faint, distant glimmer of a
smile began.

" I suppose I've disappointed you, and I'm sorry about
that. But I couldn't have been happy about it if I'd——"

She moved towards him suddenly with a queer little
gesture of protest, and, " Oh, do be quiet," she said,
" idiot, idiot! I could shake you! " She came at him
with a rush, taking him by the shoulders as though she

intended to put the threat into effect, and then, slipping
her arms under his and winding them tightly about him,
hugged him to her and hid her face in his chest. " I love
you, I love you! " she said in muffled tones against his
heart.

He didn't understand, he was hopelessly at sea. He
never would be able to make sense of it, he'd be just as
mystified about what he'd suddenly done right as about
all the things he'd been doing wrong. Maybe he'd even
come to the conclusion that she was simply female,
illogical and responsive to a firm touch, and strain his
innocent powers to keep the whip hand of her. It didn't
matter, as long as he believed her. " I love you," she
said. His arms had gone round her automatically, he
held her carefully and gingerly, as though she might break
and cut his fingers, but with the warmth of her solid and
sweet against him he had begun to tremble, astonished
into hope.

" I'm sorry about the money, Jean," he stammered,
floundering in the bewildering tides of tenderness and
fright and returning joy that tugged at him. " But we'll
manage without it between us. I know you think it was
irresponsible, but I couldn't help it, I couldn't feel it
was mine. Oh, Jean, don't cry! "

She lifted her head, and she wasn't crying at all, she
was laughing, not with amusement but with pure joy.
She put up her face to him and laughed, and she looked
like the woman in the drawing. " Oh, do shut up,
darling," she said, " you're raving! " And she kissed
him, partly to silence whatever further idiocies he was
about to utter, partly for sheer pleasure in kissing him. It
was quite useless to try to put into words for him the

revelation she had experienced, the sudden realisation of
how rich they were in every way that mattered, he and
she and the child that was coming. With so much, how
could she have fretted about the minor difficulties? How
could she have felt anything but an enormous pity for old
Alfred Armiger, who had so much and couldn't afford
to give any of it away? And how, above all, could she
ever have feared dissatisfaction or disappointment with
this husband of hers who had nothing and could yet
afford to make so magnificent a gift?

"You mean you don't mind?" he asked in a daze,
still breathless. But he didn't wait for an answer. What
did it matter whether he understood how this sudden and
absolute fusion had come about? It wouldn't pay him
to question how he had got her back; the wonderful
thing was that he had. All the constraint was gone.
They hugged each other and were silent, glowing with
thankfulness.

It was the unexpected tap on the door that broke them
apart, the prim double rap that invariably meant Mrs.
Harkness, and usually with a complaint. Leslie took his
arms from round his wife reluctantly, put them back
again for one more quick hug, and then went to open
the door.

Mrs. Harkness was looking unusually relaxed and
conciliatory, for Professor Lucas's influence still enveloped
her as in a beneficent cloud.

"A boy brought this note for you a little while ago,
Mr. Armiger. He said you were to have it at once, but
as your visitor was still here I didn't care to disturb you."

"A boy? What boy?" asked Leslie, thinking first of
Dominic, though he knew of no particular reason why

Dominic should be delivering notes to him at this hour of the evening, nor why, supposing he had any such errand, he should not come up and discharge it in person.

" Mrs. Moore's boy from just along the road. I thought it wouldn't hurt for waiting a quarter of an hour or so."

" I don't suppose it would. Thank you, Mrs. Harkness."

He closed the door, frowning at the envelope with an anxiety for which he knew no good reason. The Moore boy also attended the grammar school, and was much the same age as Dominic and probably in the same form; he might easily be a messenger for him at need. But what could be the need?

" What is it? " asked Jean, searching his face.

" I don't know, let's have a look." He tore the envelope open, still lulled by her warmth close against his arm, and aware of her more intensely than of all the other urgencies in the world, until he began to read.

DEAR MR. ARMIGER,

I've asked Mick Moore to bring you this on the dot of half past eight, because I need help with something at nine o'clock, and it's desperately important, but I daren't let it out more than half an hour before the time. If my father knew about it too soon he'd knock the whole thing on the head, but if he only knows just in time to be on the spot as a witness I hope he'll let me go through with it, I hope he won't be able to stop me. I don't want to telephone home myself because it might be Mummy, and I don't want to scare her. I don't want her to know anything about it until it's all over. So I thought the best thing was to leave this message for you.

This is what I want you to do. Please get on to my father and tell him to have the police watching the corner of Hedington Grove and Brook Street at nine o'clock. There'll be a car there waiting to pick me up and drive me back home to Comerford. Please *make them follow it*, be *sure* they do, it's urgent. I've done something to make things happen, but they *have to be there to see it*, otherwise it will all be wasted, and no good to Kitty after all.

If anything comes unstuck for me, please try to help Kitty, I don't mind as long as she comes out all right.
Thanks. DOMINIC FELSE.

" What the hell! " said Leslie blankly. " Is he fooling, or what? "

" No, not about Kitty, he never would. He's dead serious. Leslie," said Jean, her fingers clenching on his arm, " he's *frightened*! What is it he's done? "

" God knows! Something crazy, stuck his neck out somehow—— Oh, *lord*! " said Leslie in a gasp of dismay as his eye fell on his watch. He sprang for the door and went clattering down the stairs. It was eleven minutes to nine, eleven minutes to zero hour. There was no time now to do anything but take the affair seriously.

He heard Jean's heels rapping down the stairs close behind him, and turned in the open doorway to shout to her to stay where she was, that he'd see to everything, that he'd be back. But she was still close at his elbow, tugging her way breathlessly into her coat, as he wrenched open the door of the telephone booth at the end of the street.

It seemed to take him an age to locate George Felse's number, and a fantastic time to get an answer when he dialled it, and even then it was Bunty who answered. Dominic's assumption that mothers were not to be frightened inhibited Leslie's tongue no less surely. No, never mind, it could wait, if Mr. Felse wasn't there. Never mind, he'd call him again. He slammed the receiver back and tried again.

" Police, Comerbourne? Listen, this is urgent. Please do what I ask *at once*, and *then* stand by for the explanation. It's the Armiger case, and this is Leslie Armiger, and I'm not kidding. If Mr. Felse is there, get him. Never mind, then, *you*, listen——"

Jean whispered in his ear: " I'm going to fetch Barney's van. I'll be back." She shoved open the door and ran, the staccato of her heels dwindling along the street.

" Corner of Brook Street and Hedington Grove, nine o'clock," Leslie was repeating insistently. " We'll be coming along from this end to meet 'em—you see you're there to follow 'em."

It was two minutes to nine when he cradled the receiver for the second time.

CHAPTER XV

DOMINIC STRUCK the hundredth wrong note of the evening, corrected it with a vicious lunge of both normally adroit hands, and said resignedly: " Damn! Sorry! I'm making a hell of a mess of this. Wouldn't you rather I shut up?"

" I would," said old Miss Cleghorn frankly, " but your parents are paying for an hour, my lad, and an hour you're going to put in, even if you drive me up the wall in the process. I'm beginning to think I ought to revert to the old ebony ruler, though, and fetch you a crack over the knuckles every time you do that to my nerves."

Dominic flicked a phrase of derisive laughter out of the piano and made a face at her. She was plump, sixty-odd and as lively as a terrier, and on the best of terms with her pupil, indeed from his point of view she was the one redeeming feature in these Thursday evening lessons. It was Bunty who had insisted that the ability to play at least one musical instrument was an invaluable part of any young man's equipment, and kept his unwilling nose to the keyboard; a feat which wouldn't have been nearly so easy if some part of his mind hadn't come to the generous conclusion that she was probably right about the ultimate usefulness of the accomplishment.

" Ebony ruler my foot! " scoffed Dominic. " I don't believe you've even got one, much less that you ever hit anybody with it."

" You be careful! It isn't too late to begin, and it

doesn't have to be ebony. Come on now, you're not getting out of it by trying to side-track me. Try it again, and for goodness' sake keep your mind on what you're doing."

He did his best, but the trouble was that his mind was very insistently and earnestly upon what he was doing, and it had almost nothing to do with this harmless regular Thursday evening entertainment, which had merely provided the occasion for it. He set his teeth and laboured doggedly through the study again, but his thoughts were ahead of the clock, trying to speculate on all the possible developments which might confront him, and to compile some means of dealing with all of them. What worried him most was that he had had to base his actions so extensively upon speculation, that there was so much room for miscalculation at every stage. But it was too late to allow himself to be frightened by all the possible mistakes he had made, because there was no drawing back now.

" One certain fact," said Miss Cleghorn, nodding her bobbed head emphatically when he had fumbled his way to the last chord, "*you* haven't touched a piano since last Thursday, have you? Own up!"

He hadn't, and said so. He quite saw that from her point of view it was reprehensible, and the tone in which he made his excuses was deprecating. He thought it would be nice if he could believe that some day such things would again have importance for him, too. The weight of the real world was heavy on his shoulders; the little cosy, everyday world in which mealtimes and music lessons mattered had begun to look astonishingly charming and desirable to him, but he couldn't get back to it.

Like an unguided missile he was launched and he had
to go forward.

" And how do you expect to learn to play well if you
never practise? No, never mind soft-soaping me with
fancy finger-work, you take your hands off that keyboard
and listen when I'm talking to you."

He removed them obediently and sat meekly with
them folded in his lap while she scolded him. It couldn't
be said that he listened, though his eyes stared steadily
at her round pink face with a rapt attention which amply
covered the real absence of his mind. To look at her was
comforting, she was so ordinary and wholesome and un-
secret, knowing and knowable, no partner to the night
outside the closed curtains, which had begun to be
terrifying to him. He dwelt earnestly upon her invariable
hand-knitted twin set and short tweed skirt, the Celluloid
slide in her straight, square-cut grey hair, the mole on
her chin that bobbed busily as she abused him. He smiled
affectionately, cheered by the human conviction that
nothing sinister or frightening could exist in the same
dimension with her; but as soon as he looked away or
closed his eyes he knew that it could, and that he had
invoked it and could not escape it.

" It's all very well," she said severely, " for you to sit
there and smile at me and think that makes everything
all right. That's your trouble, my boy, you think you
can just turn on the charm and get away with murder."

She could have made a happier choice of words, of
course; but how could she know she was treading hard
on the heels of truth?

" I know," he said placatingly, " but this week I've
had things on my mind, and honestly there hasn't been

time. Next week I'll do better." I will if I'm here, he thought, and his heart shrank and chilled in him. He grinned at her. " Cheer up, it's nearly nine o'clock, your suffering's almost over."

" Yours will begin in a minute," she said smartly, " if you don't watch your step. You know what you're asking for, don't you? "

" Yes, please. With lots of sugar." He knew there was cocoa in a jug on the stove in her kitchen, there always was on cold nights. She got up good-humouredly and went to fetch it. " All right, pack up, we'll let you off for to-night."

It was still a few minutes to nine, and he didn't want to be even one minute early for his appointment. If Leslie had done his part the police should be watching the corner of the street. To arrive ahead of time was to risk appearing there in full view, and having an irate father descend on him on the spot with a demand that he should explain himself, and wreck everything he had gone to such pains to build up. Even reasonable fathers were queer about allowing you freedom of action in matters which infringed their authority and involved your own danger; and of the reality of the danger he had brought down upon himself Dominic was in no doubt whatever. That was the whole point. If he was not in any danger, then he was hopelessly off the track, and all his ingenuity would have proved nothing, and left Kitty as forsaken and encircled as ever. Moreover, this danger was something he must not ward off. He would have to watch it closing in, and sit still like a hypnotised rabbit to let it tighten on him. If he fought his own way out he might fail of proving what he had set out to prove.

He mustn't struggle, he must leave it to others to extricate him and hope they would be in time. He was voluntary bait now, nothing more.

"You are in a state to-night," said Miss Cleghorn, shaking him by a fistful of chestnut hair. "You don't even hear when I offer you biscuits. Why I bother, when all you deserve is bed without supper, I can't imagine. What's the matter with you? Things being tough at school, or what?"

School! That was all they thought about. If you were sixteen, whatever worries you had must be about school.

"No, I'm all right, honestly. Just one of those days, can't concentrate on anything. I'll catch up by next time."

"You'd better! Here you are, get this down you, it's freezing outside, you need something to keep you warm, waiting for that old bus. I always say that's the bleakest spot in town, that bus station."

He made his cocoa last until the dot of nine. Better give her an extra minute or two, in case she got held up at the club.

"I'll tell Mummy you said I was making steady progress," he said impudently as he pulled on his coat. "That all right?"

"You can tell her I said you should be spanked, she might oblige. Now watch how you go, I can see the frost sparkling on the road already. Only just October and hard frost, I ask you!"

"Good night!" he said, already at the front gate.

"Good night, Dominic!" She closed the door on him slowly, almost reluctantly. Now what can be the matter with that child, she wondered vexedly, he's cer-

tainly got something on his mind. Ought I to speak to
his mother, I wonder? But he's at a funny age, probably
it's something he doesn't want her to know about, and he'd
never forgive me if I interfered. No, better let well alone.
She switched on the television and put her feet up, and
in a little while Dominic Felse passed out of her mind.

He walked to the end of the street with a slowing step,
trying not to notice that it was slowing, not to let it slow.
Normality, be with me! I've got a load *off* my mind, not
on it. I've got to do it right, otherwise I'd have done
better not to do it at all. Come on, you're in it now, give
it everything you've got. Remember Kitty! He thought
of her, and the tension within him was eased as by a
sudden warmth relaxing every nerve. What, after all,
does danger matter? You're making Kitty safe. What
happens now can't hurt her, it can only deliver her. He
took heart; he was going to be all right. Even when
it came, he was going to accept it and not chicken
out.

There was always, of course, the thought that she might
not come to the rendezvous, that in all honesty she might
have thought better of it. There was the possibility that
she might come, but acting in all good faith, in which case
she would simply take what he gave her, and reassure
him and drive him safely home; and the thousand deaths
he died on the way would be no more than he deserved,
and the abject amends he owed her would be something
he could never hope to pay. There were so many pitfalls,
so many ways of being wrong; and yet all the time he
knew in his heart that he was not wrong.

And she was there. When he drew near to the corner
of the silent, frosty road, under the tinkling darkness and

sparkle of the trees, he saw the long, sleek shape of the old Riley sitting back relaxed and elegant alongside the knife-edged glitter of the kerb. She opened the near-side door for him, smiling. Never before had he noticed how silent, how deserted this quarter of the town could be at night. There was not another person in sight, and only one lone car passed along the middle of the broad road as he approached. When it had gone everything was so still that his light footsteps sounded loudly in the quietness, reverberating between the frostlight and the starlight with a terrible, solitary singleness.

" Hallo, Dominic," said Miss Hamilton, scooping up an armful of things from the front passenger seat and dumping them at random into the rear seat, scarf and handbag and a bunch of duplicated papers that looked like club notices, and a large electric torch that rolled to the far hollow of the hide upholstery.

" Hallo, Miss Hamilton! This is most awfully kind of you. You're sure I'm not being a nuisance? I could easily get the bus home."

" Don't be silly," she said placidly. " Get in. It will only take me a quarter of an hour or so, I shall soon be home. And it's much too cold to hang about waiting for buses." She leaned across him and snapped home the catch on the handle of the door. " It's getting rather worn, I shall have to have a new handle fixed. I have to lock it or it might come open, especially on a bend. And as I'm apt to be carrying rather lively passengers sometimes it could be dangerous," she concluded with a smile.

" None aboard to-night," he said, glancing at the back seat.

" I've just dropped two of them. The club's still in session, but I don't have time to stay all the evening." She settled back in the driving-seat, and looked at him with the indulgent smile that took into account both his youth and its extreme sensitivity, his helpless tears of the afternoon and his desire that she should forget them.

" Well, did you bring them? " she asked gently. " Or have you thought better of it and turned them over to your father? Don't worry, I shan't blame you if you have, I shall quite understand. It was entirely up to you."

" I've brought them," he said.

" Then the best thing you can do is hand them over right now, and I'll take them and put them away, and you can forget the whole thing. I'll never remind you of it again, and no one else can. You've not told anyone else? "

" No, not a word."

" Good, then don't. From to-night on you're to stop worrying, you understand? Kitty'll come out of it all right if she didn't do it, and we two are agreed that she didn't. That's right, isn't it? "

" Yes, of course." He withdrew from his music-case a small, soft bundle rolled rather untidily in tissue-paper, so loosely that a corner of Polythene protruded, and in the reflected light from the sodium street lights there was just a glimpse of crumpled black kid through the plastic, soiled and discoloured. He put it into Miss Hamilton's hand, his large eyes fixed trustingly upon her face, and heaved a great sigh as it passed, as though a load had been lifted from him.

Her eyes flickered just once from his face to the small package in her hand, and back again. She leaned across to open the dashboard compartment in front of him, and thrust the gloves into the deepest corner within. " Don't be afraid," she said, catching his anxious glance, " I shan't forget about them. They're quite safe with me. Do as I said, put them clean out of your mind. You need never see or think of them again. Not a word more about them, now or at any other time. This closes the affair. You understand? "

He nodded, and after a moment managed to say in a very low voice: " Thank you! "

She started the car. A motor-bike whirred by them towards the town, its small, self-important noise soon lost. A solitary old gentleman on his way back from the pillar-box turned into a side road and vanished. They inhabited a depopulated world, a frosty night world full of waiting, ardent echoes that had no sound to reduplicate. He must not look round. His head kept wanting to turn, his eyes to search the street behind them, his ears were straining for another engine turning over reluctantly in the cold, but he must not look round or even seem to wish to look round. He was an innocent, a fool without suspicions, a simpleton who had not said a word to anyone about this meeting. What should he be con- centrating on, now that she had relieved him of his burden? Naturally, the car. It was worth a little en- thusiasm, and at sixteen adults don't expect you to have any tenacity even in your anxieties, they take it for granted you can be easily seduced by things like cars.

" What year is it? " he asked, watching the competent movements of her hands as the car moved off, and capturing one genuine moment of pleasure in its smooth, quiet lunge forward. " Is it actually vintage? "

It wasn't, but it missed it by only a few years. She smiled faintly as she answered his questions, the controlled, indulgent smile of a considerate adult allowing a child his preoccupations, even stooping to share them, but distantly envying him his ability to lose himself in them as a blessing long passed out of her own experience. Precisely the kind of smile to be expected from her in the circumstances, and it told him nothing. He could have done with a few pointers. There should have been something revealing in that one glance she had cast at his carefully assembled package, something to tell him if he was on target or if he had guessed wildly astray and utterly betrayed himself; but there had been nothing, no sudden gleam, no sharpening of the lines of her face. It was too late now to wonder.

" You do keep her beautifully," he said without insincerity.

" Thank you," she said gravely. " I try."

The road had narrowed a little, the pavement trees ceased abruptly, the garden walls and fences began to be interspersed with the hedges of fields. He wished he could lean far enough to the right to get a glimpse in the rear-view mirror, but he knew he mustn't. He wished he knew if they were following. It would be hell if he had to go through all this for nothing.

" We'll take the riverside road," said Miss Hamilton, " it's shorter. I suppose you haven't started learning to drive yet? "

" Well, it would be difficult, really. I can't go on the road yet, and we haven't got any drive to speak of, only

P

a few yards to the garage. They did talk about starting
lessons at school, there's plenty of room in the grounds
there, but nothing's come of it yet."

"It would be an excellent idea," she said decidedly.
"In school conditions you'd learn very easily, from sheer
force of habit. And it's certainly become an essential
part of a complete education these days."

"But I think they're scared for their flower-beds, or
something, they swank frightfully about their roses, you
know."

It was possible to talk about these remote things, he
found with astonishment, even when his throat was dry
with nervousness and his heart thumping. He cast one
quick glance at her profile against the last of the street
lighting, the clear, austere features, the slight smile, the
sheen of the black hair and the smooth shape of the great
burnished coil it made on her neck. Then they had
turned into the dark road under the trees, and the headlights were plucking trunk after slender trunk out of the
obscurity ahead, sharp as harp-strings, taut curves of
light that swooped by and were lost again in the darkness
behind. Somewhere there on their right, beyond the belt
of trees, the shimmer of the river, bitterly cold under the
frosty stars. In summer there would have been a few
cars parked along the grass verges down here, with
couples locked in a death-grip and lost to the world
inside, and more couples strolling among the trees or
lying in the grass along the river-bank; but not now.
The back rows of cinemas were warmer, the smoky booths
of the coffee-bars had as much privacy. No one would
come here to-night. And without the lovers this was a
lonely and silent road.

It will be here, he thought, somewhere in this half-mile stretch, before we leave the trees. And he gripped the piped edges of the bucket seat convulsively, and felt his palms grow wet, because he wasn't sure if he could go through with it. It isn't just being afraid, he thought. How do you manage it when you see a blow coming, or a shot, and you mustn't duck, you mustn't drop for cover, you must just let it come, let it take you? How do you do it? He flexed his fingers, startled to find them aching with the intensity of his grip on the leather. He was strong, he could very well defend himself, but until the witnesses appeared he mustn't. They had to see for themselves what had been planned for him, his own word would never be enough. And if they weren't following, if they didn't arrive in time, then in the last resort what happened to him would have to be evidence enough to clear Kitty, Kitty who of all people in the world was safest from being blamed for whatever deaths might occur to-night.

Miss Hamilton put out her left hand and opened the glove compartment, rummaging busily among the tangle of things within until she brought out a packet of cigarettes. She had slowed down to a crawl while she drove one-handed, and she shook out a cigarette from the packet and put it between her lips with neat, economical movements which made it clear she had done the same thing a few thousand times before. She reached into the pocket again, groping for her lighter, and failed to find it.

" Oh, of course, it's in my handbag," she said, letting the car slide to a stop. " Can you reach it for me. Dominic? "

He looked over into the litter of things on the back
seat; her bag had slid down into the hollow against the
torch. The old car was spacious, with ample leg-room
between front and rear seats, and he had to turn and
kneel on the seat to lean over far enough to reach the
corner. He did so in an agony of foreknowledge, living
through the sequel a hundred times before it became
reality. Terrified, in revolt, forcing himself to the
quiescence against which his flesh struggled like an animal
in a trap, he leaned over with arm outstretched, presenting
to her meekly the back of his brown head. Oh, God,
let her be quick! I can't keep it up, I shall have to turn
round—— I *can't! Oh, Kitty! And maybe you won't even
know!*

Something struck him with an impact that made the
darkness explode in his face, and he was jerked violently
forward over the back of the seat, the breath driven out
of him with a second shock of pain and terror. Then the
darkness, imploding again on a black recoil into the
vacuum from which the burst of light had vanished,
sucked him down with it into a shaft of emptiness and
let him fall and fall and fall until even the falling stopped,
and there was no more pain or fright or anger or fighting
for breath, no more anxiety or agonised, impotent love,
nothing.

CHAPTER XVI

" I wish we knew what we were looking for," said Jean,
crouched forward into the windscreen of Barney Wilson's
Bedford van and peering with narrowed eyes to the limit
of the headlight beams. " A car—it might be any car,
we don't know whose, it could be a taxi, or anything.
We just don't know."

" It won't be a taxi," Leslie said with certainty. " He's
done 'something to make things happen.' It sounds
like a man-to-man business."

" And we don't even know that they'll be coming by
this road, it could be the main road."

" If it comes to that, we don't *know* they'll be on either.
Anyhow, the police are covering both. What more can
we do? I can only take this thing one way at a time, and
this is the quietest and loneliest. Headlights ahead there,
keep your eyes open."

The approaching lights were still two or three coils of
the winding road distant from them, and perforated by
the scattered trees, but they were coming fast. One
dancing turn carried them into the intervening double
bend, and a second brought them out of it and into full
view on one of the brief short stretches. Leslie left his
headlights undipped, checking a little and crowding the
middle of the road, setting out deliberately to dazzle and
slow the other driver. The approaching lights, already
sensibly dipped as they turned into the straight, flashed
at him angrily, and failing to get a response, stayed up

to glare him into realisation of his iniquity. He narrowed his eyes, trying to focus beyond the dazzle on the wind-screen of the car. Only one face in view there, and not much hope of distinguishing whether man or woman. In a lighted road it might have been easier.

A horn blared at him indignantly. He said: " Oh, *lord*! " as he pulled aside just far enough to let the long car by. Driven well and peremptorily, and going fast, going with purpose.

" No boy," said Jean, and instantly gasped and clutched at the dashboard as he braked hard. " Leslie! What are you doing? "

It was instantly clear what he was doing, and he didn't bother to answer her in words. He was in close under the trees at the side of the road, hauling on the wheel to bring the van about.

" What is it? What did you see? He wasn't there."

" Not in sight," said Leslie, and ran the van back-wards with an aplomb he would never have achieved in ordinary circumstances. " Didn't you recognise the car? " They came about in an accelerating arc that brushed the grass, and whirled away in pursuit of the vanishing rear lights. " Hammie's! That *couldn't* be a coincidence. Thank God I know that car so well it can't even hoot at me in the dark without giving itself away. And she doesn't know this van. She's used to seeing me driving various missiles, but not this."

Jean huddled against his arm, shivering, but not with cold. " Leslie, if it *is* her—suppose he isn't with her any more? Suppose something's happened already? " She didn't say that it was unthinkable to suspect Miss Hamilton of crime and violence, because now nothing was unthinkable, every rule was already broken and every restraint unloosed. " Could she have left him somewhere back there on the road? "

He hadn't thought of that, and it shook him badly. The Riley could be as lethal a weapon as any murderer would need. But he kept his eyes fixed on the receding rear-lights, and his foot down hard. "The police car will be coming along behind."

" Yes, but the road's so dark, that black surface——"

" She's turning off," he said abruptly and eagerly, and stamped the accelerator into the floor; for why, if she was alone and upon innocent business, should she turn off this road to the right? There was nothing there but the remotest of lovers' lanes, a dead end going down to the river-bank. Not even a lane, really, just a cart-track through the belt of trees, once sealed by a five-barred gate, though it hadn't been closed for a year or so now, and hung sagging in the grass from its upper hinge. Leslie knew the place well enough from summer picnics long ago. There was a wide stretch of open grass by the river there, where cars could drive right down to the water and find ample room to turn. But what could a woman alone want down there on a frosty October night?

He swung the van round into the mouth of the track, and pulled up. " You get out and wait here for the police car."

" No," she said in a gasp of protest, clutching at his arm, " I'm coming with you."

" Get out! How will they know, if you don't? They're nowhere in sight. Oh, God, Jean, don't waste time."

She snatched her hand away and scrambled out. He

saw her face staring after him all great wide-set eyes in
an oval pallor, as he drove down into the darkness
between the trees. She didn't like letting him go without
her. They were loose among murders and pursuits and
all the things that didn't normally happen, who could be
sure there wouldn't be guns, too? But what sort of a
team were they going to be in the future if they pulled
two ways now? She watched the van rock away down
the rutted track, and then stood shivering, watching the
road faithfully. Leslie's ascendancy was established in
that one decision, when he wasn't even thinking about
their partnership or their rivalry, and it couldn't have
been won in the face of a stiffer test. The hardest thing
he could possibly have asked of her was to stand back
and let him go into action alone, now, when she had
newly discovered how much he meant to her.

The frozen ruts of the track gripped the wheels of the
van and slewed it in a series of ricochets down into the
rustling tunnel of trees. He couldn't see the rear-lights
of the Riley now, he couldn't hear its engine; he had
all he could do to hold the van and drive it forward fast
towards the faint glimmer of starlight that flooded the
open river-bank. The trees thinned. He slowed, killing
his headlights altogether in the hope of remaining
undetected until he got his bearings, and cruised to the
edge of the copse.

She had driven the car right out on to the low terrace
of rimy grass above the water, sweeping round in a circle
to be ready to drive out again. Both doors hung open
like beetle-wings spread for flight, and midway between
the car and the edge of the bank she was dragging something laboriously along the ground, something limp and

slender that hung a dead weight upon her arms. Beyond
the two figures moving sidelong like a crippled animal
the flat breadth of the river flowed pallid with lambent
light, at once swift and motionless, a quivering band of
silver.

All down the rough ride under the trees Leslie's mind
had been working coolly and lucidly, telling him exactly
what to do. Don't leave the escape route open. Broad-
side the van across the track, there's no other way out.
Make sure she shan't get the car out again. But in the
end he didn't do any of the things his busy brain had
been recommending to him, there was no time. She had
such a little way to go to the water, and he knew the
currents there and could guess at the cold. He didn't stop
to think or consider at all, he just let out a yell of which
he was not even conscious, slashed his headlights full on
and drove straight at her, his foot down hard. Let her
get away, let her run, anything, as long as she dropped
the kid in time.

The front wheels left the track and laboured like a
floundering sea-beast on to the bumpy shore of the open
turf. Rocking and plunging, he roared across the grass,
and his headlights caught and held her in a blaze of
black and white. She was hit by noise and light together,
he saw her shrink and cringe, letting the boy fall for a
moment. She wrenched her head up to stare wildly,
and he saw a face carved in light, as hard and smooth
and white as marble, with panting mouth and gaunt
eyes glaring. The eyes had still an unmistakable intelligence and authority, he couldn't get a finger-hold on
the hope that she might be mad. Then she stooped and
seized the boy beneath the armpits, wrenching him up

from the ground with furious determination, and began to drag herself and him in a stumbling run towards the water's edge. Heavy and inert, he slipped out of her hold and she clawed at him again, frantic to finish what she had begun.

Only at the last moment, as the van swerved and braked screaming to a stop a few yards short of her, did she give up. She flung the boy from her with a sudden angry cry, and ran like a greyhound for her car. Her hair had slipped out of its beautiful, austere coil, it streamed down over her shoulders as she ran, shrouding the whiteness of her face. Leslie, tumbling from the van before it was still, snatched vainly at her arm as she fled, and then, abandoning her for what was more urgent, plunged upon the boy who lay huddled where she had thrown him.

She had all but done what she had set out to do; a few seconds more and he would have been in the river. His head and one arm dangled over the downward slope of grass, the limp fingers swinging above the edge of the water. Leslie fell on his knees beside him and hauled him well ashore, turning him so that he lay face upwards in the grass. Under the tumbled chestnut thatch Dominic's face was pinched and grey, the eyes closed. He was breathing with a heavy, short, painful rhythm through parted lips, but at least he was breathing. Leslie felt him all over with hasty hands, and began to hoist the dead weight into his arms. He was just clambering gingerly to his feet under his burden when he heard the Riley start up and soar into speed.

He'd forgotten that she had a lethal weapon still in her hands. She hadn't finished with them yet. There was room between the water and the standing van for her to drive round and come upon them at speed, and what was there now to restrain her from killing two as readily as one? He was one man, apparently alone, there was room for him in the river with the boy.

The Riley's headlights whirled round the bulk of the Bedford, straightened out parallel with the river's edge, and lunged at him in a blinding glare. Caught off balance, staggering beneath the boy's weight, he broke into a lurching run. He couldn't hope to get into the trees, where she couldn't reach them, but he jumped for the van and tried to put a corner of its bulk between him and the hurtling car. She wouldn't crash the van, she wouldn't do anything to wreck her own means of escape; she was sane, appallingly sane, and at least you can have some idea of what the sane will do. The blaze of light blinded him, he couldn't see the van or the ground or the starlit shape of the night any more, he could only hurl himself straight across the car's path into the dark on the other side.

He caught his foot in the tussocky grass and fell sprawling over his burden beneath the back wheels of the Bedford. The car missed his scrabbling feet by inches, he felt the frosty clumps of the turf crunch close to his heels. Then the light and the rushing bulk were past, and his cringing flesh relaxed with a sob of relief. He eased his weight from the boy and put his face down into his sleeve for a moment, and lay panting, sick with retrospective terror.

The roar of the car receded, swaying up the rutted track towards where Jean waited. Leslie struggled out of his weakness and came to his feet and began to run, but what was the use? A couple of minutes and the Riley would be out on the road. He cupped his mouth in his hands and bellowed in a voice that shook the frost from the trees: "Jean, look out! Stand clear!"

She surely wouldn't try anything crazy? Would she? How could you be sure with Jean, who couldn't bear to be beaten, and would die rather than give in?

Winding along the complex curves of the road from Comerbourne came the headlights of two cars, late but coming fast. Jean was standing in the middle of the road waving her arms peremptorily at the first of them when she heard the labouring sound of the Riley climbing back up the lane, and started and quivered to Leslie's shout. She ran back to stare frantically into the tunnel of the trees. Not the van, the car. What had happened down there? Where was Leslie? What was he doing? The Hamilton woman shouldn't get away now, she mustn't, she shouldn't, even if it made no difference in the end. Jean ran like a fury and wedged her shoulder under the top bar of the drunken old gate, and dragged it protesting out of its bleached bed of grass. She staggered across the track with it supported on her shoulder, and slammed it home against its solid gatepost on the other side. There was a great wooden latch that still dropped creakingly into place; she lodged it with a crash, and flung herself aside under the hedge as the Riley drove full at the barrier.

The impact burst the bars and sent the weaker gatepost sagging out of true. Wood and glass flew singing through the air, and splinters settled with a strange noise like metallic rain. The car had not the impetus to drive straight through the obstacle, it was brought up shuddering and plunging in the wreckage of the gate, the wind-screen shivered, one lamp ripped away. The engine died. Jean crouched quivering in the midst of a sudden teeming activity that shuddered with movement and purpose, but made no more sound.

She opened her eyes and uncovered her ears and crawled shakily out of the hedge. Beyond the impaled Riley the van came rocking gently up the slope; she saw Leslie's disordered hair and anxious face staring over the wheel, and in the passenger seat beside him Dominic's unconscious head lolled above the fringe of Barney Wilson's old utility rug. Both the cars from Comerbourne were drawn up along the edge of the road, and five men in plain clothes had boiled out of them and taken charge of everything. Two of them were closing in one on either side of the wrecked car. Two more were dismembering the ruins of the gate and hoisting them aside to clear the way. And the fifth, who was George Felse, had made for the Bedford and climbed in beside his son, easing the dangling head into the hollow of his shoulder and feeling with gentle fingers through the tangled hair.

Dominic came round upon a rising wave of fear and pain, to feel himself held in someone's arms like a baby, and someone's fingers tenderly smoothing out the frenzied ache that hammered at his head. Making the inevitable connection, he settled more closely and thankfully into the comforting shoulder, and feeling the rush of tears stinging his eyelids, hastened to cover himself.

" Mummy, my head hurts! " he muttered querulously. But it was his father's voice that said gently in reply: " Yes, old lad, I know. You lie quiet, we'll find you something to stop it."

The discrepancy jolted him seriously, and he opened his eyes to make sure he wasn't dreaming, but closed them again very quickly because the effort was very painful. However, he'd had time to see the face that was bending over him, and there was no doubt about it, it was his father. Well, if that was how he felt about things it didn't look so bad, not so bad at all. Dominic had expected at the very best to find himself in the dog-house. Maybe if you're really going to kick over the traces in a big way it pays to get yourself half killed in the process. Even if it does hurt.

Drifting a little below the surface of full consciousness, he remembered the one thing he had to get settled, the only thing in the world that really mattered.

"It wasn't Kitty," he said, not very distinctly but George understood. "You do know now, don't you?"

"Yes, Dom, we know now. Everything's all right, everything's fine, you just rest."

He was sinking unresisting into a stupor of weariness and relief, tears oozing between his closed eyelids into George's shoulder, when a sudden appalling sound startled him into full consciousness again. Someone had laughed loudly and angrily, a discord harsh as a scream.

He opened his eyes wide, his wrung nerves vibrating, and beyond George's head and Duckett's solid shoulders, beyond Jean and Leslie clinging hand in hand, he saw a wild creature in a torn black suit, her cheek cut by flying glass, long black hair dangling in great heavy locks round her face, a bloodstained Maenad wrenching ineffectively at her pinioned wrists, her mouth contorted as she spat defiance.

"All right, yes, I killed him. I don't care who knows

it. Do you think you can frighten me with your charges
and your cautions? All right, what if I did kill him? It
isn't capital murder, don't think you're going to kill me,
that's something you can't do. I know the law, I've had
to know it. Twenty years," she shouted hoarsely,
" twenty years of my life he had out of me! I could have
married a dozen times over, but no, I had to fix my sights
on him! Twenty years his bitch, being patient, waiting
for that hag of a wife of his to die——"

Dominic began to shake in his father's arms, and then
to sob convulsively. He couldn't help it, and when he'd
begun he couldn't stop. All that black and white dignity,
all that composure and discipline, she ripped them to
shreds and threw them in his face. He couldn't bear it.
He burrowed his throbbing head desperately into George's
shoulder, whimpering, but he couldn't shut out the
sound of her voice.

"——and then still waiting after she was dead, and
still no reward. Bide my time, I've done nothing all my
life but bide my time, and what did I ever get out of it
but *him*? And then suddenly *her* on the telephone, that
fool of a girl yelling for help to me—*me!*—and bleating
that he was planning *to marry her!* And what was I to
get, after I'd given him years of my life? Nothing, none
of my rights, just the same old round, his letters to type
in the daytime, and him in my bed when he felt like it—
and her, *her* holding the reins! Yes, I killed him," she
panted, her breast heaving, " but it wasn't enough. He
ought to have been conscious. He ought to have felt it
more—every blow! There ought to have been some way
I could kill him ten times over for what he did to me! "

CHAPTER XVII

HE REMEMBERED nothing of the drive home in the van, with George nursing him anxiously in his arms, and Leslie driving as gingerly, so Jean said afterwards, as if he had an ambulance load of expectant mothers aboard instead of just one. He was conscious but totally astray. Very slight concussion, so the doctor said, and his recollections would sort themselves out coherently enough later on; but this part of the evening never came back. They put him to bed, and dosed him with something that gradually took the pain away but took the world away with it. "He's all right," said the doctor. "We'll keep him under light sedation to-morrow, and by evening he'll be right as rain."

He woke once in the night, struggling and crying out fiercely, loosing in his dreams the resistance he had restrained by force a few hours earlier. Bunty brought him a drink, and he gulped it down greedily, asked her wonderingly what was the matter, and fell asleep again on her arm. Towards dawn he began sobbing violently in his sleep, but the fit subsided when she bathed his hot forehead and soothed him back into deeper slumber; and in the morning he awoke hungry, alert and loquacious, though still somewhat pale and tense, and wanted to talk to his father.

"This evening," said Bunty firmly. "Right now he's busy arranging about getting Miss Norris released. That's what you were worrying about, isn't it? You take it easy and stop fretting, everything's under control."

"Oh, Mummy!" he said reproachfully, almost offendedly, "you're so darned *calm*." He wouldn't, she thought, have chosen that word if he could have seen her face when they brought him home. He took a rapid retrospective glance at the memories that were beginning to assemble themselves into some sort of shape, and asked coaxingly: "You're not very mad with me, are you?"

"Well, you know," said Bunty amiably, putting away the thermometer which confirmed that his temperature was normal, "maddish."

"Only maddish? Well, look, Mummy, I overspent my expense account. Those gloves were twenty-three and eleven, I never knew they cost so much. Any good my putting in a claim?"

"We can't let the detective lose on the job," she said comfortably. He wasn't feeling quite as tough and skittish as he pretended, but it was better not to notice that. "I'm surprised you didn't just go to Haywards for them, and get them put down to my account."

"Well, hell!" said Dominic, confounded. "I never thought of that."

By evening he was pronounced fit to talk as much as he liked. Later it might be necessary to take an official statement from him, but for the moment what mattered was that he should get the whole thing off his chest to his father as soon as George came home.

"Is it all right?" asked Dominic eagerly, before George could even move up a chair to the side of the bed. "Kitty's free?" He couldn't altogether suppress the tremor in his voice when he uttered her name.

" Yes, it's all right, Kitty's free." He didn't say any
more, it was for her to do that. Dominic knew what he'd
done for her, nothing George might say could add anything to his glory, and he certainly wasn't going to take
anything away from it. " You needn't worry any more,
you did what you set out to do. How does your head
feel now? "

" Sore, and I've got a stiff neck. But not so bad, really.
What was it she hit me with? "

" You won't want to believe it. A rubber cosh loaded
with lead shot, the kind the Teds favour."

" No! " said Dominic, his mouth falling open with
astonishment. " Where would she get a thing like
that? "

" Can't you guess? From one of her club boys. She
confiscated it from him a few weeks ago, with a severe
lecture on the iniquity of carrying offensive weapons."
Alfred Armiger hadn't survived to appreciate the irony,
but by the grace of God Dominic had. " What was it
that put you on to her in the first place? "

" It was Jean's doing, really. I got to thinking how all
the people involved had known Mr. Armiger for years,
and wondering why one of them should suddenly pick
on that night not to be able to stick him a moment longer.
And I thought the real motive must be something that
had happened that very evening, something that changed
things altogether for that one person. So after we got
to know about Kitty's phone call, and it seemed likely
that the person she called might be the one, this sudden
motive thing sort of got narrowed down into something
that was said in that phone call. I made a smashing case
on those lines against Mr. Shelley, and tried it on Leslie

and Jean. And straight away Jean said no, it couldn't happen like that. She said Kitty wouldn't run to a man, but to a woman. She said," said Dominic, steeling his hesitant voice to use the adult words Jean had used, firmly and authoritatively as became a man, " that Kitty had just suffered a kind of sexual outrage, almost worse than the ordinary kind, with that beastly old man making a pass at her that wasn't even a pass, but just a cold-blooded business deal. And you see—what made it much worse——"

He turned his head on the pillow and stared steadily at the wall. He couldn't say it, even now. What made it much worse was that she was still in love with Leslie, and his father's complacent proposal must have seemed to her horribly shocking. " Jean said in those circumstances she'd go to a woman if she had to have help," he said, controlling the level of his voice with determination. He wasn't quite himself yet, he cried easily if he wasn't on his guard.

" I see," said George, remembering how in the night Bunty had reorientated him with much the same phrases and sent him off after the same quarry, though by slower and more orthodox methods. " So you thought of one woman at least who was older, who was well known to her, and who'd been on the scene with her that evening."

" Yes. And I thought what Kitty could have said to her that might make her suddenly want to kill Mr. Armiger, and you see, it was there as soon as I began looking for it." Yes, it was there to be found, though he shouldn't have known enough to go looking for it. There isn't much boys miss; even the gossip they disdain their knowing senses record accurately. " I wouldn't mind betting," said Dominic, "that Kitty's the one person who didn't even know what they said about him and Miss Hamilton. She's so *apart* from those things. Even if you told her something like that it would go in one ear and out the other. She doesn't hear what doesn't interest her."

George wasn't prepared to follow him into the shadowy sweet hinterland of Kitty's mind; there was no permanent place for either of them there.

"So you decided as we couldn't find the gloves to try a gigantic bluff and pretend that you had. How did you set about it?"

Dominic told the whole story, glad to unburden himself; it was difficult to recapture the fear now, in this familiar and secure place, but there were times when he trembled.

"I went there after I knew old Shelley'd left, and pretended I wanted to talk to him, and that it was something about the case. As soon as she bit like that and suggested I should tell her instead I felt sure I was right about her. And when I told her I'd found the gloves, and they were a woman's—letting on I thought they must be Kitty's, and wanted to suppress the evidence— well, then it began to look even more promising, because right away she said I could give them to her and she'd deal with them. Meaning me to understand, she'd destroy them. Well, I mean people just *don't* stick their necks out like that, not to a chap they've hardly set eyes on before, and don't know at all. Do they? Not without a pretty urgent reason of their own. She tried to make me tell where I'd found them, and what they were like and all that, so she could make sure whether she really had

anything to fear or not, but I laid on a sort of hysterical
act, and she couldn't get any sense out of me. And you
know, she couldn't afford to take even the least risk of
my tale being true. Even if the odds were a thousand to
one against my having anything that mattered to her,
she couldn't afford to let even that one chance slip by.
So she said give them to her. And if I'd done it then and
there I don't know what she'd have done, because long
before that I could feel her thinking that I was just as
dangerous to her as the gloves themselves, and she had
to get rid of both of us. I was acting pretty emotional,
I bet she was thinking to herself, this little ass will never
be able to keep his mouth shut, some day he'll blab to
his father. I think she'd have seen to it that something
happened to me right there in the office, because everyone
else had gone, and with the car she'd have been able to
take me somewhere miles away to dump me. But I said
I hadn't got them on me, on account of the chaps at
school being naturally a bit casual with one another's
things, and I'd bring them to her when I came in for
my music lesson at night. You should have seen her
jump at it! Nobody'd ever know we were going to meet,
and if I vanished nobody'd ever think of her. She suggested she'd wait for me at the end of the road when she
came from the club. And she impressed on me that I
wasn't to say a word to a soul. So then I was absolutely
sure. She *had* got rid of some bloodstained gloves somewhere close to the barn that night, and she *had* killed
Mr. Armiger. Why else should she prepare a set-up like
that? "

" And why," asked George gently, " didn't you come
to me then and tell me everything? Why did you have

to go through with a thing like that all by yourself?
Couldn't you have trusted me? "

The note of reproach, however restrained, had been a
mistake. " All right, I know, I know! " said George
hastily. " It wasn't proof, and you felt you had to provide
the proof. But did it have to be by using yourself as live
bait? "

" Well, having gone so far I sort of couldn't stop. And
if I'd told you you'd have stopped me from going on with
it. You'd have had to. *I* could *do* a thing like that, but
you couldn't *let* me do it. You don't blame me, do
you? "

" I don't blame you, I blame myself. I ought to have
made it possible for you to rely on me more." That
wasn't the way, either; self-reproach seemed to have a
worse effect still on Dominic. " Never mind," said George
gently. " You did what you felt you ought to do, let's
leave it at that for now. How did you know what sort
of gloves to provide? That must have been a headache.
If they were wrong, one glance and she'd know you
were lying."

" But then she'd also know I suspected her and was
trying to trap her, wouldn't she? And that would have
come to the same thing, she'd still think it essential to
get rid of me while she had this chance. So it didn't
matter. But I did try to do the best I could. I saw she
hadn't got gloves on when we left the office, so I went
along to see her to the car, and sure enough she had
them there in the locker, and they were plain short black
kid and quite new, hardly creased at the joints yet. So
I thought the safest bet was that she bought a pair as like
the ones she threw away as possible, and I rode back into

town and got some like them. I ran the tap on them and
crumpled and soiled them and tried to age them a bit,
and even then I wrapped them up so she should only
get a glimpse of them.

" And you know all the rest," said Dominic, lying back
in his pillows with a huge sigh. " I couldn't know my
note to Leslie Armiger would be held up like that, or
I'd have said eight o'clock instead of half past."

" I should think so," said George warmly. " Turned
nine when they located me at the garage near her place,
and no sign of you or the Riley by the time we got to
Brook Street. If it hadn't been for young Leslie——"
He dropped that sentence quickly, for his own sake as
much as for Dominic's.

" Suppose she goes back on her confession? Will
you still be able to get a conviction without the real
gloves? "

" Oh, there'll be no trouble there. Her car's full of
traces of blood, all the seams of the driving-seat show it.
The leather's been washed, but she made the usual mistake of using hot water, and in any case you can never
get it out of the threads. And we've recovered the zip
fastener of the black skirt she wore that night, and two
ornamental buttons from the front pleat, all metal, out
of the furnace ashes from the flats where she lives. The
jacket she must have thought wasn't marked, she sent it
to a church rummage sale, but we've traced it. The
right sleeve is slightly splashed with blood, too. Oh, yes,
we've got a case. She must have knelt on the floor beside
him, I should think—anyhow she found it necessary to
burn the skirt. No wonder the hem of Kitty's dress was
stained where it brushed hers."

Looking fixedly at the edge of the sheet which he was folding between his fingers, Dominic asked abruptly : " Did you see her to-day? "

" Who, Ruth Hamilton? "

" No," said Dominic, stiffening. " Kitty. When they —when she was released."

" Yes, I saw her."

" To speak to? How did she look? Did she say anything? "

" She looked a bit dazed as yet," said George carefully, remembering the stunned purple eyes that had stared bewildered at freedom even when it was put into her hands. " Give her a day or two, and she'll be her own girl again. At first the truth was just one more shock to her, but she was coming round nicely the last I saw of her. She said she was going out to get her hair done and buy a new dress."

Dominic lay silent. His diligent fingers lagged on the hem of the sheet. He kept his eyes averted.

" And she said she'd like to come and see you to-night, if you were well enough to have visitors."

Dominic rolled over and sat up in a flurry of bedclothes, eyes flaring golden. " No! Did she, though? No kidding? " He had clutched at the bright promise with all his might, but caution made him give it a second look. " I suppose you went and told her I had to be kept quiet," he said suspiciously. They needn't think he hadn't heard them talking about him last night, even if he'd been in no mood to argue then.

" I told her there was nothing the matter with you but a swollen head. I don't suppose she'll manage to reduce that any," said George, grinning, " but anyhow she'll be here about eight o'clock. You've got a quarter of an hour to cover the worst ravages."

Dominic was half out of bed, yelling for Bunty. George tucked him back again firmly, and brought him his new dark green silk dressing-gown, his last birthday present that was too good to be worn except on special occasions. "You stay where you are, and don't squander your advantages. You look very interesting. Here you are, get busy on the details." He dropped comb and mirror on Dominic's bed, and left him to his bliss.

He was already closing the door when Dominic suddenly cried: "Hey!" And when he looked back: "Somebody must have told her about me. I mean, about what I did. Otherwise how would she know— why would she want——"

"So they must!" said George. "I wonder who that could be?"

He met Bunty on the stairs, coming up in haste to answer her fledgling's agitated cheeping. George spread his arms suddenly, on an impulse of gratitude and relief for which he didn't trouble to seek a reason, and swung her off her feet. He kissed her in mid-air, and put her down gently on the landing above him. She kissed him back warmly before she fled. She didn't know which of them she was sorrier for; but she knew they were both going to survive. George's heart, as a matter of fact, was lighter than she supposed; it had not occurred to him until this moment that he'd been so full of pride and excitement and joy for Dominic that he had somehow mislaid the sting of jealousy that belonged to himself.

Bunty was more respectful than George had been to her son's passionate and unaccustomed concern with his

appearance. She didn't smile about it, she was as much
in earnest as Dominic himself, though she did tend to go
about it in a way that made him feel about seven years
old. She brought him George's Paisley silk scarf and tied
a beautiful cravat for him; and he was too agitated to
resent her attentions provided they produced the desired
result, and submitted to having his face sponged and his
hair brushed like a convalescent child.

" Now you're not to make her too excited," said
Bunty artfully, busy with the comb, " because you must
remember she's been through a lot, and she may be easily
upset. You be calm and gentle with her, and she'll be
all right." She was rewarded by feeling him put the
trembling tension away from him very firmly, and draw
a deep, steadying breath that filled him down to his toes.

Kitty came prompt to her hour. She was thinner and
paler than when he had last seen her, and she wore that
small, rueful smile of hers with a kind of wonder, as
though she had rediscovered it after a long separation.
She had done him proud. The new dress was a rough
silk suit of a colour somewhere between honey and amber.
The soft, floating motion of the sheaves of fair hair testified
to the care someone had spent on the new hair-do, and
the scent that shook out of it when she moved her head
was enough to turn his. She sat by his bed and stretched
out those splendid long legs in their almost invisible
nylons, and looked at the toes of her absurd, fragile shoes,
and then at Dominic.

A moment of shyness hung over them both like an
iridescent bubble, while they held their breath for fear of
breaking more than the silence. Then she suddenly
wrinkled her nose at him and grinned, and he knew that

it was all right, that it had all been worthwhile. The shadow hadn't lifted, the grin didn't ring quite true, not yet; but the time was coming when it would, and if not for him, then by his gift.

"What *am* I to say to you?" said Kitty.   "It just shows you a good deed really is its own reward. If I hadn't rashly taken a fit to give away a pint of my blood I might never have met you, and then where would I have been? Strictly up the creek!"

"They'd have found out without me," said Dominic, humbled. "Dad was on the right lines as it turned out, only I didn't know it. That's the way I am, big-headed. I thought nobody was working at it properly but me." What would George have thought, or Bunty, if they could have heard him now? Adulation from Kitty made him want to go on his knees and confess all the things that least satisfied him in himself, and beg forgiveness for not being more adequate, and shout with joy at the same time because she saw him as so much more likeable and fine than he really was.

"I know the way you are," said Kitty positively. "You're sure you feel all right now? No pain? Nothing?"

"I'm absolutely fit, only they won't let me get up until to-morrow. And what about you?"

"Oh, I'm fine. I lost ten pounds in gaol," said Kitty, and the grin was warmer and more sure of itself this time. "That's what they call looking on the bright side. Don't I look all right?"

"You look marvellous," said Dominic with unguarded fervour.

"Good! This is all for you." She leaned forward, playing with the pleated edging of his eiderdown. "I

wanted to tell you about my plans, Dominic. You're the
first person I am telling. About all that money. I don't
want it. What I should like to do is just to refuse it, but
before I do I have to make sure that *if* I do it will go to
Leslie. Otherwise I shall have to accept it and find the
best means of transferring it to Leslie and Jean afterwards.
I'm determined they shall have it, it's just a question of
which is the best way to arrange it. I'm going to see
Ray Shelley about it to-morrow."

" Leslie won't want to take it," said Dominic, rather
hesitantly because his knowledge of Leslie was so new
that it seemed cheek to presume to instruct her in what
he would or would not do.

" No, I know he won't. But I think he'll do it, because
he won't want to make me unhappy." She had almost
said " more unhappy than I am "; the boy was so grave
and so sweet and so altogether a darling that it was hard
work remembering that he was in a position to suffer,
too. " And I think Jean will let him, for the same reason.
And as for me, I'm going away. If they want me for the
trial I suppose I shall have to stay until that's over, but
after that I'm going right away. I couldn't live here any
more, Dominic, not now."

She lifted her head, and the great purple-brown eyes
looked into his, and he saw her there immured within
the crystal of her loneliness, and felt the wonderful burden
of responsibility for her settle upon his shoulders. Who
else was ever going to get her out?

" Yes," he said, swallowing the heart that seemed to
have grown too big for his breast, " I can understand
that. I think you're right to go."

" It isn't because of being in prison, or being afraid

to face people, or anything," she said. "It isn't that. It's just that I have to get away from here."

"I know," said Dominic.

"Do you? *Do* you know what it's like, loving someone who doesn't even know you're there?"

He didn't say anything to that, he couldn't; the turbulent heart was back in his throat, quietly choking him. But suddenly she heard what she had said, and understood the answer he hadn't made. She slid from her chair and fell on her knees beside his bed with a soft, wretched cry of remorse and tenderness, and caught up his hands in hers and laid her cheek on them. The swirl of her hair spread like a wave over his knees.

His heart seemed to burst, and he could breathe and speak again. He took one hand from her gently, and began to stroke her hair, and then her one visible cheek, smoothing the long, silky line of her brow, laying trembling fingertips on her mouth.

"You'll find somebody else," he said manfully. "Just give it time. You'll go away from here, and it will all be different." He listened to his own voice, astonished and awed. The words he had expected to find bitter were sweet as honey, and tasted not of renunciation but of achievement. "Don't just settle somewhere else, Kitty, not straight away. You travel. Go right round the world, give him a chance to show up. You'll find him, you'll see."

She lay still, letting him soothe her and listening to the deepening tones of the voice that was feeling its way by great forward lunges towards manhood. This was something she'd never meant to do. She had debated all day what she could bring him, what gift she could offer him for all he had done for her, and she had been able to think of nothing that would not diminish his triumph rather than complete it, so that in the end she had come empty-handed. And here without even meaning to she had made him the perfect return, her life for his life, the gift of her drifting, solitary self to be moulded and urged and cherished, and launched on a new course. He had recovered her, he had the right to dispose of her. And why not? Comerbourne wasn't the world. One man couldn't be the world, unless she shut all the rest out. I've got to live now, she thought, I'm a piece of his life, I owe it to him to live.

" You know what? " she said softly, moulding the words with her lips against his palm. " You're absolutely right. That's just what I'm going to do."

" Go to India, go to South America, all those places with the wonderful names. There are people everywhere. Nice people. You've only got to let them in."

" Even a few as nice as you," she said, and smiled up at him, cradling his hand against her cheek. She was in two minds about trying to prolong his pleasure, inviting him to plan with her where she would go and what she would do, but then she thought, no. One more thing she could do for him, and only one, and that was wind up this thing now and get out of his life clean, and leave him a perfect, immaculate, unassailable experience, safe for ever from any anti-climax. Wind it up on a high note, and finish! He'd be miserable for a while, but it would be wonderful misery. Not like mine, she thought, drawn out day after day, month after month in decline. My own fault, my own fault! I won't let that happen to him. I've been to blame. If I'd cared enough, if I'd felt enough, I could have saved all this. *He* could have been alive still, and poor, frustrated, calculating, vindictive Hammie needn't have been a murderess. But all I could see was *my* misery. Now I look at Dominic, and I no longer see myself so clearly, but I see him, he's real to me. With him I won't make any mistake.

"That's exactly what I'm going to do," she said. "And when I do find him, you'll be the first person to know."

She rose on her knees, leaning towards him, and her face was where a woman's face should be, just below the level of his own. She put out a hesitant hand and passed it gently over the back of his head, where the thick hair was clipped short. The touch of her fingers on the dressing was almost too light to feel, and very close to his, all great warm eyes and sympathetic mouth, her face swam out of focus. He drew breath hard, and suddenly his arms went round her and caught her to his heart, and he kissed her three times, beginning at her throat and ending on her lips, inexpertly but not clumsily, with an abrupt, virginal passion.

His mouth was cool and fresh and smooth, and moved her to prodigies of hope and excitement and laughter and tenderness. She knew by every touch of him that there was nothing left in the world that he wanted or needed, not even from her. She let him begin the embrace and end it. She held him tenderly while he willed it so, and as soon as he recollected his role and gently and firmly disengaged himself under the impression that he was releasing her, she took her arms away and drew back, rising and stepping back from him in one lovely, fluid movement.

" Good-bye, Dominic! Bless you for everything! I'll never forget you."

She was gone from the room, the door closing softly after her, before he managed to get out in a small, stunned voice: " Good-bye, Kitty! Good luck! " He didn't say that he'd never forget her, either, but she knew it; never until the Greeks forget Marathon.

When Bunty looked in half an hour later Dominic was curled in his pillows fast asleep, smiling a little with fulfilment and content like a fed infant.

Kitty was as good as her word. Nine months later, one morning in the height of the summer, there was a picture postcard of Rio bay by Dominic's plate at breakfast. The text said:

> I've found him, and you're the first to know. His name is Richard Baynham, he's an engineer, and we're getting married in September. Terribly happy. Bless you!
>
> Love, KITTY.

Dominic read it through with a puzzled face, frowning over a hand which was totally unknown to him. He was not quite awake yet, and the message struck no immediate chord. Nine months is a long time. At the end he said blankly: " Kitty? " And then, in a very different voice: " Oh, *Kitty*! " That was all; but he didn't leave the postcard lying about, he put it carefully in his wallet and no one else ever saw it again; and he got up from the table and went about his business with a bright reminiscent gleam in his eye and looking several inches taller, a man with a future and a past.